GET BUSY DYING

For Uncle Chris and Aunt Suzanne, with love.

GET BUSY DYING

BEN REHDER

ACKNOWLEDGMENTS

I am very grateful to all of the people who helped with this novel, including Tommy Blackwell, Don Gray, Greg Rosen, Helen Haught Fanick, Mary Summerall, Marsha Moyer, Becky Rehder, Leo Bricker, and Stacia Hernstrom. All errors are my own.

1

Where do you get a corpse when you need one? The answer was obvious, so here he was. Digging. At midnight. He'd started just after dark, which was at nearly nine o'clock this time of year. Now he was more than halfway done.

He had prepared well, and everything was going smoothly. Faster than he'd expected. One shovelful of dirt at a time, placed carefully on a large tarp. No spillage on the surrounding grass. It was important that the gravesite look untouched when he left. He couldn't leave any indication of what he'd done.

Originally, he'd been worried about getting caught, but now he realized how silly that was. Way in the back of a cemetery on a quiet county road in the middle of nowhere. Maybe six vehicles had passed by in three hours, but they were more than a hundred yards away. No security cameras. No guards. No homes nearby. Just a six-foot chain link fence that wasn't even locked. Full moon overhead, providing plenty of light, which meant he didn't even have to use a flashlight.

The first thing he'd done, several weeks ago, was search for the right place to stage the accident. He needed the perfect stretch of road. Curvy. Dangerous. As he'd done his scouting, he'd become aware of just how many small, private cemeteries were scattered all over the Texas Hill Country. He'd never noticed before, but damn, there were hundreds. Made sense. Dead people had to be buried. And how many people died every year around the world? Millions and millions. The more he thought about it, the more he was amazed we weren't overrun with graveyards on every spare tract of land.

After he'd decided on a wreck site and picked a dozen cemeteries that seemed ideal, he'd had to sit back and wait. Read the obits. Scan small-town newspaper websites. Couldn't be just any dead body. It had to be right. Couldn't be some little old lady, or some former basketball star. He needed someone average. About his age. About his height.

Thirty-six days later he had his man.

2

Bosworth "Boz" Gentry's death was tragic, if a bit of a Hollywood cliché. In the wee hours of a Saturday in spring, the twenty-eight-year-old construction worker plowed his truck through a guardrail on a winding road outside Austin and tumbled nearly one hundred feet into a canyon. There, it burst into flame. The odds of that happening — a vehicle catching fire — are actually quite slim, despite what you see in the movies, where exploding gas tanks are as common as breast implants. But that's the way the accident unfolded, and I can think of several more agreeable ways to die than burning to death. Drowning in a pool of sewage, perhaps, or being seated next to our long-winded governor at a formal dinner.

Of course, the questions were plentiful in the days after Gentry's death. Was alcohol involved? Where was he going at that time of night? Why were there no skid marks? Had he fallen asleep at the wheel? Why had his parents cruelly named him Bosworth?

Days passed, the accident dropped from the headlines, and I hadn't given it any more thought since, until Heidi called on a Wednesday afternoon and said, "You been keeping up with this Boz Gentry case?"

I was seated in my Dodge Caravan, which is beige, nondescript, and as inconspicuous as any vehicle on the road. I had a video camera at the ready, waiting for a blond gentleman to emerge from a KFC in north Austin. He was average height and weight — nothing distinguishing about him, except that he was wearing a padded neck brace. Two spaces over from his car, a stunning woman in a short skirt was trying to change the tire on a classic Mustang.

"It's a case?" I said.

"It is for me. And maybe for you and your partner, if you have the time."

Heidi is one of my biggest clients. She works at a humongous insurance company — one that's too dignified, or perhaps too stodgy, to use an animated gecko or an annoying duck as a spokesperson.

"Tell me more," I said, because I've found that it facilitates a conversation quite nicely.

"The M.E. said the corpse was about right — height and gender and all that. But he wanted to confirm it with dental records, and guess what?"

"Boz Gentry never grew teeth. He was a scientific anomaly."

"His dentist couldn't find the files. He's an old-time type of dentist — nothing is digital over there, all paper — and he said Gentry's entire folder was missing. Not just the X-rays, everything. No explanation, just not there anymore."

"Did Gentry ever see any other dentists?"

"Nope. Lived in the area all his life and saw the same guy since he was a kid."

"Huh," I said. Always insightful. "DNA?"

"The cops say the body was burned so badly, they don't know if they'll be able to pull any. Plus, it looks like an accelerant was used, in addition to the gasoline in the tank."

"'Looks like?'"

"They can't be one hundred percent positive, but they're fairly sure."

"This is sounding suspiciouser by the minute."

"And the topper: Gentry applied for a life-insurance policy just twelve weeks before the accident."

"How much?"

"Three million."

I gave a low whistle. "Not bad for a night's work."

"Of course, we haven't paid yet — not unless the M.E. issues a death certificate. But we want to make it clear that it wasn't Gentry in that truck."

"Okay, so who was it?"

"No idea. That's for the sheriff's department to figure out. Ultimately, it makes no difference to us, as long as we don't have to pay out the three mil."

"I think it's your warmth and compassion that draws me to you," I said.

"Hey, I'm as warm as the next gal when I'm not getting fleeced."

I said, "Normally I'd be thinking somebody killed Gentry and tried to make it look like an accident, but no dental? No DNA? What're the odds of that? Sounds like an episode of CSI."

"Exactly. The detective working the case agrees."

"Who's the lead on this one?"

"One guess," Heidi said, and there was something in her tone I didn't like.

"Oh, you're kidding me," I said. "Ruelas?"

"Indeed."

"Good Lord."

"Try not to let your bromance cloud your thinking," she said.

I don't hate a lot of people, but I hated Ruelas. Smug, arrogant jerk. Pretty good at his job, but still. Cocky. Obnoxious. An astute observer might point out that I've had all of those same adjectives applied to me at one time or another. But there's a difference of some kind. There has to be.

"So you want me to find Gentry," I said.

"Or provide evidence that the body in the truck wasn't Gentry. If that means finding Gentry, sure, but whatever works. Questions?"

"Uh, yeah. How long was the Cretaceous Period?"

She didn't say anything.

"I can hear you grinning," I said. "You like to pretend you're not amused, but I know better."

"Questions?" she repeated.

"Gentry was married, right?"

"You mean 'is.' He *is* married. Yes. Wife's name is Erin."

"Any indication that she was involved in this diabolical scheme?"

"Not that we know of, but you'd think she'd have to be. I mean, if he faked his own death, and his supposed widow was his beneficiary, he'd want to enjoy the fruits of his labors, right? So she'd have to know he was alive, either before or after. Doesn't mean she was involved, but she'd have to be an accessory after the fact, after he shows up and says, 'Surprise, honey, I'm not really dead.'"

"Good point."

"Other questions?" she said.

"Not at the moment, but you know how slow I am. I'm sure I'll have some later."

"I'll email you a file with everything we got, but it's not a lot."

"Before you do that," I said, "I should mention that I only have ten days to wrap this one up. Then I'm off for a month. You okay with that?"

"Vacation?"

"Yep."

"For a full month?"

"Yep."

"Jeez, Roy, how am I supposed to get along without you for a month?"

"Romance novels? Besides, Mia will take over when I'm gone, if we're not done."

"That's cool," Heidi said. "She's even sharper than you are."

"No need to go overboard."

"Where are you going?" she asked. "Wait. Doesn't matter. Just take me with you. I could use a break, too. Is it a cruise?"

"Actually, I'm not going anywhere. Got a visitor coming to town."

"Some floozy, I bet."

"No. I source all my floozies locally," I said.

"Then who?"

It felt really good to say it out loud. "Hannah. She's coming to see me."

Heidi and I have a similar sense of humor, and she can banter with the best of them, but my last remark caught her by surprise. There was a short pause, and when she responded, her tone had changed entirely. She said,

"Oh, Roy, that's fantastic."

"Yeah," I said. "It is."

When you're at a party and you say you're a legal videographer, most people simply nod, as if they know exactly what that is. They don't know, of course, but they're not interested enough to pursue it any further. I don't blame them, because "legal videographer" sounds just a little more exciting than "actuarial analyst" or "claims representative."

So, instead — assuming I want to further the conversation — I simply say, "I catch people who commit insurance fraud."

They usually say something like, "Oh, really? So you're an investigator for an insurance company?"

"No, I'm a freelancer. I work for myself."

"Like a private detective?"

"Sort of, but I'm not licensed to be a private detective. I'm a legal videographer." Then they look puzzled, so I say, "Legal videographers record all sorts of things on video — depositions, wills, the scenes of accidents. But all I do is insurance fraud. It's sort of my specialty."

"So you follow them around with a camera? I've seen videos like that on YouTube."

"Yep," I say.

"That must be kind of fun."

"It can be. Other times, not so much."

Like now, waiting outside the KFC. I had been keeping a man named Jens Buerger under surveillance for more than three days, but so far, my efforts had been futile. He and three of his pals had been rear-ended by a Mercedes, allegedly resulting in various severe soft-tissue injuries to all of them, but the accident had all the hallmarks of a classic swoop-and-squat. Plus, Buerger had pulled similar stunts before, several times.

And now here came Buerger, leaving the chicken joint, walking toward his car, carrying a red-and-white bucket. Of course, he couldn't help but see the woman in the skirt struggling to lift a spare tire out of the trunk of her beautiful red Mustang fastback. Hard to miss.

The woman — my partner, Mia Madison — said something to Buerger as he approached. He stopped and talked to her, listened to her pleas, but then he gestured toward the neck brace. *Sorry, I can't help. Wish I could, but my neck.* Mia did the thing where she reaches out and touches his arm lightly, imploringly — but it didn't work. Buerger wasn't going to give up his ruse, even for the hottest babe he'd likely seen all year. He got into his own car and drove away.

Time for Plan B: Reinflate the tire Mia had flattened earlier, and then inform her that I'd be tackling this new and interesting case while she continued surveillance on Buerger, which was somewhat tedious.

Sure, we're partners, but seniority has its privileges.

3

At eight-thirty the next morning, I was in the small town of Dripping Springs, twenty minutes west of Austin, waiting patiently in the reception area of Tyler Lutz, the insurance agent who had sold Boz Gentry his life-insurance policy. A wall of windows to my right looked over a wooded area behind the office complex.

Meanwhile, Candice Klein — Lutz's receptionist — was brewing coffee, straightening magazines, watering plants, and generally getting the front office in order. Candice looked to be about 25 years old. Maybe five-six in flats. She was wearing a navy skirt, a cream-colored blouse, and rimless eyeglasses.

I had spoken to Candice the previous afternoon, when I'd arranged the appointment. Heidi had called before that, giving Lutz clearance to speak freely to me about Boz Gentry's insurance policies.

"Mr. Lutz should be here any minute," Candice said at eight-forty, as she took a seat behind her desk. "He rarely runs more than a few minutes late."

"No hurry."

"I'm sure he'll help you however he can."

"Great. Can he rebuild the transmission on my van? It's been slipping lately."

She gave me an indulgent smile that said, *You're quite the rascal, aren't you?* Or, possibly, *Are you always such an idiot?*

Before I could continue the conversation, the door opened and in walked a reasonably handsome, tanned, early middle-aged man in a suit. Candice made a gesture with her hand, like *And here he is now.*

He closed the door and turned to me, grinning. "Roy Ballard?"

"Tyler Lutz?"

We shook hands. He said, "Now that we both remember who we are, come on into my office."

"I have to admit I didn't see this one coming," Lutz said. "Not until Heidi called yesterday afternoon. I've been in this business for nearly twenty years and, well, this is a first. It's just so damn ballsy. And stupid. Who would try something like this?"

"What, you've never had a client fake his own death in an elaborate scheme to collect three million dollars?" I said.

He laughed. "Not that I know of. So they know for sure that's what he did?"

"Well, not one hundred percent, but everybody is sort of operating on that assumption."

"Cops, too?"

"Yeah."

"Nobody tells me anything," Lutz said.

We were in his office with the door closed. It was neither posh nor shabby. Just an office, with semi-comfortable furniture and forgettable art on the walls. How did people do this sort of work? If I had to sit in here eight hours a day, I'd probably slowly lose my sparkling personality and end up buying some wingtip shoes.

"My job is to track Gentry down," I said. "Provide evidence that he's still alive. Video, preferably."

"That's what Heidi said. You're a legal videographer."

"I am. Try to contain your excitement."

"Also, I'll be honest — I recognized your name from the news last year, when you found that missing girl."

I knitted my brow. "You sure that was me?"

He grinned. Lutz wasn't having any of my false humility.

"You're a goddamn hero in my book," he said. "You took the bull by the horns and maybe even saved that girl's life."

I'd experienced my share of Lutzes since the incident — people who think what I did was so magnificent, so brave, they don't even want me to joke about it. They're too busy patting me on the back, literally or figuratively. I can say with absolutely no false humility at all that it becomes tiresome.

"That's nice of you to say. Got lucky. So you think you can help me with this?"

"I'll sure try."

"I appreciate that," I said. "I need our conversation to remain confidential."

"No problem. I'd like to see this get resolved one way or the other. If Boz really is dead, well, I feel bad for his widow, and she deserves to receive the benefits. Right now the poor gal is in a holding pattern. That's not the way it's supposed to work. So if you have questions, fire away."

"How long have you been his agent?" I asked.

"Maybe ten years or so, going back to when he graduated high school and moved out of his parents' house. I've known him a long time. We both grew up here, although I was six or seven years ahead of him. Then he married Erin and they moved to her old family homestead off Bee Caves Road. I carry the policy on that place, too."

"So I'm guessing you sell insurance to a lot of people you know. Other people who grew up here."

"Exactly. I'm pretty much the only agent in town, or I used to be. Couple of others have popped up the past few years. Boz bought all his policies from me — everything across the board. Home. Health. Disability. Auto. He had a motorcycle and a jet ski, and I covered those, too."

"And life insurance," I said.

"Well, yeah. You knew that already."

"Is it normal for such a young guy to be so responsible? How many guys his age have disability insurance? Who thinks about that when they're so young?"

Lutz grinned. "I take that to mean you don't have all the coverage you need, but I'll refrain from giving you a sales pitch. No, you're right, lots of people — not just his age but older — don't cover themselves as well as they should. They're either uninsured or underinsured. Boz had a good head on his shoulders. Well, that's what I thought until now. He never struck me as a con artist."

"Did it seem weird that he wanted that much life insurance? Guy like that, with no kids?"

"Not really, no, because I always stress the importance of locking in your insurability early on, when you're young. See, he could get that much coverage now, but if he tried later, he might've been denied. It's easier to get higher limits when you're young. I encourage my clients to do that. Most agents do."

"So how does a transaction like that actually take place?" I asked. "Did he come into the office, or did you do it all by phone?"

"Oh, he stopped in, and then he had to pass a physical exam. Wasn't a problem. He was in great health. Is, I guess."

"Did he seem odd about it? Nervous?"

"The exam?" Lutz said.

"No, when you met with him about the policy. Did he say anything peculiar? Ask any strange questions?"

Lutz was already nodding his head. "You know, he seemed like the same old Boz, except for one thing. After I heard about his accident, I remembered a remark he made that day here in my office. I told the detective about it. Boz said something like, 'Does Erin still collect if I decide to drive off a cliff on my way home?' Weird — like he was kidding, but maybe he really wanted to make sure there weren't any loopholes he needed to know about. I told him he was fully covered as soon as he signed the contract."

"Interesting," I said. "Were you and Boz the kind of friends where he'd feel comfortable making a joke like that?"

"No, not friends, but I always knew him, like I said, and he knew me. Small town, so I'd see him around, and every couple years we'd sit down and review his policies. We had a beer once or twice, but we didn't have a lot in common, even when we got older. He ran in different circles. He was into, like, dirt bikes and hunting deer and wild pigs with a bow. Rambo stuff. He'd tell me about camping for days without any food, so he'd have to kill his own dinner. He was sort of a survivalist. Oh, he loved to talk about seceding. Stuff like that."

"Seceding?" I said.

"Yeah, he was big into the idea that Texas should secede from the nation. I'm not making fun of him. I don't want to sound like that."

"Yes," I said, "because seceding from the union is completely rational. It worked out so well the last time."

"He was a decent guy, really," Lutz said. "Maybe a little out there."

I noticed that we were both occasionally referring to Gentry in the past tense. Hard to shake that, once you think someone's dead, even though he probably wasn't.

I said, "Who does he hunt with? Any idea?"

"Just some of his friends. They all hunt. Pretty much all the men who grew up around here do, and some of the ladies, too. Tell you what — I'll write down a list of his buddies."

He reached for a pen.

"That would be great," I said.

"I insure several of them, too," he said as he wrote. "I'm curious. How do you go about solving a case like this? I mean, if the cops haven't had any luck..."

"Well," I said, "it helps that the evidence I produce doesn't usually have to survive the same kind of scrutiny that a cop's does. They are, uh, limited by physical and legal boundaries that don't affect me quite as much."

He grinned. "Okay, I won't even ask what that means. Probably better if I don't know." He slid the written list across the desk to me, along with a business card.

"Really appreciate your time," I said.

"You have any more questions, my cell phone is on there. Call anytime. And, hey — not trying to be a pushy salesman, but if you want to sit down and discuss your coverage sometime..."

4

Mia walked into Trudy's Four Star on Highway 290 just a few minutes after noon. I was seated at a table on the far side of the dining area, so I could see her coming from a long distance. It's always entertaining to watch Mia cross a crowded room. Not because of anything she does — she behaves like any other woman who is confident and poised — but because of what the other people in the room do.

Other women notice her instantly. Then those other women turn to their husbands or boyfriends to see if *they've* noticed Mia. The men always have, and they get caught watching her, which usually prompts a throat clearing or a discreet kick under the table. It's comical. Today Mia was wearing pressed blue jeans and a well-fitting three-quarter-sleeve henley T-shirt in light blue. Simple, but wow.

Fortunately, she's also intelligent, creative, clever, patient, easygoing, loyal, and willing to put up with my nonsense. The perfect partner.

"Hey," she said now, pulling out a chair.

"You can't help it, can you?" I said, alluding to the men in the room still checking her out.

"Help what?" she said, and then, when she caught my meaning, she rolled her eyes.

"Any luck with Buerger?" I asked.

She was scanning the menu and held up a finger in a give-me-a-minute gesture. After thirty seconds, she closed the menu and said, "How are you?"

Simple pleasantries. I was still learning that I shouldn't skip right past them. "I'm great. How are you?"

"Not bad. Thanks for asking. As for Buerger, he didn't leave his apartment all morning. Frustrating."

And, yes, we both knew there was a chance Buerger might go out somewhere while Mia was here with me, but that was the nature of the business. You couldn't watch a subject 24 hours a day. You had to take breaks, just for reasons of sanity, and if that meant you missed an opportunity to shoot a revealing photo, well, you kept up your surveillance and waited for another time. If a guy dropped his charade once, he'd almost certainly do it again.

"How'd it go with the insurance guy?" Mia asked.

I quickly brought her up to speed on my meeting with Tyler Lutz, and just as I finished, the waiter arrived to take our orders — Cholula honey chicken for Mia, chicken-fried steak for me.

When the waiter left, I said, "I've been wrestling with something."

"An oiled-up stripper?"

"Haven't done that in weeks. No, I'm trying to decide if I should approach Gentry's wife and friends, or just put one of them — probably the wife — under surveillance from the get-go."

Mia thought about it for a few seconds. "You don't want to tip 'em off, but they probably already know the cops are watching them. So what difference will it make if they think you're watching, too? They're already conducting themselves with the assumption that they're being watched."

"True, unless they're really dumb," I said.

"And we've encountered that before."

"Seems to be the rule rather than the exception, thank God. First, though, I need to go home and do some research."

"Meaning take a nap in your underwear?" Mia said.

I looked at her. "Have you hidden a camera in my apartment?"

We walked out to the parking lot, and I was following Mia over to her vehicle — not her Mustang, which was way too flashy for surveillance, but a used Chevy Tahoe — when I heard someone shout, "Say cheese!"

We both looked toward the person, and there he was, less than twenty feet away, standing in the open driver's door of a sedan that had been backed into its parking spot. He was holding a camera. And wearing a neck brace.

Jens Buerger.

He held the camera up and snapped our picture. "How does that feel? You like having someone following you around, taking your picture?"

We were totally busted. No point in denying it, so we walked in his direction. When we got within about six feet he said, "Y'all thought you were clever, huh? Thought I didn't know what you were doing? Wrong again."

I spread my hands. "Just doing our job, Jens."

"Stop following me."

"We're just trying to verify that you really are injured," Mia said. "You shouldn't have a problem with that."

"Harassing me is what y'all been doing. My neck is all fucked up, and now the insurance company is trying to weasel out of paying for it, so they sent y'all to harass me. I know exactly who you are. Knew it all along. Assholes."

"Hey, hold on a second there, Jens," I said. "Sure, I'm an asshole, but my partner here most certainly isn't."

"I'm more of a bitch," Mia said. "Or even a whorebag."

"Y'all are a laugh riot," Buerger said. "Stop following me or next time I'll take a big shit on your car seat."

Lovely guy. This was going nowhere, so I decided to try a different tactic. "Was your face injured in the wreck, Jens?"

"What? No."

"Oh, wow. It's always been that way? That's a shame."

Mia picked up on what I was doing.

She said, "Your poor nose. Have you considered surgery? They could probably do…something. Maybe."

Buerger raised one hand toward his face, self-conscious, but he caught himself halfway and stopped. "Hey, fuck both of y'all."

I said, "Imagine that. To go with your looks, you have the vocabulary of an eighth-grade dropout. I bet your prospects in life are limitless."

"I know I can hardly resist him," Mia said. "Who needs Brad Pitt when this guy is roaming the streets?"

The goal was to piss him off enough for him to get physical with me. Even if he simply shoved me, that would do the trick. Mia already had her cell phone in her hand, ready to record.

Buerger sneered at us. "Y'all are just pissed because you suck at what you do."

"Speaking of sucking," I said, but it was too late. He had ducked into his car and closed the door.

He cranked the engine and began to pull out of the spot. Mia made a placating gesture with her hands, asking him to stop, because now that the ploy had failed, we needed to change direction yet again.

Surprisingly, Buerger stopped. His window was open, and Mia stepped closer to speak to him.

"Okay, we apologize for hassling you. It's obvious you really are injured, and that's all we were trying to determine from the beginning. Believe it or not, some people fake injuries to collect money they don't deserve. Now we know for sure that you aren't doing that, so we won't be following you anymore."

He looked suspicious. "Then what was all that stuff you just said? About my face? Seems like y'all are just a couple of jerks."

Mia said, "We wanted to see if you'd respond to that sort of provocation like an injured man — and you did. An injured man would resist getting into any sort of physical altercation, and that's what you did. That will go into our report."

Our report? Ha. She was laying it on thick. It was smooth and believable, but Buerger was too angry to care.

"You know what?" he said. "Fuck you both anyway. Sideways." He squealed the tires, shooting the rod as he left.

"Well, that was a fine start to the afternoon," Mia said. "Don't know how he made us."

"Probably figured it out at the KFC."

"I guess."

"Buerger has played this game before."

"So if he figured it out at KFC, that meant he would've been watching for me to show up again," Mia said. "And he spotted me parked outside his apartment this morning. Crap."

"It happens. Don't worry about it."

"What now?" she asked.

"One down, three to go," I said, referring to the other men who had been in Buerger's car when it was hit. "They all went to the same quack doctor. If we can prove one of them is faking, all four claims will collapse."

5

Sometimes you just have to go with your gut — I'm a big fan of that approach — and that's why I knocked on Erin Gentry's front door at about four that afternoon.

The Gentrys lived off Bee Caves Road — more precisely, off Riverhills Road, west of Austin. Some longtime residents still called it "the Pier road," because there used to be a fantastic lakeside beer joint called The Pier at the bottom of the winding blacktop. Imagine rocking to the Fabulous Thunderbirds, with the Texas sun shining down through towering cypress trees, while hundreds of scantily clad people — young and old, hippie and college student — dance and mill around in the grassy areas beside the lake. Picture dozens of boats anchored just off shore, enjoying the music. Sound like I miss it? Only because I do. I wasted a few summer days there myself.

Going back eighty or a hundred years, these wooded hills were home to a specific subgenus of central Texas redneck known as the cedar chopper. Those folks did in fact make a living by chopping Ashe juniper trees — called cedar around here — for charcoal (yes, you can turn cedar into charcoal) and for fence posts. Over the decades, as development gradually came this way, the cedar choppers were slowly forced out by rising property taxes, or they were enticed by the promise of a big payday from selling. There were still remnants of those days here and there. Between a couple of high-end gated neighborhoods, you might glimpse an old homestead tucked back in the trees. These were the hangers-on. The ancestors of men with nicknames like "Skeeter" and "Axe" and, of course, "Bubba."

It appeared the Gentrys fell into this category. Or I guess Erin Gentry did, and Boz Gentry married into it. The driveway onto their property was caliche, and the house appeared to be at least sixty or seventy years old, but it was actually in decent shape. A coat of paint wouldn't have hurt, but at least the roof wasn't caving in. There were no appliances on the front porch. A dirty Ford Focus with peeling paint was parked in a bare spot in the yard.

I climbed the wooden steps and knocked, and a dog somewhere behind the house began to bark. Big dog, from the sound of it. A few seconds later, I sensed movement to my right, and when I looked, Erin Gentry was peering through a gap in the curtains. I recognized her from photos Heidi had emailed.

Erin Gentry let the curtains fall shut, and then I heard the deadbolt slide out of the frame. The door opened, and there she was. You looked at this young woman and you immediately thought: *Tough, sassy, country girl.* She was also pretty darned cute, despite the cigarette in her left hand. Shoulder-length blondish hair. A handful of freckles. Sunburned nose. A mole on her right cheek, a la Cindy Crawford or Marilyn Monroe. Erin Gentry couldn't have weighed a hundred pounds. Wearing a red bikini top with a faded denim skirt, as if she'd been to the lake. She had no shoes on. I saw no smudge-faced toddler peering from behind her hip, although it would have completed the picture perfectly.

"Yeah?" she said, standing in the open doorway.

"Mrs. Gentry?"

The dog was still barking.

"What're you? Reporter? Cop? You know you're trespassing?"

"Actually, I…well, you appear to be the type of woman who

appreciates the value of Tupperware. Am I right?"

"A salesman? You've gotta be shittin' me."

I gave her my best smile, which has been known to melt hearts and make women reconsider their marriage vows. "Yeah, I am. I'm not selling anything. I'm from the insurance company."

Her eyes went skyward, as if she were looking for patience. "You people, I swear. What now?"

Considering her attitude, I decided to clarify my position. "I'm not actually one of their employees. I'm a freelancer. Name is Roy Ballard."

The dog wasn't letting up. Erin Gentry took a drag on her cigarette, exhaled the smoke in my general direction, and said, "Bring a check with you?"

She used her right hand to cup her left elbow, propping her cigarette conveniently close to her mouth. The move also conveniently squeezed her perky breasts together, creating some distracting cleavage. Even more distracting than the dog. I managed to retain my wits.

"Uh, sorry, no," I said. "See, I'm a videographer. In fact, they've hired me to see if I can get footage of your husband. Still alive."

"What?"

"So they can reject the claim permanently."

"Oh, for fuck's sake." Now she was pointing her cigarette at me and raising her voice. "You've got the balls to show up at my house and —"

I raised my hands, palms out. "I'm not saying he's alive. Hell, maybe he's not. But if that's the case, instead of helping the insurance company, I could end up helping you. I might end up getting your money for you."

I was stretching it, but I could tell that I'd calmed her down and piqued her interest.

"Blackie! Hush!" she hollered over her shoulder. Girls like her don't yell, they *holler*. The unseen dog finally fell silent. "How's that gonna help me?"

"The more I look for him, and the more I can't find him, that's all the more reason for them to admit he's dead. I've looked at the files myself, and frankly, it seems pretty clear to me. You do think he's dead, right?"

"Hell, yeah. Got no reason to think otherwise."

And you look real broken up about it, I thought. If she wasn't in on the scam and she really did think he was dead, she wasn't exactly overcome by grief.

"Okay, good. Wait. Sorry, I didn't mean it to sound that way."

"What way?"

"That it's good that you think he's dead," I said.

"What's your name again?"

"Roy Ballard," I said.

"Roy, you're cute and all, but you wanna get to the point?"

"Okay, yeah, what I'm saying is, if that was really your husband in the truck, the best thing you can do for yourself is answer my questions. I need to know where to look for him, and once I've checked all the possibilities, I can report back that he's nowhere to be found. Not to brag, but I'm known for being really good at what I do. If I can't find your husband, my client will be more inclined to admit that he's dead and approve the payout. Make sense?"

"What about the cops?" she asked.

"What about 'em?"

"Don't they have to agree that Boz is dead? Same with the coroner? And that don't seem likely anytime soon, 'cause the cops keep coming at me like I'm in on some kind of big con job."

"Annoying detective named Ruelas?"

Ruelas had a first name, but I never used it — when speaking to him or about him — because I didn't want to accept that sort of familiarity. In fact, I was always hoping I'd never see him again. He was a prick. A jerk. He used too much hair product.

He also refused to believe me when I was convinced that I had seen a missing six-year-old girl in the company of a mutt named Brian Pierce. Ruelas had been patronizing. Condescending. Dismissive. And usually stylishly dressed.

Then, later, after Pierce had been killed, and when I'd finally determined where the little girl was being held, I gave Ruelas a chance to help me get her out. Instead he sent a cop to try to stop me. I busted through the door anyway and found the girl, and even though making Ruelas look bad had no bearing at all on why I'd done it, it sure was a nice little perk of the job.

"That's him," Erin Gentry said.

I nodded. "He's an asshole, huh?"

"First he came on tough, then he tried flirting, and then he went back to being tough. I finally told him I wasn't answering no more questions. Tyler said I wouldn't get the money until there was a death certificate, and that won't happen until the cops finish up with their so-called investigation."

"That's true, yes. So the more people looking for your husband, the better, right?"

She didn't appear convinced, but she said, "I guess." She flicked her cigarette butt into the yard.

"So you don't mind a few questions?"

Right then, I heard something I didn't expect. A sound, from somewhere deep in the house, like someone closing a door or a cabinet. Apparently she had a visitor. Then again, maybe it was another dog. Or a noisy appliance of some sort. Erin Gentry didn't seem to notice it.

Instead, she said, "You can ask. Don't know if I'll answer."

Excellent. She was going to cooperate.

"I'm hoping you can give me the names of his closest friends. Places where he hangs out. Like, where would he go if he wanted to fake his own death? Things like that. Anything you think might be helpful."

She stared at me for a few seconds, obviously wondering if it would be worth her time. Or maybe wondering if she could trust me. Then she started talking, and it was good stuff. Even better, most of it matched up with what was in the files Heidi had sent me, and with what Tyler Lutz had told me.

When she was done talking, I asked for her phone number, in case I had questions later. She gave me a cell number. Then, before I left, she said, "So that's it, huh?"

"Unless you have something else," I said.

"Ain't you gonna even ask if he's here?" Almost a dare.

"Who, Boz?" I said.

"Well, who else?" she said.

"I was thinking Vladimir Putin," I said.

"Everybody else seems to think I was involved, so you might as well ask," she said. "You know you're wondering. You're thinking, 'Why won't she let the cops search her house if he's not in there?'"

"Because it's your constitutional right," I said.

"Damn right, it is," she said. "Speaking of which, I know how guys like you work."

"You do?"

"You follow people around with a camera, right? When they're not watching?"

"Sometimes," I said.

"Okay, well, I'm telling ya — you follow me around or hide a camera on my place, I'll find it and kick your ass." She was giving me the slightest smile to soften the blow.

"I wouldn't doubt it for a minute," I said. "You have my word — no cameras."

And I stuck to my word. No cameras. But I did sneak back after sundown and attach a GPS tracker to the underside of her aging Ford Focus.

6

While I was interviewing Erin Gentry, Mia was having a bad day. Of course, I wouldn't hear about it until the following morning, because she didn't want to tell me about it that evening. Her reasoning was that it would've made me angry — and she was right. And that it would have kept me from sleeping well that night — and she was right about that, too.

Here's what happened: One of the men in the car with Jens Buerger during the alleged accident was Craig Evans, who was claiming to have a herniated disc. Evans was only twenty-two, but he had a fairly impressive record, including burglary and assault. On the other hand, unlike all three other members of the group, Evans had no prior history of insurance fraud, so Mia decided he might be the least wary of the group. The least likely to be on the lookout for anyone watching him. Same conclusion I would've reached.

So, after lunch, Mia set up at a shopping center where she could watch the main boulevard coming out of Evans's neighborhood. She got lucky, because he drove past in his truck less than an hour later. He was pulling a trailer with a load of landscaping timbers on it, which seemed a hopeful sign. Hard to move lumber with a bad back.

But the day started going poorly when Evans hopped onto Interstate 35 and went south, past the city limits. It's never fun when your subject decides to leave town. You have to decide whether or not to follow. Will it be worth the time investment? Mia followed. Evans passed through San Marcos. Then New Braunfels. Then into San Antonio. Mia was following at a discreet distance, but traffic was heavy, so she couldn't fall too far back or she might lose him. She was starting to wonder if Evans would keep going all the way to Laredo, but then he took an exit on the east side of San Antonio.

He jumped on a major thoroughfare for a couple of miles, and Mia couldn't help noticing that it wasn't the nicest part of town. Trash was gathered around buildings. Weeds were growing on medians. Some businesses were boarded up. Lots of people walking slowly — almost shambling around — as if they weren't headed anywhere in particular, and they didn't have to get there anytime soon.

Then Evans ducked into a residential area — again, everything was sort of seedy and run-down — and he took a couple of turns before parking along the curb in front of a house with waist-high weeds in the front lawn. Mia had no choice but to drive past. She went deeper into the neighborhood for a few minutes, hit a dead end, then turned around and approached the house again. Pretending to be lost, or at least confused. Like she was looking for a certain address.

She didn't see Evans. She didn't see anybody.

Then a man — not Evans, but a larger, taller, older man in overalls — suddenly stepped into the street from between Evans's truck and trailer and held up his hands in a *STOP* gesture. Mia had no choice. She stopped. There was no traffic coming from either direction. She waited. Now she recognized the man as Zeke Cooney, one of the other men involved in the fraud scam. Older than the other three players by about twenty years. Apparently, we hadn't had his latest address.

And right behind Cooney came Evans, from behind his truck, where he had also been waiting. He casually walked in front of Mia's SUV and came around the driver's side, approaching the open window.

By this time, Mia had slipped her hand inside a zippered pocket of her specially designed purse, and her palm was wrapped around the grip of a .38 Special. She had her concealed-carry license, of course. That was one thing I had insisted on when she became my partner. What we do for a living is rarely dangerous — except for those times when it is. Sometimes the subject figures out who you are and what you're doing, and then reacts poorly.

Like now.

Evans bent toward the window and grinned. In person, he didn't look as young — or as friendly — as in photos. "I know who you are. Jens told me you'd be poking around. So I'm just gonna say straight out that you'd better quit fuckin' following me. You understand?"

Mia and I had discussed the appropriate ways to react when confronted under various circumstances. Right now, she was alone, she was outnumbered, and she didn't have any sort of recording device running. There was little to gain in egging Evans on, as we'd done with Buerger, or to have any sort of conversation at all. Better to simply leave.

So she said, "Your friend is blocking the road. Please ask him to move."

"Who the fuck do you think you are?"

"He's impeding traffic, which is against the law," Mia said.

"So is invading my privacy, you smug little bitch."

"Your friend needs to move so I can be on my way."

Now his eyes drifted downward to the hand inside her purse. He incorrectly assumed she was reaching for a cell phone. "Gonna call your faggy partner? Jens told me about him, too."

I can't recall anyone ever referring to me as "faggy," but if someone was going to call me either "faggy" or "a lot like Craig Evans," I'd take "faggy" every time.

I'm sure Mia was tempted to show him exactly what she had in her hand, but you don't ever, ever, ever pull a gun unless you or someone else is in danger and you fully intend to shoot the bad guy. You don't pull it just to scare someone away. You don't pull it to shut someone up, or to show him that you aren't scared. You pull it to use it. Period. Also makes sense from a tactical standpoint. Why let a potential attacker know what you're packing? Better to keep the element of surprise.

Mia said, "At this point, you are keeping me against my will. That's a felony."

Well, maybe. She could still drop it into reverse, but as she admitted later, she was too rattled by then for that to have occurred to her. This was her first real confrontation with a subject. Worse yet, there was nobody else in sight except those two goons, so there would be no witnesses if anything should happen.

Evans placed his hands on the window opening and leaned in closer. "You know what? I got an idea. I didn't mean to be so ugly. How about you pull over and come party with me and Zeke?"

"You and Zeke?" Mia said.

"That's right."

"You want me to party with you and Zeke?" Mia said.

"You get high? Zeke has some good weed. You got a boyfriend?"

"You absolutely cannot be serious."

"We could have a lot of fun," Evans said.

"But you're not physically capable. You're injured, remember? Wasn't it a back injury?"

Evans grinned. "Oh, right. Almost forgot. I'm sure I could get by. You should come on inside."

"Sorry, can't," Mia said. "Besides, just twenty seconds ago, you told me to quit following you."

"That was before I got a good look at you, and damn, girl. You wanna party or what?"

"I didn't bring any penicillin. Now get your hands off my car."

"Do what?"

"Remove. Your. Hands," Mia said. "Now."

"Stuck-up bitch," Evans said, and he made a grab toward her. Mia stomped the accelerator. She felt a thump — Evans's arm hitting the doorframe — and heard him yelp.

Good ol' Zeke stayed in the street as long as he could stand it, but he lost his nerve and finally jumped out of the way. Good thing, too, because as Mia told me later, she fully intended to run him over if necessary.

7

First thing I did the next morning was grab the laptop on my nightstand and see whether Erin Gentry had gone anywhere after I'd attached the GPS device to her car. She had, and her travels were all nicely illustrated on a map.

The tracker was smaller than a cell phone, and arguably every bit as powerful. It was known as a "slap and track" unit, and that described it perfectly. It had a magnetic case, along with a built-in antenna and battery, so you could slap it underneath a vehicle in seconds and begin tracking immediately.

Flexible, too. You could use one of these units to track someone online in real time, with a live update of their location every ten seconds. Or the tracker could record data for up to 90 days, so you could look backwards in time and see where the subject had gone. In other words, you didn't have to physically follow a subject if you followed them electronically.

Sometimes this was the ideal solution. If I was conducting

surveillance on a subject who was suspected of committing fraud, I would almost always follow him or her in person, so I could shoot incriminating video or photos, if the opportunity presented itself. But this case was different. I had no idea where Boz Gentry might be. I was hoping Erin Gentry would lead me to him. I didn't necessarily need to follow her — not yet — I just needed to know where she went.

The GPS data informed me that she had left her house at 1:12 a.m. Interesting. Odd time for a bereaved widow to be out and about, unless she was simply battling insomnia — maybe taking a drive to ease her anguish.

Actually, I couldn't assume Erin Gentry was in the vehicle — especially considering that I might have heard someone else in her house when I'd interviewed her. But whoever was driving, her Ford Focus followed Riverhills to Bee Caves Road, went east toward Austin, then turned right less than a mile later on Barton Creek Boulevard, the main drag through a very ritzy area that centered around Barton Creek Country Club.

Erin Gentry's Focus then turned left on Chalk Knoll Drive, which led into a gated community, which meant the driver had to have entered a punch code on a keypad to gain entry, or maybe had some sort of clicker device like a garage door opener. The secrets of the wealthy.

Bottom line, it didn't really matter how the gate had been opened, but it had, and the Focus took Chalk Knoll down to a street called Portofino Ridge. Pulled into a driveway on the right, stayed for four and a half minutes, then followed the same path all the way back to Erin Gentry's house.

It appeared someone or something had been dropped off. Or picked up. But who? Or what? Who lived at that house?

I jumped over to the website for the Travis County Appraisal District, keepers of the tax rolls, and did a property search for the address. Owner was named Alex Albeck. Also interesting. Because Alex Albeck was one of the names given to me by Erin Gentry. She'd told me that Alex Albeck was Boz Gentry's best friend, buddies since kindergarten.

I was just about to start speculating about the possibilities of this new development when Mia called. And this was when she described what had happened to her the previous afternoon — the incident with Craig Evans and Zeke Cooney.

When she was done, I wanted to immediately track Evans down and talk to him. With a crowbar. But I remained calm and said, "You handled it well. Glad you're okay." I'd learned through a painful trial-and-error period, during the first few months of our partnership, not to start sentences with "What you should've done was…" or "If it had been me…"

"Thanks," she said. "Evans seems like a harmless punk, and I think he was just trying to scare me, but you never know."

"That's exactly right. You just keep assuming that asshole is dangerous, please."

"Worried about me, Roy?"

"Worried about you winding up in prison for busting his head open. You could be charged with cruelty to animals."

"It won't come to that," she said.

"If he's lucky."

I wanted to offer advice on what she should do next, but she didn't ask, so instead I told her what I'd been up to, including my recent discovery regarding Alex Albeck. We did this often — just talking about our cases, brainstorming — because more often than not, one of us would think of something the other had overlooked.

"Tell me more about Albeck," Mia said.

"He's a Taurus who likes Michael Bolton songs and long walks on the beach."

"Hey, just like you," Mia said.

"Albeck pretty much grew up in the same circles as Boz Gentry, but Albeck seems to have done a lot better for himself than all his buddies."

"How do you define 'doing better for yourself'?"

"You know, like setting goals and actually achieving them. Working hard. Helping old ladies cross the street. Staying off crack."

"What line of work is Albeck in?"

"Real estate developer. He and his partners have built several high-dollar neighborhoods in the last decade or so. They buy ranches and cut them up. He's made a bundle."

"So he's wealthy."

"Lives near Barton Creek Country Club on a street named 'Portofino Ridge.' That right there just exudes class, don't it?"

"Married?" Mia asked.

"No, I'm divorced, but it's against company policy for me to date a fellow employee. Alex Albeck, on the other hand, is single."

"Wealthy and single. What's that address again?"

I gasped. "Gold digger!"

"You know me."

"I do know you. I should mention that he lives in a gated community, which keeps harlots like you at bay."

Gated communities were always a problem in our line of work. Worse than fences, dogs, alarm systems, even nosy neighbors. The worst possible scenario is a gated community with a competent guard at the entrance around the clock.

"You probably already thought of this, but there's no way to know if Erin Gentry was actually driving," Mia said, following the same thought process I'd followed earlier. "How certain are you that you heard someone inside her house?"

"I'm only certain that I heard *something*. Wouldn't wager that it was a person. It was probably nothing."

We were both quiet for several moments. This was typical. Just thinking.

Then Mia said, "Well, let's get the most obvious scenario out of the way first. If Boz Gentry is alive, it wouldn't surprise anyone if he's hiding out with his best buddy, at least part of the time. Maybe she was dropping him off late last night."

"Or picking him up."

"What kind of read did you get off Erin Gentry?" Mia asked.

I thought about that for a few seconds. "She's no dummy. She picks up on things real quick."

"So she very well could have understood that your whole pitch — 'help me help you' — was a crock."

"Absolutely, but she answered all my questions anyway. So she either truly does not know whether her husband is dead, or she has a great poker face."

"Got a gut feeling?" she asked.

"Oddly, no. Could go either way. This late-night trip to Albeck's house is kind of suspicious, though."

"How about this?" Mia said. "Erin and Albeck are having an affair.

One or both of them killed Boz Gentry. They're sneaking around at night because they can't let anyone see them together."

"Albeck killed his best friend?" I said.

"It happens."

"Okay, true — and an interesting hypothesis. But in that case, whose body was in the vehicle?"

"Could've been Boz," Mia said. "They still haven't confirmed that it *wasn't* him, right?"

"Yeah, but come on. No dental. No DNA. Fishy as can be."

"Still. Until there's confirmation one way or the other…"

"I know, I know," I said.

"Hey, here's a question. What happens if you end up proving it *was* Gentry in the car, and our biggest client loses three million because of it?"

"Bite your tongue," I said.

I've learned time and time again that if you want access to the most intimate details of a person's life, you just can't beat Facebook. People will post almost anything there — no matter how outrageous or improper. It's a very strange phenomenon.

Just learned that my grandfather was an actual Nazi.

Here's a video of my dog eating its own vomit.

Does anybody know how to get rid of genital warts?

It's also surprising how little most Facebook users know about the privacy settings. Believe it or not, you can use Facebook and actually maintain a fairly strict level of privacy. But, yeah, it does take some effort to understand which posts can be seen by your friends only, or by friends of friends, or by the public.

For instance, anytime you post a new profile photo, the privacy level is automatically set to Public. Anybody on Facebook can see it, and they can see any comments people make about the photo. If you want more privacy, you have to get in the habit of immediately changing the setting when you upload a new profile photo. And timeline cover photos? Those — and the comments they receive — are set to Public, and the setting can't be changed.

Some Facebook users want a great deal of privacy, but they simply don't understand how to maintain it. Then there are others who simply don't seem to care one way or the other. They'll post just about any damn thing for anybody to see. No filters, no boundaries.

And I love that, for obvious reasons.

That's why one of the first things I do on any case is troll Facebook to see if I can learn anything helpful or interesting about my subject. I did that now, checking to see how many of the people on Boz Gentry's list of close friends had Facebook accounts. I found five out of seven, including Alex Albeck. Most of them had their privacy settings fairly tight. I could see some comments under various profile and timeline cover photos, but nothing useful.

Which led me to the next step I usually take. I sent all of them a friend request from one of my fake Facebook profiles — Linda Peterson. Linda is an eye-catching lady, without appearing to be a spammer or some sort of con artist. Her privacy settings allow a guy like Alex Albeck to see just enough to think she's a real person that he must somehow know. Maybe she's a former coworker or classmate or something, right? Why not say yes? Ridiculous how often Linda's friend requests are approved.

Then another very obvious question finally occurred to me. Did Boz Gentry have a Facebook account? Turned out he did, and the privacy settings were about as loose as they get, but he wasn't much of a user. The few likes he'd listed told me that he was a Dave Matthews fan and a motorcycling enthusiast, and that his favorite movies were *The Shawshank Redemption* and *The Godfather*.

I spent a few minutes sifting through his timeline, but the bulk of the recent postings were from friends and loved ones lamenting his death. In fact, there was Erin, just yesterday, writing a tear-jerking missive about how much she missed him, and she had received a bunch of supportive comments, riddled with typos, from friends.

I pondered sending Boz Gentry a friend request from Linda Peterson, too. I figured, why not? You just never knew what would pan out and what wouldn't. Sometimes I had to toss out a dozen fishing lines, figuratively speaking, knowing only one would get a strike. Granted, if Gentry was alive, he'd have to be a real moron to accept the request, but morons kept me in business.

If he did accept it, that might give me access to some of his friends' pages, if they'd selected friends-of-friends as a default privacy setting. Again, many Facebook users didn't understand the implications of that setting. If you had 500 friends and you chose the friends-only setting for a post, that meant 500 people could see it. But if you had 500 friends, and each of your friends had 500 friends, any post you made visible to friends of friends could be seen by 250,000 people. You can understand why I love that privacy setting. If one of my surveillance subjects didn't accept my friend request, sometimes I could get one of their friends to accept a request, and that would gain me access to my subject's posts.

After I was done with Facebook, I couldn't think of anything else to do at the moment — so I broke down and made a phone call I didn't really want to make, to arrange a meeting with a person I'd just as soon kick in the groin.

8

"Well, look who the fuck it is. The great fraud expert. How's it hanging, fraud expert?"

It was the voice of Detective Ruelas, dripping with sarcasm. Reminding me that I was a simple videographer, whereas he was an Important Bigshot who investigated Serious Crimes. He'd managed to sneak up on me while I was looking at a menu. We were inside a Chili's in Lakeway, not far from the sheriff's substation where Ruelas officed. An early lunch. He'd picked Chili's. He was a Chili's kind of guy, and that wasn't necessarily a compliment.

There were a thousand places I would have rather been, but I should have known that in my line of work, Ruelas was unavoidable. Interacting with cops in general was unavoidable. Occasionally I learned things that I was ethically bound to tell them. Conversely, I always hoped I built up enough goodwill that the cops would sometimes tell me things I needed to know. Back scratching.

"Detective," I said, as Ruelas sat down on the other side of the booth without shaking hands. "Charming as ever."

"You like charming men?" he said. "I never knew that about you."

"There's a lot you don't know. I finished high school, for instance. You should try it."

He smirked, then he looked down at my shirt. "Still shopping at Goodwill, I see. It's amazing what you can find for three dollars."

"Coincidentally the same price as your haircut," I said.

He grunted and picked up a menu. That was something I'd learned about him: As offensive as he might be, it was almost impossible to offend him back. It bounced right off. Probably because, as a cop, he'd heard much worse — including outright threats that were meant in earnest, from murderers and rapists who'd give most of us bad dreams. Or maybe he had brothers. These back-and-forth putdowns were almost like a form of entertainment for him. I'll admit it made me want to pour a bottle of ketchup onto his head. He was irritating. So was the fact that he was a reasonably good-looking guy, and successful, which made me dislike him even more. I wanted him to be a fat, balding slob with a poor complexion, crooked teeth, and no professional skills.

After about twenty seconds, Ruelas slapped his menu shut and said, "I hope you aren't gonna waste my time today."

"Yeah, because it's so valuable," I said, which wasn't one of my best comebacks. "I have some useful information about Erin Gentry."

"Yeah?"

"But I'll need something in return."

"Like what?"

We were both keeping our voices low, even though there wasn't anybody sitting nearby. The restaurant was no more than half full at the moment, and I had asked for an out-of-the-way booth.

"I want to know what you know about Boz Gentry," I said. "Specifically, whether or not that was his body in the truck. If it *was* him, I'd rather know now than later. Save myself a wasted search."

I knew what Heidi had told me — that it was unconfirmed — but Heidi didn't necessarily have the latest news. A guy like Ruelas wouldn't feel compelled to keep her up to date. He wouldn't even feel compelled to tell her the truth, because, admittedly, there were times when cops needed to keep certain facts to themselves, so as not to compromise an investigation.

"Don't you watch the news?" Ruelas asked. "We haven't figured that out yet." Sarcastic.

"No problem," I said. "In that case, I can keep what I know to myself."

A waiter — a guy about twenty years old — showed up and asked what we wanted to drink. Ruelas said he wanted iced tea, and that he was also ready to order. He'd take the bacon burger with fries. No onions. I asked for a Dr Pepper and the grilled chicken sandwich.

The waiter left and Ruelas said, "Okay, I'm willing to share, but I ain't promising much."

"Does that mean you don't know much or that you won't share much?"

"Guess you'll have to take your chances."

I'd have to go first, taking the risk that he had nothing of value to tell me. There was no way around it. So I said, "Late last night, after midnight, someone drove Erin Gentry's car to one of Boz Gentry's friend's houses."

Ruelas didn't appear to have the slightest interest, but that had always been his typical response to almost anything I told him. There was no way of knowing whether this was a surprise to him or not. He asked, "Which friend?"

Good. That told me that Ruelas didn't know what I knew. He wasn't keeping tabs on Erin Gentry so closely that he'd gotten a warrant to put a tracker on her vehicle. See, he needed a warrant, whereas I wasn't encumbered by all those pesky legal technicalities. Oh, sure, I was breaking the law when I attached the unit to Erin's vehicle, because I'm supposed to have the permission of the vehicle's owner, but I didn't mind committing a misdemeanor. I wouldn't lose my job if I got caught. I'm my own boss, and I wouldn't fire myself. Even if Erin Gentry found it, she'd have a tough time proving I'd put it on there. In fact, I wasn't aware of any cases where anyone had actually been charged with illegally tracking someone with a GPS unit.

"My turn," I said, ignoring Ruelas's question. I knew he'd screw me if he could, so I had to hold back the most important part until I'd gotten something in return. I said, "Tell me about the corpse. Was it —"

I fell silent as the waiter arrived with our drinks, then left us alone again.

"Was it Boz Gentry in the wrecked truck?" I asked.

Ruelas said, "Since you don't know who was driving her car, I'm assuming you weren't tailing the vehicle. You woulda seen who was driving. So that means you got a tracker on it. Shame on you."

"No comment."

He made a face, like he was trying to decide whether it was worthwhile to continue this conversation. But I knew he'd want to know which friend's house I was talking about. He understood the implications. Maybe it was even a missing piece of the puzzle in his investigation. Maybe he already had phone records, emails, or credit card bills showing that there was an affair between Erin Gentry and Alex Albeck. Or something entirely different. Or maybe he had nothing.

"Here's my best offer," Ruelas said. "I'll tell you what we got from DNA, but first you gotta tell me which friend."

Surprisingly, that seemed fair, assuming he meant it. So I said, "That doesn't seem fair."

"Fair as it's gonna get."

The waiter arrived with our food, then scuttled away.

"You'll owe me one," I said.

He didn't say anything.

I waited.

He still said nothing. In fact, he picked up his burger and took a bite, nonchalant as hell.

You have to know which battles are worth fighting, so I said, "Alex Albeck."

Ruelas didn't react, nor did I expect him to. He said, "How long was the car at Albeck's place?"

"You have to talk with your mouth full?" I asked.

"How long?"

There was no harm in answering that. "Four and a half minutes."

"So she was probably dropping someone off or picking someone up," Ruelas said. "Or maybe Albeck wasn't home."

"You're quick. You should become a contestant on a game show." I picked up my sandwich but didn't take a bite yet.

"Where'd the car go after that?" Ruelas asked.

"Back to Gentry's place."

"Any activity since then?" Ruelas asked.

"That wasn't covered in our agreement," I said. "But no. No further activity. Now tell me about Boz Gentry."

Ruelas took another bite of his burger, making me wait while he chewed. Then he said, "We put a rush on the first test, but it came back inconclusive. Now we're waiting on a more advanced test. Takes less material to work with. But the lab is backed up. Those assholes are always backed up. In the meantime, they're saying don't hold my breath."

"Meaning?"

"Meaning expect inconclusive again," he said.

"That's it?" I said.

"Yep."

"Well, crap."

"Warned you I wasn't promising much."

"And that's what you gave me."

He stopped eating and actually seemed a little miffed. "Hey, douche bag, I told you exactly where it stands — and you wanna get pissy about it?"

"All right. Okay."

He kept eating. And I kept pushing.

"What does your gut tell you?" I asked. "Was it Gentry in that vehicle?"

"Hell, no." There was juice running down his chin. The man was a slob. I bet he didn't eat that way when women were around. "Too handy that the dental records went missing. What're the odds?"

"So whose body was it?"

"No idea."

The noise level was rising as the restaurant started to fill up. "Any idea where Gentry is?" I asked.

Ruelas said, "If I knew that, I wouldn't be sharing this special moment with you."

"Think he's at Albeck's house?"

"That'd be great for you, huh?" Ruelas said. "Then you could act like you solved the case for me."

"So Albeck wasn't involved?"

"Didn't say that," Ruelas said.

"He was involved?" I asked.

"Don't think so."

"Why do you think that?"

Ruelas stopped chewing for a minute. "Tell you what. Why don't I just make a copy of everything I got and send it over? What do you need? Forensics reports? Witness statements?"

I finally took a bite of my sandwich. Not bad, for Chili's.

Then I said, "Did you search Albeck's house?"

"On what cause?" he said.

"Hey, don't ask me. You're the cop."

"I can tell you he came in willingly for an interview. No red flags. Talked for an hour until one of his lawyers got wind of it and shut us down."

"What about Gentry's other friends?"

Ruelas shook his head. "I'd say we're about even."

"I'm assuming you talked with them all and got nothing," I said.

"Assume whatever the hell you want."

I said, "Make a deal with you. If I get another solid lead, I'll let you know, and you do the same. Off the record. We could save each other some wasted time that way."

Ruelas made a scoffing sound. "Fuck no. If I get a lead and don't tell you, I'm just doing my job. If you get a lead and don't tell me, you're committing a crime. I'll tell you one thing: Finding Gentry — if he's alive — ain't gonna be as simple as sticking a tracker on Erin Gentry's car. If she's involved, she's not that dumb. I assume you've met her?"

"I have. She's sharp."

"Looks like a pretty good piece of ass, too, doesn't she?" Ruelas said. "Speaking of which, how's your partner?"

I stared at him for a long moment, and he looked right back, smirking. He wasn't intimidated in the least. He had said it purely to goad me. In fact, I knew that he liked and respected Mia, but he understood that making a crack about her was the best way to get under my skin, and it worked.

The previous year, when we'd been searching for the missing girl, Ruelas had flirted with Mia, and eventually asked her out. Not very professional, because he was working the case and Mia was a potential witness. She turned him down, but still, it pissed me off, and, yeah, I acknowledge that there is a certain electricity in the air between Mia and me — an unspoken "what if?" that we both contemplate on occasion. A decent therapist might even say that's what makes me dislike Ruelas so much. He's a threat to my relationship with Mia. Or he was. Maybe. I don't know.

Right now, I weighed my responses, then I said, "One of these days you're going to lose some teeth over a remark like that."

He wiped his mouth with a napkin and tossed it onto the table. "Yeah, well, maybe, but it's not gonna be you who does it. I have to hit the john."

And with that he was up and gone. I hated the fact that I was seething. Why did I care what that jerk said? And while I was sitting there, I made up my mind that I'd had enough. When he came back, I'd tell him it was time to take it outside. And we would, and I'd take his fucking head off. Maybe I'd get arrested, but I didn't care.

A minute passed.

I glanced over my left shoulder, toward the restrooms — and then I saw him through a window. He was outside, walking toward his unmarked unit. He was leaving.

Son of a bitch.

He wasn't worried about what I might do if he came back to the table. I knew that. He was leaving because he thought it was funny. It was his way of making me wait around like an idiot, then sticking me with the check.

I wished I'd thought of it first.

9

I was angry, but at least I'd learned something useful. Boz Gentry was probably still out there somewhere. All I had to do was find him. So what next? Truth is, I had no idea how to proceed.

I sat in my van outside Chili's for a few minutes and tried to think like Boz Gentry. Tough, because I didn't *know* Boz Gentry. The critical question: If I were going to fake my own death, where would I go? The answer was disheartening. I'd leave the country. I would plan far in advance and create a flawless fake identity — which was still possible, even in this digital age — then I would flee to someplace like Costa Rica.

But I didn't know if Gentry was smart or creative enough to construct that sort of elaborate getaway. It seemed more likely that Boz Gentry was somewhere close by, so he could rendezvous with Erin on occasion. Then, when the money came through, they'd take off together, or attempt to. Good chance they'd flee in such a clumsy fashion that they'd be rounded up in a few days. But, again, that wasn't my concern. I just needed to provide evidence that Boz was committing fraud.

So, for now, I decided to assume he was somewhere nearby.

Where? How to find him?

In an ideal world, I'd have GPS trackers on the vehicles of Boz Gentry's closest friends, Albeck included. Then I could see if any of them traveled anyplace out of the ordinary. But physically locating that many people could take days. And some of them would likely own more than one vehicle. I didn't own that many trackers. Besides, it would likely be wasted effort, because it was probable that none of them knew anything about Boz Gentry's whereabouts.

If any of them did know, it would be Albeck, right? Albeck was Gentry's best friend, and I had to wonder why Erin had driven over to his house so late at night.

There was also the fact that Albeck — being wealthy — had plenty of resources to help Boz stay off the radar. That made me think of the case from last year — the missing girl, Tracy Turner. She had been stashed in an empty rental house. Not around the world or across the country, but just a few miles from her home.

I had to wonder: What real estate holdings did Albeck own? Where might Gentry hide? I decided to go back to my apartment to do some research on Albeck, but as so often happens, a different idea popped into my head, and I went off in that direction.

The office of Bernard Wilkins, D.D.S., was located in Dripping Springs, in a small building across Mercer Street from The Barber Shop. (The Barber Shop wasn't a barber shop, but was actually a small brew pub. Made me wonder if anyone was tempted to open an actual barber shop and call it The Brew Pub.)

The dentist's office had last been updated in the late fifties, if one were to judge by, well, everything in it. The dark walnut paneling in the waiting room was something you'd have seen in Ward Cleaver's study. The Danish furniture was so out of date that it was now back in style. Who needs Wi-Fi and flat-screen televisions when you can have *Reader's Digest* and *Highlights* magazine? What were Goofus and Gallant up to now? There was even a dusty book of illustrated Bible stories, because what better time to ponder the mysteries of man's creation than when you were about to get all jacked up on nitrous oxide? On the plus side, the office smelled minty fresh.

There was only one patient in the waiting room — an elderly man who appeared to be dozing — but that was one more than I'd been hoping to see. When the woman behind the halfway-opened frosted partition asked if she could help me, I said, "I was wondering if Dr. Wilkins could see me today. I hear he's giving out those miniature floss dispensers, and who can resist a sweet deal like that?"

The woman smiled. She was maybe 55, with short salt-and-pepper hair and striking green eyes. "They are handy, aren't they? I keep one in my purse and one in my car. Never know when you might need some floss."

"Couldn't agree more. I spend an inordinate amount of time flossing. In fact, I listed flossing as a hobby on my resume."

That really seemed to tickle her. "Well, now you're just being silly. Do you have an appointment?"

"I'm afraid not. I've never been here before. Truth is, despite all my flossing, I have this toothache that's been driving me nuts. Any chance you could squeeze me in?"

As I spoke, I grimaced just a bit and lightly cupped my jaw with the palm of my left hand. *See, I have a toothache.* Where do I pick up my Academy Award?

The woman — Shelley Milligan, according to her nameplate — said, "It'll be about thirty minutes. Is that okay?" A small sign next to Shelley's partition informed me that they didn't take credit cards and the office was closed on Mondays.

"Better than a kick in the shins," I said.

Shelley grabbed a clipboard and passed it to me over the counter.

"Okay, I'll need you to fill out a New Patient form," she said. "Front and back, and please include a current phone number, mailing address, and insurance information if you want us to file a claim." Very efficient, this Shelley. Like a well-oiled machine. She'd given that little speech a thousand times.

Just behind Shelley, against a wall, were five filing cabinets. Metal. Gray. Utilitarian. Four drawers each. Heidi was right — this place had thus far successfully avoided the digital revolution. Boz Gentry's file had lived in those filing cabinets until it disappeared.

"Thank you, Shelley," I said, and I could tell that she appreciated the fact that I'd called her by name.

She nodded, and I took a seat. The old man was still snoozing. I pretended to fill out the form, but actually I was just biding my time. Waiting. Fortunately, I didn't have to wait long.

After less than seven minutes, I could hear the murmuring of a conversation — a male and a female, behind walls, but coming closer — and then the door to the rear portion of the office swung open and a middle-aged woman appeared. She was clutching a small paper bag that likely contained a miniature floss dispenser, a miniature tube of toothpaste, and a toothbrush. Freebies for every patient. She made some small talk with Shelley as she paid her bill and arranged her next appointment.

Then she walked out, and less than a minute later, Shelley stood up and left her counter, disappeared from view for a moment, then opened the same door and said, "Mr. Goodwin, come on back."

The elderly man groaned softly as he hoisted himself out of his chair, and then he disappeared through the doorway. The door closed behind him with a loud click.

Now I was alone in the waiting room. As it turned out, I was alone for a solid twelve minutes, which told me there were only two employees who worked here — Shelley and Dr. Wilkins. Which meant Shelley wore many hats: receptionist, office manager, and dental hygienist, or at least dental assistant. This wasn't one of those high-dollar operations that felt more like a day spa than a dental office. This was bare-bones.

I used the twelve minutes wisely. After Shelley and the old man disappeared, I got up and tried to open the door through which they had just passed. Nope. It wouldn't open from this side. That meant the file cabinets were not easy pickings for anyone alone in the waiting room. That narrowed down the possibilities.

Next, I took a closer look at the lock on the door coming in from the parking lot. I am by no means an expert on locks, but I know which brands and models are fair, which are good, and which are excellent. This old office — maybe precisely because it was old, and things were built to last back then — had an excellent lock on the door. There didn't seem to be any evidence of a break-in, and now I was fairly sure that the person who had stolen the file hadn't picked the lock. That narrowed down the possibilities even further.

I turned and faced Shelley's counter again. She'd left the frosted partition open. The window was about two feet wide. Would someone have had the balls to climb over that counter, through that narrow space, and steal a file from the metal file cabinets? Could they have done it gracefully, without making a great deal of noise? Without being caught by Shelley? Without a patient arriving and wondering who that was behind the counter? Plus, the cabinets had locks. Not great locks, but the average Joe wouldn't know how to open them. It just didn't seem likely that someone had vaulted the counter, stolen the file, and left, without getting caught.

I sat back down and checked my email on my iPhone. Nothing important. None of Gentry's friends had accepted my friend requests on Facebook. A friendly Nigerian man informed me that I had won a lottery, but that would have to wait.

Then I saw that I'd missed a call from Laura, my ex. There was a voicemail waiting. I was about to listen to it when Shelley came back, settled in behind the counter, and gave me another warm smile. "How's that form coming along?"

"Honestly, I hate filling out forms. It's like pulling teeth."

She shook her head, but she couldn't help grinning. "You are terrible."

"The laughter helps me endure the pain."

"You know what kind of award the dentist of the year gets?" Shelley asked.

"No idea," I said.

"Just a little plaque," she said, and I gave her an authentic laugh.

Now that we'd made a connection, I raised the clipboard and said, "Actually, Shelley, I have a question for you about this form."

"Yes?"

I rose from the chair and approached the counter, and she looked so pleasant and eager to help. Just me and Shelley out here. Nobody would hear anything, but I kept my voice low and leaned in a bit.

"I have to be straight with you," I said. "I don't really have a toothache."

Now Shelley was truly puzzled. It said so all over her face. But she wasn't afraid or nervous — just confused — because she had no idea what was coming.

I said, "I'm the guy who paid you for Boz Gentry's file."

Shelley's pretty eyes widened with surprise and her face went as white as the lab coat she was wearing.

10

I have to admit, it was uncomfortable to watch her react. Suddenly she wouldn't make eye contact. She fumbled around on her desk, as if she were looking for something. This was not a woman who was used to deceiving people. Then she actually said, "Pardon me?" as if she hadn't heard what I'd said.

I spoke even softer — now just a whisper. "Shelley, don't freak out on me, okay? What I just said isn't true. But judging from the way you reacted, I'd say it's pretty obvious someone *did* pay you —"

She started to speak, but I held up my hands and kept talking, because I've found that once someone denies their guilt, it's almost impossible to get them to admit otherwise. Maybe they don't want to add being a liar on top of whatever else it is they've already done.

I said, "Look, I'm not a cop, okay? I'm not here to cause trouble for you. The insurance company hired me to prove Boz Gentry is still alive, because they aren't convinced he's dead. That's it. I don't care who did what, or why, or for how much money. I don't care where the file went.

But unless Dr. Wilkins himself did something with that file, there aren't many other ways it could've disappeared. There wasn't a break-in. I'd say someone contacted you discreetly and offered a nice chunk of money for it. Believe me, I can understand how tempting that would be. What's one file, right?"

Shelley had gone from pale to bright red. Shame was settling in. She was not proud of what she'd done.

"It's just me here, Shelley. Anything you tell me won't go any further. Promise."

I was lying. I'd tell Mia. Also, depending on what Shelley revealed — if she revealed anything at all — it might be the type of information I'd be morally bound to share with Ruelas. Speaking of Ruelas, it was obvious he hadn't grilled Shelley, because if he had, he would've seen the guilt on her face. He would've pressured her, and she would've caved. If she found me intimidating, and I think she did, imagine how she'd feel about a homicide cop. It was a sloppy oversight on Ruelas's part. Meanwhile, Shelley was just about to talk. I could tell. But she needed one more push.

"Just tell me how it went down," I said, "and then you'll never see me again. It'll stay between you and me. Or you can stay quiet, but I'll call the sheriff's department and tell them you're withholding information."

She placed one hand across her lower forehead, looking down at the desktop, totally stressing out. I think she was starting to cry, which didn't make me feel real great, to be honest.

I waited. I could hear the muffled murmurings of Dr. Wilkins talking to the patient in some other room.

I waited some more.

"It was so stupid," she said.

I didn't say a word. She sniffed. I could hear a drill. The elderly man was getting a filling.

"I needed the money," she said. "Our thirtieth anniversary is coming up — me and Edgar — and we've been talking about a trip to Paris."

"How much money?"

"Five thousand dollars."

More than I would have guessed. But five grand wasn't much if it helped Boz Gentry and his wife score three million dollars.

"If it makes you feel any better," I said, "most people would take the money. Including me."

She looked up at me for just a second with a rueful smile, then lowered her head again.

"It started with a letter in the mail."

First thing I did when I got back in the van was listen to the voicemail from Laura.

Hey, give me a call when you get a minute, please.

Short. To the point. I listened a second time.

My reaction? This was not good. Was it fair to draw such a conclusion based on a message that brief? Well, she *had* been my wife for six years, and I could still remember that particular tone. Trying to sound casual and agreeable, but in reality there was something she wanted to worry or complain about. I called her back.

"Hey," she said, picking up after one ring.

"How's it going?"

"Oh, you know. Everything's fine."

"Yeah? That's good," I said.

"But there's something we need to talk about."

Who would have guessed?

"What's up?" I asked. "Is Hannah okay?"

"Oh, yeah, it's nothing like that. It's just…" She let out a big sigh. A delaying tactic. "It's about her visit. I've been thinking about it some more, and I'm not so sure it's a good idea."

To my credit — even though I'd wondered if something like this might happen — I did not overreact. I simply said, "Okay, well, what is it that's causing you to be concerned?"

"Just…I don't know. The way she's acting lately. I don't think she wants to go."

"Has she said that?" I asked. "Has she said she doesn't want to go?"

"No, not directly. She's just all moody. Like she's pissed off, because the date is getting closer, and it's making her unhappy. When I call her on it, she goes into the whole silent treatment thing, you know?"

"I'm sure that's no fun to deal with," I said, "but isn't that typical teenage behavior?" Laura didn't respond right away, so I said, "When we started talking about this visit — what was it, seven, eight months ago — I remember you saying it might straighten out her attitude a little bit. That you two were getting on each other's nerves."

More silence, but I was starting to fill in the gaps myself. Hannah didn't have the problem. Laura did. I couldn't blame her, though. The last time I'd spent time alone with our daughter — I mean serious time alone, just the two of us — I'd made the mistake of leaving her unattended at a dog park. It wasn't any more than two minutes, but when I returned to the car, she'd vanished. That was nearly ten years ago. She was five years old at the time. We didn't know it, but Hannah had been abducted by a very sick man. We quickly learned that if she wasn't found in the first few hours, she'd probably never be found — at least, not alive.

But our sweet Hannah had been found. Alive. Unharmed.

Unfortunately, our marriage hadn't been able to withstand the aftermath of the ordeal. Laura blamed me for failing to watch our daughter closely enough, and I can't fault her for that. Her anger festered into a lingering resentment and distrust that ultimately eroded our relationship. Bottom line: She asked for a divorce a year later, met a new guy, then moved with him to Canada when Hannah was eight years old. My daughter lives in a different country, more than two thousand miles away. She is nearly fifteen years old, and I haven't seen her in person — Skype doesn't count — for seven years.

I could feel myself starting to lose it. I wanted to lash out, but that would have been the worst thing to do.

"Please, Laura," I said calmly. "I know this is a big step, and I know it's not easy for you, but please don't take this away from me. I promise you everything will be fine. I'll take good care of her. Once she gets here, she'll be glad she came, and so will you."

Call waiting beeped. Ruelas was on the other line. Probably wanting to razz me about the free lunch. I ignored it.

I said, "You've never been apart from her for that long. It's natural to get a little emotional about it."

I stopped talking before I made it worse. We sat in silence for a solid minute.

Then Laura said, "Okay. Okay. I just need to get my head around this a little more. I'll talk to you later."

Before I could respond, she hung up. I wasn't sure what she'd meant. Was the visit back on?

I checked my phone and saw that Ruelas hadn't left a voicemail, but as I was looking at the screen, he called again.

I answered, saying, "I didn't appreciate that little stunt at lunch, asshole."

Ruelas said, "Yeah, well, one of our units responded to a possible assault in a parking lot about an hour ago. Turns out the victim was your partner. Thought you might want to know, asshole."

11

Despite appearances, my Dodge Caravan can really move when it needs to. Two minutes after hanging up with Ruelas, I was flying west on Highway 290 toward Oak Hill.

Mia was not injured; that was the important thing. I didn't know many details, but I knew she had not been hurt.

Ruelas had said a resident in an apartment complex had seen a long-haired man shouting at a woman — Mia — in the parking lot. He had her trapped between two cars and a brick wall. The resident called 9-1-1, but the long-haired man left before the cops arrived. Mia told the deputy she didn't want to file a report and she had not been assaulted. The deputy kept pushing, and Mia eventually revealed that she was tailing the long-haired man because of a fraud investigation and he had gotten angry about it. End of story. No big deal. But she did ask the deputy to call me. She needed a ride. Ruelas got wind of it and made the call.

So I'd asked Ruelas for the address of the apartment complex, then I'd immediately hit the road. Now I was wondering: Why hadn't Mia called me? And why did she need a ride? Why hadn't she simply driven away from the scene?

Twenty minutes later, I pulled into the complex and immediately spotted Mia sitting on a curb on the far side of the lot, near the cleverly named Building B. She was dressed in loose khaki shorts and a white T-shirt — the kind of outfit she wears for surveillance, not for enticing some dumb fraud suspect into lifting an eighty-pound bag of cement. She had her hair tucked under a baseball cap and she was wearing very little makeup. There weren't many vehicles in the lot — everyone was still at work — and I didn't see her Chevy Tahoe anywhere.

I pulled into a parking spot two spaces over from a white Honda and Mia immediately opened the passenger door and climbed inside the minivan.

"Sorry for the hassle," she said. "Thanks for coming."

"Are you okay?" I asked.

"Fine. He didn't hurt me."

"Did he try to?"

"No, not really."

"What happened?" I asked. "Why didn't you call me?"

She was shaking her head. "I don't have my phone. Or my car keys."

"Start at the beginning," I said.

"Okay, well, Shane Moyer was the only one of the group who hadn't spotted us yet, so I decided to focus on him. I figure his buddies told him I drove a Tahoe, so I borrowed a friend's car."

She gestured toward the white Honda Civic parked nearby. It wasn't too bad as a surveillance vehicle. A common car, and it had tinted windows.

She continued, saying, "This morning, after we talked, I came over here and scoped the complex out. See that little freestanding building over there?"

"Yeah."

"That's the laundry room. I went inside and saw a clipboard where residents sign up to use one of the washers and dryers at a specific time. Moyer always uses them on Friday afternoons at around three, so I figured that was perfect. Catch him carrying a loaded basket of laundry when he's supposed to have a shoulder injury. He's in Building A, and I can see the steps to his apartment from way over here."

"Pretty good set-up," I said.

"So I came back at two o'clock," Mia said. "He must've been watching the lot, because he made me big time. Plus, I screwed up. I was in the process of sending you a text — just wondering how your case was going — when Moyer suddenly opens the passenger door and climbs in. I never saw him coming."

"Mia," I said, about to give her a rare lecture. I try to avoid this, but she's still a rookie in this profession, and how is she going to learn if I don't point out her mistakes? I make plenty of mistakes of my own, and I encourage her to point them out when I do.

"Yeah, Roy, I know," she said. "I should've had the doors locked. The doors should always be locked during surveillance. I screwed up."

"Fair enough. Remember that scumbags like Moyer and Evans are more likely to confront a woman than a man. It's just a sad truth. They'll pull shit with you that they wouldn't pull with me. You have to *always* remember that."

"I know. You're right. Anyway, he immediately starts saying all the same stuff that Evans and Buerger said: 'Why are you following me?' Calling me a bitch. So I put up with that for about three seconds."

"What'd you do?"

"I got out of the car. Left him sitting there by himself."

"Smart." I was proud that Mia had kept her wits about her. She hadn't gotten rattled. Then again, she'd once been a bartender. A beautiful bartender. So she'd had plenty of experience dealing with obnoxious jerks.

She said, "Only problem is, I grabbed my purse when I got out, because my gun is in there, but I dropped my phone. He grabbed it, and apparently he took the keys from the ignition. Then he came chasing after me and trapped me between a couple of cars. He started yelling at me, and then he started coming toward me…"

For the first time since I'd arrived, she was starting to seem shaken up by the incident. My own palms were sweating. I was getting angry.

"And?" I asked.

She took a deep breath. "I pulled my gun, Roy. I did. I pulled it, and I was going to shoot him. I felt threatened. This was the first time I was truly scared on this job. He backed off and ran away as soon as he saw it come out of my purse."

I placed a hand on her shoulder. "I don't blame you for a second. Nobody would. He's lucky you didn't pop him." I was holding my own emotions back — chiefly a desire to seek quick vengeance. But now was the time to be calm and rational.

She smiled at me, staying brave and strong. "Thanks."

"What happened next?"

"A woman came over and said she'd called the cops. I could hear a siren about a minute later. They were fast."

"Did this woman see you pull the gun?"

"No."

"Did you tell the deputy you pulled the gun?"

"No."

I pondered the situation for a second. "Why didn't you tell him Moyer stole your stuff?"

"Who, the deputy?"

"Yeah."

"The deputy was a woman."

"Okay, but same question."

Mia spread her hands. "It was a snap judgment. I was thinking: Can I catch this guy if he's locked up? Will he claim that I was hassling him on behalf of the insurance company? Plus, frankly, I don't want the sheriff's department to fight my battles. I want to take care of this myself." She looked at me. "What would you have done?"

I grinned. "Same damn thing."

"Yeah?"

"Yeah."

"Would you have pulled a gun on Moyer?" she asked.

I hesitated for a moment. "That's not a fair question," I said.

"Why not?"

"Goes back to what I said earlier. He wouldn't have the same physical advantage over me that he'd have over you, so he probably wouldn't approach me to begin with. I know that sounds sexist, but in this case, I think it's true."

She grinned again and said, "Sexist pig."

"Sexy pig, yes. Very sexy."

"But you're right," she said. "I have a gun and I have pepper spray, but there are times when it would be good to have a *physical* advantage. To be able to take care of myself without scrambling for my purse. So, while I was sitting there waiting for you, I made a decision."

"About what?"

"I'm going to take a self-defense class," she said.

"That's a great idea."

"I am going to become an ass-kicking machine. Or I guess an ass-defending machine."

"You have a great ass to defend."

"Why, thank you. And then I am going to stop carrying a gun."

I didn't answer right away. I wasn't sure I liked that decision. "How about one step at a time?" I said. "Take some classes, and then decide about carrying."

She nodded. "I love this job, Roy. And working with you. I can't tell you how great these past ten months have been. I look forward to getting out here every day. But I don't want to shoot anybody."

"Nobody does," I said. "And you didn't have to. Next time, you have to remember —"

"Lock the doors, I know. Don't be a nag."

I started to come back with something extraordinarily witty, but then something occurred to me that must have changed my expression so suddenly that Mia said, "What?"

"Oh, good Lord," I said. "I should have thought of this ten minutes ago."

"*What?*"

"Remember when we bought those new iPhones? Remember how much fun we had playing around with them the first few days?"

"Yeah?"

"Remember that feature that allows you to find a lost or stolen phone? We can use my phone to find your phone."

Mia suddenly appeared positively mirthful. "We can track that jackass down."

12

He wasn't far away, or at least Mia's phone wasn't.

We used the Find My iPhone app on my phone, plugged in her password, and the little map quickly told us that her phone was currently located in a little rundown bar in a little rundown strip center off South Lamar. Place was called The Joint. I'd never heard of it, but the name alone sounded like it catered to ex-cons, so I had a pretty good idea what sort of clientele to expect. When we pulled up, it was almost five o'clock, but there were only a couple of cars parked out front. Her phone hadn't budged.

We'd brainstormed on the drive over, and we'd realized this forthcoming encounter represented more than an opportunity to get the phone and car keys back. Maybe we could use it to close this troublesome case. As an added benefit, Mia would then be able to help me with the Boz Gentry case.

So we sat outside in the parking lot for a few more minutes, plotting, until we had a plan that was as finely honed as it was going to get. Maybe it would work, maybe it wouldn't. Either way, at a minimum, we weren't leaving without Mia's phone and car keys.

I went inside first, as a spotter. The place was dark and cool — they definitely didn't skimp on the air conditioning. I was wearing sunglasses, which I removed, and a ball cap, which I left on. To my left was a long bar, with an unsmiling and unshaven bartender behind it and three customers spaced evenly at the stools. They looked at me for five seconds, then went back to their drinks. To my right were a dozen tables sparsely occupied by men. There wasn't a woman in the place.

I didn't bother pretending to be an actual customer by ordering a drink, but instead glanced down at my phone, looking like every other jerk who constantly checks his email in public. In reality, I was still using the phone-locating app. Amazing how accurate it is. It told me that Mia's phone was directly in front of me, toward the tables. I took a few steps forward.

And there he was, sitting in the darkness at the farthest table to the rear. Shane Moyer. I recognized him from photos in the case files. A twenty-four-year-old punk. A fairly large punk, admittedly. But you know what? Size doesn't matter nearly as much as everyone thinks.

The trick is to get the first punch in — and don't hold back. Bring your shoulder around, put your entire torso into it, and drive your fist directly into the center of a man's face. Big or small, most men don't want any more after that. If you're desperate, as in worried-about-getting-killed desperate, or if you're outnumbered, punch to the throat. Hard. Now *that* will take the wind out of anybody's sails, when they suddenly can't breathe. The only drawback is you might actually kill a guy.

As angry as I was with Moyer — as much as I wanted to walk right up, cold-cock him, and then give him a thorough and lasting beating — I had to restrain myself. For now. We had a job to do.

It was nice that we had the element of surprise. He was completely oblivious to the world around him, because he was busy exploring Mia's iPhone. I watched him for a few seconds. He appeared downright giddy. Why not? After all, he had a very expensive gadget to play with. There was a full mug and a half-empty pitcher of beer on the table in front of him.

I waited, still pretending to look down at my phone. Nobody was paying any attention to me. I didn't have to wait long, because we'd agreed that Mia would follow me inside exactly one minute later. I would have preferred to take care of this situation myself, but Mia wanted to take part and I wasn't going to stop her. Hell, I probably *couldn't* stop her.

Right on cue, the door to the bar opened, and here she came. The bartender and the men on the stools looked up, and of course their eyes lingered, but Mia walked right past them.

She joined me, and without a word, we walked to Shane Moyer's table, her on one side, me on the other. He was so transfixed by his new toy that he didn't even notice us until Mia leaned over and yanked the phone from his hand.

"Hey!" Moyer protested, but when he saw who had grabbed the phone, his expression turned to stunned, wide-eyed surprise.

I immediately said, "Wanna go to prison, Shane? You committed felony theft, you worthless turd. This would be your third strike."

Moyer remained seated. We had him boxed into a corner.

"With a record like yours," Mia said, "you're looking at ten years."

Moyer said, "But you —"

"You're a stupid fuck," I said, leaning forward and pointing a finger at him, acting as street as I'm capable of acting. "Your future's in her hands, so you should shut your damn mouth and listen."

"You stole my phone, Shane," Mia said. "That was incredibly stupid. I came *this* close to shooting you."

"You got brain damage?" I asked.

"Or no brains at all?" Mia asked.

"Ever been to the Walls Unit in Huntsville?" I asked.

"You're not big enough to fight off the gangs," Mia said.

I could see it in his eyes already, darting back and forth from me to Mia. Shane Moyer was no tough guy. Just a punk.

"They'll turn you inside out just for fun," I said. What did that even mean?

"They'll love your long hair, but they'll knock your teeth out so you'll give better blowjobs," Mia said, and I had to struggle to keep a straight face.

"Hey, you *gave* that phone to me," Moyer managed to say, trying to show some attitude.

"Oh, shit, really?" I said, laughing. "She *gave* it to you? That's how you're gonna play it? We are two respected professionals in our field. We have sterling reputations. The cops know us. Judges know us. We will testify against your sorry ass. Plus we have a solid witness at your apartment complex. You, on the other hand, are a known scumbag."

Mia said, "The only break you got is that I didn't tell the deputy you stole my stuff. I have a brother like you. Total loser when he was your age, but he managed to get his life together. Maybe you can do the same."

"She's giving you a break, Shane," I said. "Even though I was in favor of kicking your ass."

"*You*," Moyer said. "*You* were gonna kick my ass? That's funny."

"I'm losing my patience," I said. "We need the car keys back. Right now." I stuck my palm out.

"Go to hell."

Shane Moyer might have been intimidated by our threats of prison, but he obviously wasn't too worried about losing a bar fight to a guy twenty pounds lighter than he was. Guys like him rarely are. Plus, I guess he figured he might keep some of his macho façade if he didn't give the car keys back. Which was perfect.

"You want me to take them from you?" I asked.

"I'd like to see you try."

"You're a tough guy, huh?"

"Tough enough."

"Then you wouldn't have any trouble, say, beating me at arm wrestling. Right?"

I held my breath. Would he fall for it? Was he that stupid?

"Not even if you used both hands," Moyer said.

"Seriously?" Mia said, looking at me like I was being as big a jerk as Moyer was — a couple of men in a pissing match. She pulled it off perfectly.

We both ignored her.

I said, "Tell you what. You win, she doesn't press charges. I win, she does press charges. Either way we get the car keys back."

He was looking at me with suspicion.

"Best offer you're ever gonna get," Mia said. "You've been such an asshole today, I should call the cops right now. But if you two studs want to prove how big and bad you are, go for it."

Moyer was still looking skeptical. "After I win, what's to stop you from pressing charges anyway?"

I said, "See, there's this thing called integrity. Most people have it, but the space where your integrity was supposed to go is filled with rat droppings. Either that or you're a scared little pussy."

"Fuck that," he said, as he pushed the pitcher out of the way and brought his right arm up onto the table.

I grabbed a chair and sat down. Then we clasped hands. I'm not sure whose palm was clammier.

"Gotta keep your elbow on the table at all times," I said.

"I've done this before."

I was going to lose. He was a big guy. But the outcome didn't matter — except to my ego, because Mia was watching.

"Ready?" I asked.

He nodded, and our arms immediately went rigid. In less than five seconds, he had my arm halfway to the tabletop. But I held on. And held some more. Thirty seconds passed. His face was contorted with concentration and effort. I guess mine was, too. I could feel sweat breaking out on my forehead.

Then I managed to regain some ground. Our arms were vertical again. He was grunting. My elbow was beginning to ache a little, but overall, I felt pretty good. I was glad I regularly lifted weights three times a week.

We held it like that for another solid minute.

Then he began to let out short little bursts of air. No breath control.

And I began to feel his strength sapping.

"Come on, tough guy," I said.

He didn't reply.

"I think my partner could beat you," I said.

I could feel him summoning one last burst of effort. Veins were popping on his forehead.

And then the resistance completely disappeared and I slammed his hand onto the table.

"God damn," he said, rubbing the deltoid muscle in his upper arm. My bicep was burning, but I ignored it. I stood up again, because I wanted that advantage, in case I needed it.

I stuck my palm out. "Keys."

He grudgingly dug into his pocket and tossed the keys onto the tabletop. I grabbed the key ring and handed it to Mia.

"Here's a little something you should know," I said, pointing toward my hat. "See the little circle in the middle of the logo? That's a video camera."

He closed his eyes momentarily. He'd been suckered. I had the arm wrestling recorded. Evidence that his insurance claim was a scam.

I wouldn't have guessed that he had any fight left in him, but then his eyes popped open and he came out of his chair, making a grab for my hat. I was ready for it, of course. That's exactly why I'd told him about the hat. I *wanted* him to make a grab for it. I deflected his arm with my left hand and then — remember what I said about punching earlier? — I drilled him with a punishing right cross directly to the bridge of the nose. It connected hard.

Moyer fell back into his chair, moaning and clutching his face. Blood began to spill from his hands.

"No fighting in here!" shouted a voice from behind me. Had to be the bartender, but I didn't look.

"That's all on video, too," I said to Moyer. "You just tried to steal my hat. Have you learned nothing about theft today? If you're lucky, I won't report it."

"Take it outside or I call the cops!" It was the bartender again.

Moyer was done, so Mia and I turned and headed for the door. The bartender glared at me, but he didn't say anything more. The three guys on the stools had turned to see the action, but they lowered their eyes as I walked past.

I needed to get somewhere quick and start icing my hand.

13

"Why is it so damn crowded in here?" I asked. "Why aren't all these people at work?"

"It's Saturday, Roy," Mia said.

"Oh. Right."

When I'm working, I tend to lose track of things like that.

It was the following day — nine in the morning. After what Mia had been through with Shane Moyer, and after we'd had the showdown at the bar, I'd suggested we call it a day. Normally we work long hours when we have an active case — because there is plenty of involuntary downtime between cases — but I think we were both ready for an evening off.

The good news was, Heidi had left me a voicemail earlier in the morning saying the attorney for Moyer and his pals had withdrawn their claims. Of course, they'd be lucky if they didn't end up in jail for insurance fraud. That included the doctor who had "diagnosed" all four of them, who might also catch some heat from the state medical board if Heidi complained loudly enough.

Mia and I had decided to meet at La Madeleine in Westlake Hills, on the western outskirts of Austin. We had already placed our orders at the counter, and now we were waiting for our food to arrive. We had a table as far in the back as possible, which gave us the tiniest bit of privacy.

"How's your hand?" Mia asked.

I shrugged. "Forged from the finest steel, just like the rest of me."

"Uh-huh. Really?"

"Well, okay, it aches a little."

She gestured for me to reach my hand across the table, so I did.

"Your other hand, you dope," she said.

So I gave her my right hand, the one I'd punched Shane Moyer with. She took it in both of hers and held it gently.

"Quite a bit of swelling," she said.

"I'll say."

She looked at me and shook her head. "Why are you always so gross? What're you, twelve years old?" Then she looked at my hand again. "Some bruising, too. Have you taken any Advil?"

"Took two last night, two this morning."

"Can you make a fist?"

I did. It hurt.

"Can you straighten all the fingers?"

I did. That hurt, too.

"I don't think anything's broken," Mia said.

It was another one of those oddly intimate moments we have on occasion. She was holding my hand and I liked it. No denying it. I could almost feel an electrical charge flowing between us. I wondered if she felt it, too. I wondered if I was an idiot for never pursuing these feelings. And, yeah, I wondered how our partnership would fare if we became more than partners — assuming she was even interested in me, which was a fairly sizable assumption. I'd never asked her if she was. She'd never said she was. Maybe I'd misread previous signals. Maybe the electricity was flowing only one way. Maybe I should stop with the electricity metaphor. Maybe Mia was holding my hand because she honestly wanted to make sure it wasn't seriously injured. Maybe we —

Mia let my hand go, because a woman wearing a green apron was just now stepping up to our table with our food. I drew my hand back across the table. Like many times before, the moment was gone.

After the server left, Mia said, "Tell me about your trip to the dentist."

I talked as I drizzled some syrup on my French toast. "Shelley, the hygienist there, got an anonymous letter in the mail at home. It said the sender would pay five grand for Boz Gentry's file — but if she told anyone about it, they'd burn her house down while she was sleeping. And they'd know if she contacted the cops, because police reports are part of the public record."

"Is that true?"

"In general, yeah, but in a case like this — with a death threat involved — I'm pretty sure the cops could seal it, or at least redact her name. But she didn't know that, so she was scared. And I guess the money was pretty tempting, too, because she did it. She took the file home and stuck it in her mailbox, as instructed."

"Her mailbox? Really? That's not a very elaborate type of money drop."

"Agreed. Unless there's something we're missing, whoever picked up that file would've been easy pickings if the cops had been waiting. On the other hand, the blackmailer might've paid some kid a hundred bucks to get the file out of the mailbox. That way, if the kid was grabbed by the cops, the extortionist would know Shelley had squealed."

"Did you really just say 'squealed'?" Mia asked.

"It slipped out."

Mia said, "So, let me guess — Shelley never got the money."

"That's what I would have guessed, too, but she did get it. They took the file and left the money, just as they'd said they would."

"Maybe they figured Shelley would be more likely to keep her mouth shut for the long term, because even though she was being extorted, she *did* take money for the file, and that has to be a crime, right?"

"Probably," I said. "And then she used some of the money to put a down payment on a trip to France. Doesn't exactly sound like someone who was an unwilling participant."

I dug into my breakfast. Pretty tasty. I was finding it easier to hold the fork with my left hand.

Mia began to eat, too, but I could see that she had something on her mind.

"What?" I asked.

"Do we need to tell Ruelas about this?"

"This romantic breakfast? Why make him jealous?"

"No, about Shelley and the file."

I sipped some coffee and took a moment to respond. "I don't think so. See, the thing is, there's no way to know who the extortionist was. That ship has sailed. There aren't any phone records. Shelley tossed the original envelope and letter. The money she received was all used twenties, so that's no help. If we told Ruelas, all we'd be doing is getting Shelley in trouble."

"And there's also the fact that you don't like Ruelas," Mia said, "so your judgment in matters like this could be clouded."

"Well, yeah, there's that," I said.

Mia gave me a look I'd seen before. *You sure that's the right decision?*

"Sometimes this is a tricky business," I said, "filled with moral dilemmas and ethical conundrums. We make our way the best we know how."

"You are so full of bullshit."

"In all honesty, I don't feel obligated to tell Ruelas anything. He already knows the file disappeared. If he's not enough of an investigator to interview Shelley, that's his own fault. Besides, my opinion is that he wouldn't learn anything useful from her."

Mia didn't say anything.

"No comment?" I asked.

"You are rationalizing out the wazoo."

"I've found that it's the best orifice from which to rationalize."

She went silent again, but she had something to say, I could tell.

"What's on your mind, Mia?"

She set her fork down. "Okay. Please don't get mad, but there are times when I feel like I have to coerce you into doing the right thing."

"Ouch. You think you have to do that a lot?"

"No, not a lot," Mia said. "Just occasionally."

Truth is, her comment stung a little, but it would have stung more if I'd agreed with her. I ate a few more bites of French toast, then pushed my plate aside.

"I didn't mean to hurt your feelings," Mia said.

"Hey, you didn't, and you gotta be honest," I said. "You think I'm crossing a line, you tell me. Always."

"And you do the same," she said.

"I will. And I'd like to point out that there's a difference between doing the 'right' thing and doing what's legal. Those two concepts don't always overlap perfectly."

"I understand that," Mia said.

"And there are times when we might simply disagree as to what the 'right' thing is."

"I understand that, too."

I said, "Think back to the Tracy Turner case. If I'd done the 'right' thing that night, I would've obeyed that cop and never gone inside that house. Which means I wouldn't have found her. Which means she might not have been found at all."

"Okay. Okay. I didn't mean to open a can of worms."

"Besides, I already told Ruelas about Erin Gentry's late-night trip to Albeck's house. Do we have to tell him everything we learn? Technically, every little scrap of evidence could be useful to him, so shouldn't we just keep him posted on our daily progress?"

"Roy, don't be a smartass."

"Sorry, I really don't mean to be — but what I just said is true. We're basically investigating the same case he is, and we're bound to learn some things he might not know. But we can't tell him everything, because it goes against our own best interests, and also because we'd put ourselves out of business. You see that, right?"

"I do, yes," Mia said.

I said, "On the other hand, if we had information that would unquestionably solve a possible murder, or whatever this case is, then we'd give it to him. Personally, I don't think this stuff about Shelley qualifies — not even close — but we're equal partners, so I'll leave the decision up to you. If you think we need to tell Ruelas about Shelley, give him a call. I won't be upset. Seriously."

She was still working on her quiche Florentine. I drank some more coffee and gazed out the window to the parking lot. It was going to be a beautiful spring day in central Texas.

Mia finished with her breakfast a few minutes later, dabbed her mouth with a napkin, and said, "You are one of the most ethical people I know. I just want to make that clear. I didn't mean to sound judgmental."

"Thanks. But we all have lapses on occasion," I said.

"True," she said.

"Like the time I worked as a gigolo in that women's prison."

"Those poor ladies," Mia said. "Talk about cruel and unusual punishment."

I had to smile. "I walked into that one."

She placed her napkin on the tabletop and said, "Okay, what now? How do we proceed?"

"Honestly, I'm not sure. You got any brilliant ideas?"

"Brilliant? No."

"Any completely uninspired ideas?"

"Oh, sure. But can we get out of here? It's getting too noisy."

14

"We're keeping track of Erin Gentry by way of GPS," Mia said. "We don't need to follow her in person. So I think one or both of us should focus on Alex Albeck. I still say there's a good chance Boz Gentry is hiding out at Albeck's house."

We were sitting in the rear of the Caravan, which was, all in all, a fairly comfortable and practical rolling office. The rear windows were tinted so dark that passersby couldn't see us.

"Ruelas said he didn't think Albeck was involved," I said. "But can we trust what he said?"

"Oh, I think he'd lie in a heartbeat if he thought Gentry was at Albeck's house," Mia said. "Just to keep us out of the picture. Doesn't mean Gentry is actually there, though."

A twentyish woman who had just parked in the space beside us opened her door and dinged the side of the van. I was tempted to rap loudly on my window and give her a scare, but I refrained.

"Ruelas said Albeck was willing to talk until his lawyer stopped it," I said. "And that they couldn't come up with probable cause to get a search warrant for Albeck's house."

"But Albeck is still worth watching," Mia said. "Do you agree?"

"I can't think of anything better to do, so I guess the answer is yes."

That was often how our cases progressed — without any obvious steps to follow next. Instead, you had to just keep picking away, coming at it from any angle that might prove fruitful, until you learned something valuable. Keeping an eye on Albeck seemed like a reasonable angle.

After a few more minutes of discussion, we agreed that Mia would put Albeck under surveillance — but we couldn't figure out the best way for her to do that. Should she try to gain access past the gate into his neighborhood? Then what? She couldn't linger in a high-dollar area like that without being noticed. Which meant a security guard would show up moments later in a little golf cart and ask what she was doing.

Finally Mia said, "We don't have to figure out a plan right now, do we? How about we just agree that I'll investigate Albeck in whatever way I think works best?"

"Sounds good to me."

"What're you going to do?"

"Sit back, eat bonbons, and wait for you to wrap this thing up."

"Hard to beat a good bonbon," she said.

"Actually, I had an idea yesterday, before I talked to Shelley. It involves Albeck, too. I started wondering how many properties he owns."

"Lessons learned from the Tracy Turner case," Mia said.

"Exactly. I have to wonder if Boz Gentry could be hiding out in a house or a condo or some other place that Albeck owns."

"Hmm," Mia said.

"What?"

"Boz Gentry is an outdoorsman, right?" she said. "He likes to hunt and fish and camp and ride dirt bikes."

"Yeah?"

"Okay, so where does he do all those things? Where does he hunt, for instance?"

"I guess a lease somewhere."

"Why not a ranch that one of his friends owns?" Mia asked.

I grinned and started nodding slowly. "Makes sense. Albeck buys ranches and develops them for a living. A guy like him — a country boy with money — I bet he's bought a ranch for himself. Why wouldn't he? He's a hunter. And his best friend would hunt there, too."

"Probably has a house or a cabin on it," Mia said.

"That's smart, Mia. Really smart."

"Thanks," she said. "But it's only smart if Albeck or one of his other friends does actually own a ranch somewhere."

"I'd say the odds are pretty good. Damn, I'm starting to feel like a piece of luggage this morning."

"Luggage?" she said. "What are you talking about?"

"You're carrying me."

It was nice to see her face beam like it did after that remark.

After Mia left, I stayed in the van and got comfortable with my laptop. There were times when it simply didn't pay to drive all the way to my apartment to do online research. I might uncover a key fact in, say, five minutes, and that fact might put me right back on the road again. Besides, my laptop gave me broadband access everywhere I went, so it made sense to surf right there, in the parking lot.

First, I checked my email. Nothing important. Then I checked to see if Erin Gentry's car had traveled anywhere since yesterday morning. It had not. Bit of a surprise, but then again, she was supposed to be in mourning.

Then — because I couldn't resist any longer, even though I knew I should be as patient as possible — I sent Laura a text.

Have you reached any decisions about Hannah's visit?

I sat quietly for a moment, hoping to hear back from Laura right away, but my phone remained silent. Five minutes passed. I had to put it out of my mind and focus on the task at hand.

I opened Facebook — the account for my Linda Peterson alter ego. None of Boz Gentry's friends had accepted my friend request yet. Not unusual. Sometimes that ploy worked and sometimes it didn't.

But that didn't mean checking Facebook was a waste of time. I had learned from my research the day before that Boz Gentry's Facebook privacy settings were loose, and I had spent a few minutes scrolling backward in time on his timeline. But I hadn't gone very far. Now it was time to be more thorough. My objective: Find out where Boz Gentry did his hunting.

I might have been a little slow lately in coming up with specific ideas where Gentry might be hiding, but my research skills were as sharp as ever. After less than eight minutes online, jumping from Facebook to various county government websites, I was on the road, totally jazzed, heading west on Bee Caves Road.

My destination? Blanco County.

15

It turned out Alex Albeck did own a ranch, exactly as Mia had suggested, which I had quickly learned from some of the photos on Boz Gentry's timeline from the previous fall.

They were hunting photos — Boz, Albeck, and some of their other friends, dressed in camouflage. In some of the shots, they were showing off dead trophy deer, in others they were hanging around a campfire, drinking beer, and in others they were posing with rifles or bows, or smiling down from towering deer blinds. The album was labeled "Opening Day at Albie's place," so I was quick to figure out where it had all happened.

Well, I figured out where — meaning I knew it was on a ranch that Albeck owned — but where exactly was that ranch located? I could tell from the rolling hills and the cedar in the photos that it was likely someplace in central Texas — north, south, or west of Austin, but not east, because in that direction lay mostly flat farmland. So I visited the tax rolls of various nearby counties until I hit pay dirt. Took me just a few minutes, because I've done that same type of research hundreds of times.

Albeck's ranch was in the southeastern portion of Blanco County, off Farm Road 165, which runs from Henly to Blanco. The drive was no more than 45 minutes, but I continued on 165, only slowing to identify the gate to Albeck's place, before proceeding toward Blanco, simply because I had no plan whatsoever and needed time to think.

I'd run into this same type of situation in the Tracy Turner case the previous year. The isolation of a possible subject on a large piece of land always made things difficult. In fact, it presented the same hurdle as Albeck's gated neighborhood. How do you approach without being obvious? In this case, the challenge was amplified, because Albeck's ranch was nearly 800 acres, meaning I couldn't even attempt to conduct surveillance from the road.

But there were other strategies. There always were.

In Blanco, I followed Fourth Street to the Blanco Bowling Club, home of half a dozen nine-pin bowling alleys and a pretty decent café. I went inside, found a table, and ordered a cup of coffee and a slice of pecan pie. It was just after eleven o'clock, not yet lunchtime, so the place wasn't very crowded. While I waited, I pulled out my iPhone — more discreet than hauling my laptop inside — and began to check a few things online.

Many of the people who think you can't have a Facebook account and maintain your privacy are the same folks who don't seem concerned by other sites that provide access to your personal information. Take Google Maps, for instance. It doesn't matter if you have a ten-foot privacy fence around your property; anyone can still use the satellite view to get a good look at your backyard and see, for example, whether or not you own a swimming pool. They can get a feel for how many head of cattle a rancher owns. A burglar might use it to determine the best way to approach your house. And so on. Nobody raises much of a ruckus about that — which was fortunate for me, because Google Maps was one of my most powerful tools.

Looking at it right now, I could see that there was only one visible cluster of buildings on Albeck's place, almost dead center in the middle of the ranch. I already knew from the tax rolls what those buildings were: the three-thousand-square-foot house, a detached garage, two utility sheds, and a large pole barn. I saw no indications that Albeck owned any horses, cattle, or any other type of livestock. Excellent. That meant he was less likely to have a ranch foreman or manager who lived on-site.

There was a long, winding caliche road leading from FM 165 to the house. Had to be two miles long. There were other, less worn roads all over the ranch. I figured those led to hunting blinds in various strategic locations around the property. I zoomed in tighter. And tighter still.

A plan was brewing.

I traced one of those lesser caliche roads as it progressed along a fence line, past a water tank, and finally came to a stop. This was where a hunter would park. I studied the area closely. Just clumps of trees scattered among wide-open pastureland. I scrolled to the right, away from the fence. Nothing but more trees. I went farther still, away from the truck. And there it was. The metal roof of a deer blind, tucked in the shadows between two trees, most likely cedars.

Okay, good. If I could find —

"And here you go," the waitress said suddenly, setting a plate down in front of me. I had been so focused on my phone, I'd almost been in a trance.

"Hey, thanks," I said.

"Want me to freshen that up?" she asked, nodding toward my coffee mug.

"Thanks, but I'm good."

She went away, and I went right back to my phone. If I could spot one deer blind on the map, I could find the others. I started near the house, because nothing would be more ideal than a blind that gave me a good view of the house. But no such luck. The closest blind was at least five hundred yards away.

The next-best location would be a blind that provided a view of the main road from the highway to the house. I'd decided that I would stake out the ranch house — maybe even overnight — and I figured I'd be more comfortable in a deer blind than hunkered behind some bushes.

And I caught a break.

There was indeed a blind that appeared to have a great view of the main road — maybe seventy yards away. I wasn't much of a hunter myself, but I knew enough that I could be fairly sure nobody would be using the blind this time of year. Deer season was in the fall. Yes, someone could be out hunting wild hogs, because it was open season all year on those beasts, but I hadn't seen any photos of dead pigs on Gentry's timeline. Plus, I was pretty sure I could ascertain whether or not the blind was occupied before I attempted to climb inside. If the windows were closed, nobody was inside. If the windows were open, I'd be able to see someone moving. Pretty simple.

But my plan still had holes. How would I get to the deer blind? Where would I park the van in the meantime?

While I was pondering those questions, I took a bite of the pecan pie. Wow. Great stuff. Brain food, if I was lucky.

I could leave the van right here in town, parked outside the restaurant. Or move it to the square around the courthouse. That was probably the way to go. It would be fine overnight. That would leave me with a hike of about six or seven miles out to Albeck's ranch, plus another mile onto the ranch, all the while carrying necessary equipment, plus food and drink. I wasn't crazy about making a hike that far, but it wasn't out of the question. At least the temperature was agreeable — in the mid-seventies. In July or August, that sort of trek would be absolutely miserable.

I finished my pie while I tried to come up with a better plan. Hitchhike? Nope. If I got picked up by some local, he or she might wonder what business I had at Albeck's ranch. Call a cab? Yeah, right. No cabs in Blanco. Steal a horse? Around here, that was a hanging offense. Good thing I was wearing comfortable shoes. At three miles an hour, I'd make it to the ranch in about two hours. Not so bad.

A gallon of water weighs a little more than eight pounds. It was tempting to take just one gallon, but I knew I'd regret it, so when I made a stop at a nearby convenience store, I grabbed two gallons of purified drinking water for ninety-nine cents each. Then I grabbed some overpriced beef jerky, a bag of peanuts, and a big can of stew that I could eat tonight at room temperature. No fresh fruit was available, so I picked a can of sliced peaches.

By the time I added those items to the backpack that contained the equipment I'd need to take with me, I figured I'd be toting more than thirty pounds. For two hours. No problem for a Marine, but not as easy for a guy who was somewhat less fit, especially when said guy had an injured hand.

I was starting to question the wisdom of my plan. Then I stumbled into some good luck. When I exited the convenience store, I saw a teenage boy riding around the parking lot on a bike. Not going anywhere, just turning lazy circles. It wasn't a fancy mountain bike or a ten-speed; more like the type of bike you see leaning against a used refrigerator at a garage sale. Rusty. Paint chipping away. Single speed.

I walked toward the kid, carrying my two bulging plastic sacks of provisions.

"Nice bike," I said.

He gave me a look. *You crazy?* "Not really," he said, still circling.

"Want to sell it?" I asked.

He dropped one shoe to the ground and skidded to a stop. Apparently the brakes didn't work.

"How much?" he asked.

Within the first few hundred yards, I knew why the kid had sold so easily for twenty bucks. The bike had a bent pedal crank arm that knocked against the frame with every revolution, and for reasons I couldn't determine, the chain kept popping off the front gear. I had to stop about every quarter-mile on the grassy shoulder to slip the chain back into place. Now my hands were slick with grease, and my injured hand was starting to throb. I had managed to fit one gallon of water into the backpack, but I was having to carry the remaining gallon in the plastic sack, swinging from the handlebar grip.

Despite the balmy temperature, sweat was running down my neck and torso. It was a little unnerving every time a vehicle would zoom past, because the road had no shoulder to speak of. But I was making progress, and it was still better than walking. I figured that if a county deputy should happen to drive past, he or she would be less likely to get curious about a bicyclist than a man walking with a backpack.

I was about halfway to the ranch when I heard the Commodores singing "Brick House" — my alert tone for Mia. I coasted the bike to a stop, lowered the plastic bag to the ground, and pulled my phone from my pocket.

"Lance Armstrong," I said, planning to explain my super-hilarious joke in the moments to follow. But I don't think Mia even heard what I said, or she didn't care.

"Roy? Oh, my God." The connection was poor, but something was plainly wrong. Her voice was frantic.

"Mia?"

I could hear background noise, but she didn't say anything.

"Mia? What's going on?"

"I can't believe this." She was crying, and she also seemed distracted, as if she were driving, or maybe walking.

"Tell me what's happening, Mia! Are you okay?"

"One of my neighbors just called. My house is on fire."

16

She said something after that I couldn't make out. Jesus. Was she *inside* the burning house?

I hopped off the bike and moved away from the road, so I wouldn't have to pay any attention to any passing traffic.

"Mia!"

I heard a scrambled, unintelligible reply.

"Are you in the house right now?" I asked.

I walked upward on a small rise between the road and a barbed-wire fence, and suddenly, like flipping a switch, reception improved.

"— not in the house, Roy," Mia was saying. "I'm on my way over there right now." *Thank God.* "Regina called and told me what was happening. She saw smoke coming from my backyard, so she went over there, and the sunroom was on fire. So she called 9-1-1."

I could picture that cute little attached sunroom, and the rest of the small house, quickly going up in flames. Mia would obviously be heartbroken. She had inherited the house just eight or nine months ago, from a divorced, childless uncle. Prior to that, the house had been owned by Mia's grandparents, and by her grandfather's parents before that. It was in an older part of the city called Tarrytown, and it had been in the family since the 1920s. I had been meaning to ask Mia if the electrical system had ever been updated.

"How bad is it?" I asked.

"I don't know."

"Is the fire department there yet?"

"I don't know."

I didn't know what to say. Obviously, I'd need to turn around and go back to the van, then return to Austin.

"I guess maybe I won't have to worry about the taxes now," Mia said, making a sad joke.

Her house was small and modest, like a lot of the old homes in that neighborhood, but the location — with the lake to the west and downtown to the east — made the land itself worth a small fortune. I could remember sitting on her back deck late last summer, after helping her move in, and toasting her new place with a glass of champagne. She'd been giddy about this new chapter in her life, but she'd also been worried about keeping up with the property taxes.

"I'm heading your way," I said, "but it's going to take me about an hour and a half to get there."

"Where are you?" she asked.

I told her in as few words as possible.

She said, "Roy, there's no point in you coming back."

"I should be there."

"What're you gonna do, put the fire out? No, you keep doing what you're doing. I'll call or text as soon as I know more."

"You sure?"

"Yeah, I'm sure, but thanks. I do have one piece of good news. About five minutes before Regina called, I managed to put a tracker on Albeck's SUV. I staked out the entrance to his neighborhood, and he left about ten minutes after I set up."

"That's lucky." I tried not to sound too excited, considering the circumstances.

"It was. He met one of his partners for brunch in Westlake, then went back home."

A car went past, so I waited for the noise to subside, then I said, "I'm really sorry about your house, Mia. I hope everything's okay."

There was a long pause, then she said, "I can't help wondering what caused it. You think it was arson?"

It was a reasonable question. Shane Moyer and his group of lowlifes immediately sprang to mind. Would Moyer have been so upset about the incident yesterday that he'd do something so drastic? One of his buddies could've gotten Mia's license plate number, and after that, it wouldn't have been difficult to obtain her address. The thought of that possibility made me feel guilty about being so aggressive with Moyer. Maybe if I hadn't punched him in the face...

"Roy, I gotta go," Mia said, before I could answer her question. "Regina's on the other line."

"Keep me posted, okay?"

"I will."

"If you need me for anything at all, call me."

But she had hung up.

I kept riding on FM 165, making slow but steady progress. Ten minutes after Mia called, an old rancher in a truck slowed and asked if I wanted a ride. It was tempting, but I couldn't ask him to drop me at Albeck's gate, could I? So I said thanks, but I needed the exercise. I hit a few hills that were steep enough that I dismounted and walked. The worst part was the damn backpack. My shoulders were beginning to ache. And the plastic bag with the lone gallon of water in it would swing to and fro from the handlebar and occasionally throw the bike off balance. Still, I reached the gate to Alex Albeck's ranch in about an hour.

As I'd been riding, I'd been pondering what I'd do next, and it wasn't that complicated to figure out. Lift the bike over the gate, climb over after it, then ride the remaining mile to the deer blind I'd selected. So that's what I did, and before I could get back on the bike, I heard "Brick House." I quickly checked my phone.

Damage limited to sunroom and adjoining wall leading into house. Very good news. Will call later.

I exhaled with relief. I quickly walked the bike about fifty yards, so I was no longer visible from the road. Then I sent a text:

Do they know the cause?

I waited right where I was until she replied.

Not yet. Will let you know.

The windows of the deer blind were closed. It was obvious nobody was inside. Sixty or seventy yards away was a feeder — a fifty-gallon barrel mounted on three legs — and there were plenty of native grasses and weeds growing directly underneath it. That meant the feeder hadn't been throwing corn for quite some time — probably since the end of the deer season in January.

Perfect.

I shrugged the backpack off my shoulders, and boy did that feel nice. Then I rolled the bike into a cluster of cedar trees and laid it on its side.

I returned to the deer blind and, before I wasted time hauling all my stuff up the ladder, I wanted to make sure the view would be as good as I was hoping it would be. So I climbed up the ladder and, while I was still standing on the second-to-highest rung, I swung the blind door open cautiously. I wasn't worried about people. I was concerned about wasps or rats or raccoons or anything else that might've decided the blind was a nice little place to live.

No signs of life.

I stepped to the highest rung, then ducked inside the blind. It was in good shape, with fairly new indoor/outdoor carpeting that would likely serve as my bed later tonight. There was a lone plastic patio chair shoved into a corner. I unlatched a window and eased it open. Nice. I could see over the tops of all the scrubby cedar trees in the area. If anyone drove in or out of the ranch, I'd be able to see the vehicle easily.

So I went back down the ladder and grabbed my stuff, then climbed up to the blind again and got comfortable in the chair. I unpacked the three key pieces of gear: binoculars, a Canon superzoom camera, and my night-vision goggles. I opened one of the gallons of water and guzzled at least a quart of it. Then I opened the bag of peanuts and had a snack.

It was twenty minutes until two. I was fully aware that I might sit here until tomorrow morning and see nothing at all. That wouldn't be unlike the hundreds of other times I'd conducted stakeouts that were a total waste of time. You had to keep a positive attitude. Instead of thinking of it as a waste of time, you had to think of it as one less place where your subject might be hiding.

Another text arrived from Mia. She'd sent a photo of the rear of her house. Half of the sunroom was a charred skeleton, and the door from the sunroom into the house appeared to be scorched, but other than that, it didn't look too bad. The house itself was undamaged. There were a couple of firefighters milling around, but it appeared that their work was done.

She'd added a message.

After Regina called 9-1-1, she went after the fire with a hose. She saved my house.

I had never met Regina, but I made a mental note to send her a dozen roses and a bottle of champagne.

I was writing a reply when Mia sent another note.

Still don't know the cause.

She'd answered my question, so I wrote a different note.

So glad it wasn't worse. Call me when you get a chance.

I spent the next few hours stewing, getting angrier, and feeling more guilty. Last year, when I'd asked Mia to be my partner, I'd warned her of the risks. Sometimes a subject doesn't like being put under surveillance, for obvious reasons. Sometimes they make threats, or they actually take action. If I had to lay money on it, I'd say this was one of those cases.

Now I was wondering if I'd stressed the dangers as much as I should have. For instance, I should have insisted that Mia have surveillance cameras inside and outside her house. Might not have stopped an arsonist wearing a mask or operating under cover of darkness, but we'd never know.

I should have encouraged her to take a self-defense class, as she was now planning to do of her own accord. Maybe I should have even suggested that she put dummy plates on her vehicle when tailing a subject. Illegal as hell, but who gives a damn?

I sat for another hour and tried not to think about Mia and her damaged house. At one point, a white-tailed doe with a swollen, pregnant belly emerged from the cedars, walked to the feeder, nosed around in the dirt for a minute, then continued on her way.

Maybe I was just restless because of Mia's situation, but this stake-out was starting to feel like a goose chase. What were the odds that Boz Gentry was hiding in the ranch house? This was a total waste of time, wasn't it? I should be with Mia, helping her deal with her burned house. Surely I could help somehow. I had nearly convinced myself to climb down when she called.

"Okay," she said, "the firemen just left, but there's still a couple of investigators here."

"And?"

"They took samples of the burned wood and some of the remaining siding from the sunroom, and they even took some soil samples. They're going to run some tests to see if there was an accelerant, but one of the guys already told me, off the record, that it was arson. He said he could tell from the origin and the burn pattern — that it looked like an amateur job, that whoever did it didn't know what they were doing. Apparently they threw a small amount of gas onto the wall of the sunroom and lit it. You can smell it."

"The gas?"

"Yeah."

"Son of a bitch," I said.

There had been a nice breeze through the windows of the deer blind all afternoon, but now I was starting to feel hot.

"Shane Moyer or one of those assholes," I said.

"We don't know that."

"Had to be," I said.

"We can't assume that, Roy."

I wanted to argue, but she was right. I needed to refrain from jumping to conclusions.

I said, "Did any of your neighbors see anybody coming or going?"

"Lucian — the guy across the street — said he saw a jogger a few minutes beforehand," Mia said. "Nobody else saw anything."

"Broad daylight on a weekend. That's pretty ballsy."

"Yeah."

"Was there damage inside the house?" I asked.

"You saw the door from the sunroom into the house?" she asked.

"Yeah."

"There's a guy who helped me with some repairs last year, and he's going to help me install a new door, when I'm ready. Other than that, there's a little bit of wet carpet, but that's not a huge deal. Regina had the fire out before the fire department even got here. I love that woman. Oh, I should mention that the place stinks like you wouldn't believe from the smoke. They let me in for a minute and I just about gagged. I have a call in to a company that's supposed to help get rid of the smell. Insurance will cover it, and the repairs."

"After your deductible," I said.

"Yeah, but it's only five hundred bucks," Mia said, "which isn't too bad. So I'll see what that guy says, but I can't do anything until they let me back in there. Right now, it's a crime scene."

"For how long?" I asked. I knew from previous cases involving insurance fraud that her answer wasn't going to be good news.

Mia let out a sigh. "Until the lab tests come back, which will be several days, at a minimum. Could be a week or two."

"Will they let you grab some things? Some clothes?"

"Not yet. Don't know if they will. Pretty sure they aren't supposed to, but we'll see."

"What are the investigators' names?"

She told me, but I didn't recognize them. Nobody I had dealt with before.

"I'm sorry this is such a hassle," I said.

"Thanks. Could've been a lot worse. I guess I'll grab a room at a hotel tonight."

"Don't do that," I said. "Stay at my apartment. I won't be there, but you have a key."

"You sure?"

"Of course. Use my spare bedroom. If you want to."

"There won't be, like, any wayward women hanging around?"

"Just the one," I said.

"Meaning me." She laughed, and that was nice to hear.

"Right."

"I might take you up on it," she said.

"Please do. Believe it or not, the place is reasonably clean, and there's plenty of food in —"

And I stopped talking, because I suddenly saw something totally unexpected. Movement. A person was walking along the caliche driveway. Coming from the direction of the gated entrance. A woman. I'd been expecting a vehicle, if anything, not a person on foot.

"Roy?" Mia said.

"Hang on." I said it quietly, even though the woman was at least eighty yards away. I'd have to shout to draw her attention.

"What's going on?" Mia asked.

I was trying to grab the binoculars while keeping the phone to my ear. "I see a woman," I said.

"Where?"

I told her.

"Sure it's a woman?"

"I guess it could be a man who likes wearing skirts."

I lifted the binoculars to my eyes, but everything was blurry.

"Do you recognize her?" Mia asked.

"Hold on a sec. I need to set the phone down."

I did, and now I could bring the field of view into focus, with crystal-clear ten-power magnification.

I zeroed in on the woman — and, yes, I did recognize her. It took me a moment to place who she was, because she was so out of context in this environment — but then I had it, and I felt a rush. I watched her for a full half-minute, just to be sure I wasn't mistaken. She was moving from left to right, and I had plenty of time to make a positive ID. Then I grabbed my Canon superzoom camera and quickly snapped a dozen shots. A moment later, the woman disappeared from view behind some trees.

I set the camera down and picked up the phone again.

"Well, that just blew my mind," I said.

"Who was it?"

"Her name is Candice Klein. She's Tyler Lutz's receptionist."

17

At ten the next morning, I was seated, by coincidence, at the same table in Trudy's Four Star that Mia and I had occupied three days earlier. Of course, Tyler Lutz turned far fewer heads walking through the open dining area than Mia had.

"Morning," he said, shaking my hand, which was aching more now than it had been yesterday. My bike ride had aggravated it. "Good to see you again." He was wearing crisp khaki pants, a dark-blue polo shirt, and black loafers.

By comparison, I was feeling like a slob, since I hadn't had a chance to shave or shower. I'd called Lutz an hour earlier, after riding the bicycle back to Blanco, hoping he'd be available sometime today. He'd suggested brunch, and I'd taken him up on it. Fortunately, I keep some moist towelettes, deodorant, and a spare set of clothes in the van, so I wasn't totally objectionable.

"Thanks for meeting me on short notice," I said.

"Oh, sure, no problem. Ready to talk about disability insurance? Just kidding. I'm glad you called. Any excuse to skip church."

"I hear that. I've been skipping every Sunday for about thirty-seven years now."

He smiled. "Let me guess. You're thirty-seven years old?"

"You got it," I said.

"Well, I usually feel like I should go, but it doesn't always work out that way, and then I feel guilty."

"About what?"

It appeared that he needed to ponder that for a few seconds. "I guess I feel like I need to maintain my relationship with God. It kind of keeps me centered, you know? Makes me a better person. I mean, for instance, if you don't go to church, where do you get your morals?"

"I buy mine online. I usually get free shipping."

His grin widened. "Maybe I should try that instead. What're you having?" He had picked up a menu and was now scanning it.

"Think I'm going with the *chilaquiles*," I said.

"Oh, nice. That sounds good." He set the menu down. "So what's up?"

The young waitress who'd brought my tea five minutes earlier appeared and took our orders. After she left, I said, "You mind a few more questions about Boz Gentry?"

"Not at all. I assume you haven't tracked him down yet, because that would be all over the news."

"Nope, no luck so far."

"Okay, well, fire away."

I wasn't sure how to play this, but as always, I was going to reveal as little as possible. On the other hand, I did need to figure out the connection between Lutz's receptionist and Boz Gentry — or perhaps her connection to Alex Albeck, since I'd seen her on his ranch — and I knew I might have to lay all my cards on the table to figure out that connection.

Fifty minutes after Candice had walked past the deer blind yesterday afternoon, she'd walked past again in the opposite direction. That told me she'd gone to the house, spent about ten minutes looking around, then given up and left. She hadn't found anything. Neither had I, when, after sundown, I'd climbed down from the deer blind and done some exploring. I took my night-vision goggles along, but I didn't really need them. There was plenty of moonlight. When I arrived at the ranch house, there was no sign of life whatsoever. No light from any windows. The place was locked down tight. I even checked the electric meter and it was not showing any usage at all.

I returned to the deer blind and hung around the rest of the night, but I didn't learn anything new. I was able to log on to the account Mia and I shared for the GPS tracking units, but neither Albeck nor Erin Gentry went anywhere on Saturday afternoon or evening.

I did discover that you never want to spend the night in a deer blind. Try sleeping in a space that is four foot square. You can't stretch out. And mosquitoes drive you nuts that time of year. Mostly I dozed in the chair, and when I was awake, nobody else showed up. Didn't matter. Seeing Candice had made the stakeout well worth it. Maybe. Now I just needed to figure out what it meant.

"Can we talk confidentially again?" I asked Lutz.

"Absolutely."

I contemplated the best way to approach the topic so that I might not tip my hand. "I'm kind of at a dead end right now," I said. "When that happens, I generally just keep asking questions — shooting in the dark — to see if I can learn anything new. One thing that occurred to me…I know you and Boz weren't exactly friends, but did you ever get the feeling that he might be stepping out on his wife?"

"Cheating on Erin?"

"Yeah," I said.

"Is that what he was doing?"

"No, I'm not saying he was, and I don't want to start any rumors. I'm just asking if he seemed like the type."

The waitress dropped off our plates of food, refilled our iced tea, then left us alone again.

Tyler Lutz picked up his fork, but he held it for a moment, staring into space, thinking. Finally he said, "Well, if he was, I wouldn't know anything about it. We just didn't have that kind of friendship. Sorry."

"What if you had to guess?" I asked.

"I wouldn't be comfortable doing that. Have you talked to the people on that list I gave you? His friends? They'd know better than I would."

"I've talked to a lot of people," I said, skirting the question, "but I'm not sure they've been totally honest with me. People are usually reluctant to make their friends look bad, which is understandable."

Of course, I'd been tempted to speak to all of Boz Gentry's friends, but if one of them was hiding Gentry, I might scare him away from the area for good. It was possible that I'd talk to them all eventually, when I'd run out of better options, but I hadn't yet decided that was worth the risk. Plus there was the distinct probability that Ruelas had already spoken to them, and while I didn't think much of him personally, he was a good enough investigator to ferret out any involvement on Gentry's friends' part.

"I don't really like to gossip..." Lutz said, but I got the sense that he wouldn't mind doing exactly that if he thought other people were doing it too. Maybe he thought that was why I was asking about any potential affairs on Gentry's part — that I'd already heard it from others.

I said, "I can understand that. It's one of the things I like least about my job." I said it as if it were all very distasteful, the way I had to dig into people's personal lives. "But it's something I have to do sometimes to help my clients either approve or reject a claim. Like you said, it isn't really fair to leave Erin hanging. If Boz *is* dead, she deserves the money coming her way."

Lutz said, "What have Boz's friends said about him?"

I pretended to be reluctant. "Well, to be blunt, it sounds like he was sort of a player, but I could be wrong. What's your take on that?"

Lutz said, "I'd have to say that's probably accurate."

"Yeah?"

He picked at his food, but didn't eat. "Have you ever been around a guy who is constantly checking out every woman in the room? It's like he thinks that's what he's expected to do, because he's a man. Showing how macho he is, maybe making comments."

"What kind of comments?" I asked.

Lutz shrugged. "It's one thing to tell a woman she looks pretty today, or maybe even do some flirting, but I'm talking about when a woman passes by, and a guy says something crass to his friends, like, 'Did you see the rack on her?' That kind of thing."

"Not speaking *to* her, but *about* her."

"Right."

"I hate that kind of crap," I said.

"I know, right? And maybe it's not fair for me to jump to conclusions, but I figure a married man who behaves like that would probably follow through if he had a chance." Lutz shook his head. "If we all still thought he was dead, I probably wouldn't be saying any of this. Doesn't seem right to be bad-mouthing a dead man, especially a client."

"But he's probably not dead," I pointed out.

"Right."

"And it appears he's attempting to commit fraud."

"Yeah."

"So we can totally trash him," I said, grinning, because I wanted Lutz to keep talking.

He laughed and dug into his food without saying anything more. It was obvious he wasn't completely comfortable with the topic. It had occurred to me that if Candice and Boz had something going, and Lutz knew about it, he might be reluctant to spill the beans. That sort of thing would make his agency look bad.

I ate a few bites, then said, "When you'd hear Boz make comments like that, where would you be?" I asked.

"Where?"

"Yeah. Home Depot? The grocery store? Church?"

"No, more like if I'd see him out somewhere having a beer, and especially if he was there with a couple of his buddies. You know how men act when they're in a group."

"A testosterone festival."

"Exactly. Then you add alcohol and they become jerks."

I dropped the next question as casually as possible. "What about in a more professional environment? Like, would he ever say anything about your receptionist?"

That seemed to catch Lutz by surprise. "What, Candice?"

"Yeah."

"Why would you ask about her?"

I was watching him closely. He seemed genuinely puzzled.

I said, "It was just a random example. I figured if Boz was the type to make comments about women, maybe he said something to you about her. Or would he only make remarks like that to his close friends?"

"I don't remember him ever saying anything about Candice. You're right, I guess it's a little different when you're in an office instead of a bar. Plus he probably figured I wouldn't respond well to any of his comments, which I wouldn't have."

A disappointing answer. I'd been hoping Lutz would say something like, "Oh, I could always tell Boz had a thing for Candice." But he obviously had nothing more to share. I wondered if I should tell him where I'd seen Candice the previous afternoon. I decided against it.

18

Four hours later — after a shower and a two-hour nap at my apartment, followed by a couple of phone calls that got me nothing but voicemail — I walked up the cobblestone sidewalk toward one of the most meticulously maintained homes I'd ever seen.

The place was postcard-perfect in every detail, from the lush green lawn and the immaculate flowerbeds to the green shuttered windows and the gabled front porch. The house appeared to be as old as Mia's, and not much larger, but it had obviously received loving care throughout its history. That, or someone had sunk a lot of money into a total restoration.

I rang the bell and a dog immediately began to bark. Okay, "bark" might not have been the right word. "Yap" was probably more accurate.

I waited. The dog continued to yap.

I rang again, and after about thirty seconds, the dog went quiet, then the door swung open to reveal a slender blond man in his forties, wearing a T-shirt and some sort of silk lounging pants or pajamas. He appeared every bit as well groomed and maintained as the house, and so did the fluffy white dog that was now in the man's arms.

"Yes?"

"Are you Lucian?"

"I am."

"Sorry to bother you this morning, but my name is Roy Ballard. I'm Mia's partner."

"Oh, right."

"And when I say 'partner,' I mean that she does most of the work and I watch."

Lucian grinned. "How is she?" He glanced past me, over my shoulder, toward Mia's house, which was across the street and down one door. The house had been staked off with yellow crime-scene tape.

"Doing fine, considering. She's out shopping for a new door right now." I hadn't seen her at my apartment, but we'd exchanged a few texts. I'd told her to take as much time as she needed to get her life back in order.

"So upsetting, what happened," Lucian said. "Do they know any more about what caused it?"

Mia had said the fire investigator's conclusion of arson was off the record, for the time being, so I said, "They're running some tests."

"But they're thinking arson, right?"

"It's a possibility."

The dog had been staring at me suspiciously — and silently — but now it let out a single yap.

"Gwendolyn!" Lucian said, shushing the dog.

Gwendolyn?

"What kind of dog is that?" I asked.

"Cavapoo. A cross between a Cavalier King Charles Spaniel and a poodle."

"Interesting," I said. "I think I've seen them in the wild."

"Ha. This little girl would last about two seconds on her own. She eats better food than I do. Don't you, Gwendolyn?"

She continued to scowl.

"Listen, Lucian, I understand you saw a jogger shortly before the fire started."

"I did, yes. You want to come inside and have a cup of coffee?"

"I don't want to be any bother," I said.

"Nonsense. Come on in. We can talk."

"I didn't really think much of it," Lucian said, "because we have joggers in this area all the time. Joggers, walkers, bicyclists. But after the commotion, I realized I had seen this guy just moments before the fire started."

The inside of the home was as immaculate as the outside. Hardwood floors. Crown moulding. Vibrant abstract paintings on the walls. I was seated on a black leather couch. Lucian was seated on the matching chair. Gwendolyn was sleeping on a dog pillow that looked more comfortable, and more expensive, than my bed. She was snoring loud enough that we both had to speak up.

"Which side of the street was he jogging on?" I asked. I had turned down the coffee.

"The far side. Mia's side."

"Going which direction?"

"Uh, heading away from me." He pointed. "Up the street."

"So west?" I said.

"If you say so," Lucian said. "Well, yeah, I guess it is west, because that's where the sun sets."

"Can you describe him?"

"Yes, but it's going to sound very generic. Average height and weight. Just another jogger."

"Color of hair?"

"I'd guess dark blond or light brown, but he was wearing a baseball cap, so I don't really know for sure."

"Could it have been dark brown or black?" I said, to see how confident he was in what he'd seen.

"It could have been, yeah," Lucian said.

Crud.

"How old was he?"

"Sorry, no idea," Lucian said. "He was too far away. He moved like a fairly young man, but that doesn't mean he was."

"Clothes?" I asked.

"Blue shorts and a white T-shirt," Lucian said. "Positive about that."

"Was there anything memorable about him at all? Was he juggling chainsaws or missing a leg?"

Lucian appeared reasonably amused. "The only thing memorable — and I don't know if it actually qualifies — is that he was carrying a water bottle, like one of those squirt bottles that bicyclists use. Do joggers usually carry water bottles when they run?"

"I'm not sure," I said.

"You don't jog?"

"I don't carry water bottles."

Lucian smiled and said something, but the dog snored with such force, I couldn't make it out. Lucian said, "Gwendolyn," rousing her enough that the snoring stopped. "She has a deviated septum. Can you believe I'm considering spending a thousand dollars to get it fixed?"

"I have a Dremel you can use," I said.

"What's that?"

I shook my head. "Never mind. Bad joke. So did this jogger appear interested in Mia's house? Did he slow down as he went past?"

"Honestly, I'm not even sure he did go past, as opposed to going into Mia's backyard. I was outside, grabbing the newspaper, and I saw him, just for a moment. Then I turned and came back inside. It couldn't have been more than three or four minutes later when I heard Regina yelling. She's right next door. She was yelling for someone to call 9-1-1."

"And did you come outside then?" I was starting to sound like an attorney questioning a witness on the stand.

"I did, and at first I didn't see or hear anything, but then I saw the smoke rising up from behind Mia's house. I went over there, and Regina was already hosing it down. There was only the one hose, so I ran back over here to grab a fire extinguisher. But by the time I got back, Regina had it under control."

"Any sign of the jogger when you came outside the second time, after Regina started yelling?"

"Nope."

"Anyone else hanging around?" I asked.

"At first, no, but eventually some other neighbors started coming out of their houses, especially after the fire trucks showed up. A crowd gathered in front of Regina's house."

"You recognized everybody?" I asked.

"I did, yes."

"Did any of your neighbors mention seeing the jogger, or any other stranger hanging around?"

"I'm afraid not."

Gwendolyn started snoring again.

I was running out of questions. The description Lucian had given me could have matched either Shane Moyer or Jens Buerger. Or maybe twenty thousand other youngish men in the city.

I said, "Does everyone on the street get along okay? Any feuds or arguments?"

Lucian didn't react to the implications of those questions, but that was probably because the cops had already asked the same thing. "No problems at all, as far as I know. Everybody gets along great."

I sat for a moment, thinking. Lucian waited patiently. I said, "If I think of more questions later, can I call you?"

"Absolutely."

I was starting to feel guilty. I was investigating the arson when I should have been concentrating on locating Boz Gentry. Mia would be pissed, because she wouldn't want her personal troubles to hinder our latest investigation, and I could understand that.

On the other hand, screw it.

If you drive west from Mia's house — as I did now — after three blocks, her street dead-ends at Lake Austin Boulevard, which, as the name implies, runs along the edge of the lake. Now I was directly across from a small park with a boat ramp. I turned left, then turned left again, to enter a large parking area for the waterfront restaurants across the street. One was a popular place called the Hula Hut, always hopping with tourists, frat boys, hipsters, and enough young, attractive women that crass types sometimes called it "the Butt Hut."

I found a spot and parked. Here in this lot — this was my guess as to where the arsonist had left his vehicle. He'd be a lot less noticeable here than parking along a curb in the adjoining neighborhood itself. Easier to blend right in with the crowds. Even right now, well after lunch and hours before dinner, there were lots of customers making their way from the parking lot to the restaurants.

I'd been here plenty of times myself, but now I was looking at the area from a different perspective, and with particular questions in mind. If I were the arsonist, what would I do with the container that had carried the gasoline? Toss it or take it with me? On the one hand, I'd be tempted to carry it away from the scene, so that it wouldn't be found later. But I'd also be paranoid. What if I got pulled over with the container in my vehicle?

I strolled around the parking lot, searching for a discarded water bottle — like the squirt bottles that bicyclists use. Couldn't find one. Then I even poked around in a few garbage cans, prompting one passing group of sorority girls to make various sounds of disgust. They thought I was an indigent, and it made me consider my clothing choices. I called out that I'd found half a burrito and I was willing to share. No takers.

At one point, my phone rang, but caller I.D. didn't reveal who it was, so I didn't answer. The caller didn't leave a voicemail. Probably a wrong number.

I left the parking lot and began walking back toward Mia's house, studying each home closely as I went. Most of the homes were fairly small and not ostentatious, but the location alone jacked up the appraised value. All in all, it was a nice, quiet neighborhood, with a different type of class than, say, Alex Albeck's gated community.

I was less than a block from Mia's house when I finally spotted what I was looking for. A small limestone home on the south side had a security camera mounted on the garage, and it was aimed straight out the driveway toward the street. If it was a real camera, not a dummy, and if the homeowner actually had it turned on, then there was a chance the jogger had been recorded as he passed by. If he hadn't turned at the intersection between here and Mia's house. Okay, that was a lot of ifs, but it was worth checking.

I knocked. Nobody answered. Knocked again. No luck. I left a brief note — one that might've accidentally given the recipient the impression that I was an investigator with the city — saying I would be grateful if they would give me a call.

19

I bought a six-pack of longnecks on the way back to my apartment. It still felt somewhat odd to walk into any establishment and purchase alcohol. After all, my probation had ended less than six weeks ago. My second term of probation, to be specific.

I'd had some legal troubles a few years ago and I was lucky that I hadn't served any time.

It had started when I was still working as a news cameraman. My boss was a colossal dickhead, and I occasionally have a short fuse, and those two factors proved volatile one afternoon when he called a female reporter a cunt. I hate that word. Always have. So much misogyny and sexism crammed into four little letters. So I broke the weasel's nose with a microphone stand. I'm not going to lie — it felt great. Getting arrested didn't. Neither did getting fired. I received probation on a plea deal because the boss didn't want his rich history as a minor-league sexual harasser to be brought up during a trial.

Fine by me.

It turned out for the best, because unemployment forced me to be creative in my career choices. I branched out in a new direction. Legal videography. Self-employed, of course. Who needs another boss?

I cruised through that probation period with no problems, but not long afterward, I got pulled over for suspicion of drunken driving. Fortunately, the Breathalyzer showed that I was under the legal limit. But the cops found some pills in my van — pills that I had been taking on a few occasions to stay awake during late-night stakeouts.

How dumb is that?

Probation was longer this time, but once again, I sailed right through. Now I was free and clear. I could drink a cold beer or three when I was so inclined, and there were times when I did just that. But I was also pleased to find that I didn't crave it as much as I used to. Drinking beer wasn't as much of a habit or a routine as it had been before.

I walked through the door of my apartment, and a few seconds later Mia stepped out from the spare bedroom. She was holding her cell phone, as if she'd just completed a call, and she had an expression on her face that I didn't quite know how to interpret. Amusement? Bafflement? Confusion?

I stopped in the doorway, key still in hand. I wasn't ready for more bad news.

"Everything okay?" I asked.

"Yeah..."

"What's going on?" I asked, closing the door behind me.

"You'll never guess who just called me."

"Uh, Mickey Thomas, my old friend from Cub Scouts? That would be weird, because I haven't seen him in 25 years, and you don't even know —"

"It was Laura."

I frowned. "Laura?"

"Your ex-wife?"

"No, I know — but why did she call *you*?"

"She wanted — I think she was trying to get a third-party opinion on whether it was a good idea to go through with Hannah's visit. Like, reassurance that everything would be okay. Remember, it's been a lot of years since she last saw you. She doesn't know what you're like now. I can understand her apprehension, to be honest."

I guess I could, too. I took this to be a good sign.

I said, "So you told her…?"

"That you were a meth addict who frequented underage prostitutes. You big dork. What do you think I told her?"

I pulled a bottle of beer out of the carton, twisted the cap, and handed it to her. "That I am perhaps the finest man you've ever known?"

She took a drink, keeping her eyes on me the entire time. Was it my imagination, or was she a little flushed in the face? Was that because I'd guessed what she'd actually told Laura?

She lowered the bottle and said, "Yeah, Roy, that's exactly what I said. Then I pointed out that the only thing that eclipses your integrity is your rugged good looks."

"Which is odd," I said, playing along, "because even though I am sort of a Tom Selleck, Matt Damon, and George Clooney all rolled into one, why would that even matter in this situation? Why would my stunningly handsome appearance factor in?"

"Well, you know how women get when they're around you."

"I do."

"We can't think straight. We might start out talking about your rock-solid character and your finely tuned moral compass —"

"And how humble I am," I added.

"Exactly. But pretty soon we're giggling like pre-teens and raving about how dreamy you are. We can't help it."

"It can be quite embarrassing," I said.

"No doubt," Mia said.

It was a nice moment, this teasing back and forth. When Laura and I were married, we never had moments like this.

I opened a bottle of beer for myself, and Mia said, "Is your hand still bothering you?"

"A little."

"You just winced when you opened that beer," she said. "You need to ice it."

"The beer? Good idea."

She rolled her eyes. "Why do I bother?"

"What did you really tell Laura?" I said.

"Seriously? You want me to recount my glowing description of you word for word?"

"No need for that," I said. "A brief written synopsis will suffice. Or even a list of bullet points."

She shook her head. "Maybe I should call her back and revise my opinion."

Take one step forward, I was thinking. *Put your arms around her. Kiss her. See how she responds.*

But I couldn't do it. Amazing how gutless I can be. What's the worst that could happen? That I would be wrong about how she felt?

"Roy?"

"Yeah?"

"You okay? This funny look suddenly came over your face."

"No, I'm fine, sorry. I was just thinking about Hannah. I really want to see her."

It was Mia who took the step forward. She placed her left hand on my right arm, patting it. A consoling gesture.

"This is only a guess," she said, "but I'm pretty sure Laura is planning to go ahead with it. Based on some things she said."

"Yeah?"

"I think so."

"Well, I really appreciate you talking to her."

There was a moment of silence, with Mia standing so close I swear I could feel the heat coming off her body.

Do it. Kiss her.

My phone came alive with the opening bars of "Taking Care of Business" by Bachman-Turner Overdrive. My ring tone for Heidi. Maybe I was mistaken, but it appeared Mia was disappointed by the interruption. I know I was. But I had to answer. If Heidi was calling late on a Sunday afternoon, there was probably a good reason for it.

"Hey, there," I said.

"I'm not one to resort to clichés, but are you sitting down right now?" Heidi asked.

"No, I am currently in the downward dog position," I said.

"I just got a call from one of my bosses, who got a call from the Hays County sheriff."

"What's up?"

"Boz Gentry's insurance agent, Tyler Lutz? He was found dead a few hours ago."

20

Mia drove her Mustang while I sat in the passenger seat, surfing the web, trying to learn more. I also had my iPhone scanner app tuned to the Hays County Sheriff's Office, but I doubted we'd get any new details there, because the cops were usually tight-lipped over the airways.

Heidi had had very little information to share, beyond the fact that Tyler Lutz was dead.

"How'd he die?" I'd asked.

"Don't know."

"An accident?"

"Don't know."

"Where'd it happen?"

"That I do know. His house."

So Mia and I were heading over there, with the hopes that we could hang around on the periphery and maybe ask a few pertinent questions of the investigators. Not Ruelas, because this wasn't his county, but I knew a handful of Hays County cops, and with luck, one of them would have caught this case.

"The *Statesman* is saying 'Man found dead outside Dripping Springs home,'" I said. "He hasn't been officially identified. 'Police have not determined the cause of death, but homicide detectives are classifying it as suspicious.'"

Mia kept driving.

"Same with KXAN and KVUE," I said. "Nobody knows anything yet."

"Can't be a coincidence that Lutz is dead," Mia said. "Has to be tied in with the Boz Gentry case."

"Agreed."

We stopped at a red light in Oak Hill. There was plenty of traffic, even on a Sunday evening. The sun wouldn't set for another two hours.

"If Boz Gentry is alive, as we suspect..." Mia said, and she left that thought hanging in the air.

"And if Boz and Lutz were working together on the fraud — except it wasn't working out right, and so Boz got pissed...Or maybe Boz decided he needed to get rid of the one person who can finger him. Is that where you were headed?"

Mia said, "No, actually, I was thinking maybe Boz got mad that Erin hadn't received the money yet, so he took it out on Lutz — but I like your angle better."

Mia stayed left at the Y, following U.S. Highway 290 west toward Dripping Springs.

"Those are all good hypotheses," I said. "I can imagine a scenario where Boz Gentry comes up with this hare-brained idea to fake his own death — with or without Lutz's help — but then the cops don't buy it. So now he's really screwed, because Erin doesn't get the money, and he can't return to his normal life without getting arrested. And it's hard to start over somewhere else without any money."

"Think Erin knew what he was planning?" Mia asked.

"Good question."

Mia said, "Boz had to know the cops would interrogate the hell out of her, so he'd almost be doing her a favor if he didn't let her in on it until after the money was in the bank. That way she wouldn't be pretending to be a grieving widow, because her reactions would be genuine."

"Cruel, though, making your wife think you're dead," I said.

Mia laughed. "Depends on what type of husband he was, now doesn't it? She might've been thrilled that he was dead and that three million was coming her way. If and when he reappeared, she might've been disappointed."

"Good point," I said. "So what we've decided is that Boz might've worked alone, he might've worked with Lutz, he might've worked with Erin, or all three of them might've worked together."

"Don't forget Albeck," Mia said.

"Depressing. We haven't really made any progress at all. One thing we do know," I said, looking at my laptop, "is that Albeck's SUV hasn't gone anywhere today, and neither has Erin's car. For what that's worth."

We had finally made it through the congestion of Oak Hill, onto open highway, and Mia kept the Mustang at a steady 65. I loved the rumble of that car's big engine.

I said, "I talked to Lucian earlier this afternoon."

Mia glanced over at me. She was giving me a look like a schoolteacher who was disappointed in a pupil's misbehavior — but she wasn't outright angry. "I appreciate your concern," she said, "but you need to focus on this case, not my personal troubles."

I didn't reply. We drove another mile in silence.

"But you might as well tell me if you learned anything," she said.

"I learned that Lucian has impeccable design sense and a dog that snores louder than I do. Other than that, not much."

We had the windows down and the air was crisp and cool.

"You know what else just occurred to me?" I pulled out my phone.

"What?" Mia said.

I looked at the list of incoming calls and found the one from earlier, when I'd been searching the parking lot near Hula Hut.

"Know any numbers with a 393 prefix?" I asked. "That's San Marcos, right?"

"I think so."

San Marcos — the Hays County seat. I Googled the incoming number. My hunch was right. The first hit listed was a link to the sheriff's office.

"They're going to want to talk to me," I said, "because I had brunch with Lutz earlier today. I called him this morning. They're probably calling everyone who comes up on his phone."

"Ooooh," Mia said. "You are so busted. You killed him, didn't you?"

"Please don't tell anyone." I pointed. "You'll need to turn right in about a hundred yards."

There were half a dozen county vehicles — some marked, some unmarked — outside Lutz's home, along with several news vans. We parked beside a curb forty yards away and walked toward the house. Crime-scene tape had already been stretched across the driveway and along the front of the property. Two uniformed cops were stationed at the foot of the driveway, keeping people off the premises.

I saw news teams from three different stations either shooting B-roll footage or simply waiting for something to happen. They had probably delivered live reports for the six o'clock newscast, and they might hang around to give an update for the ten o'clock newscast. One of the teams was from the station I used to work for. I recognized the cameraman who had replaced me, but we hadn't ever met.

As was the case with any crime scene I have ever visited, there was a cluster of neighbors lingering in a yard across the street. The majority of them were in their forties or fifties. Most of them would stay right there and watch until the last cop had left the premises. It's just human nature to be curious or even entertained by morbid events.

Mia and I tried to casually blend in with the crowd, but we were strangers, so the conversation came to a halt as we got closer. The residents were wondering who we were. Cops? Employees from the coroner's office? Evidence technicians?

"Any news?" I said to a man on my right. Act like you belong and people will generally go along with it.

"Uh...I'm sorry, who are you?" he asked.

Or sometimes they don't.

Everyone else was waiting to hear what I said.

I stuck a hand out and the man shook it. "Roy Ballard. This is my partner, Mia Madison. We do freelance work for various insurance companies. I just met Tyler a few days ago...and now this. Damn shame."

The man's eyes were still on Mia as he said, "Ted Barber. Nobody seems to know what happened. Just that Tyler is dead."

"Who called 9-1-1?" I asked.

A bearded man in his fifties said, "None of us did."

"I think it was Carla," said a tall blond woman.

"Who's Carla?" I asked.

"She left," said Ted. "About thirty minutes ago."

"My next-door neighbor's cleaning woman," said the blond.

"Where do you live?" I asked.

"We saw her talking to one of the cops earlier," said the bearded man, "but that doesn't mean she made the call."

"Could've been Gary," said Ted. "He and Tyler were friends."

"I haven't seen him since yesterday," said yet another man in khaki shorts and a Hawaiian shirt. He had a can of beer in his hand.

"I thought Gary moved away," said a petite brunette girl behind me. She was in her late teens or early twenties. Maybe somebody's daughter.

"No, Gary *Tate*. Not Gary Brauner. The new Gary. He moved in last year."

"Oh."

"On the corner with the blue boat?"

"I think so. His wife is Diane."

"No, that's *my* wife," said Ted. He looked at me and shrugged. "Some of us are just meeting for the first time tonight."

The bearded man said, "All of us know some of us, but none of us know all of us." He gave me a big grin, pleased with his own wit.

"Did anybody hear or see anything?" I asked.

"Are y'all investigators of some kind?" the man in the Hawaiian shirt asked. I noticed he was a little unsteady on his feet.

"We investigate insurance fraud," I said, "and that's how I met Tyler."

"Like Magnum?" the bearded man asked.

"Who's Magnum?" said the petite brunette girl.

"I don't think Magnum investigated insurance fraud," said a slender man with a receding hairline.

"I don't mean *exclusively*," said the bearded man.

"I remember an episode like that," said the man in the Hawaiian shirt. "A rich old broad supposedly had all her jewelry stolen, but it turned out she gave it all to some young dude she was banging, and she didn't want to tell her husband."

The blond woman looked at me and rolled her eyes. Not a fan of the man in the Hawaiian shirt.

"There's one of the cops from earlier," the bearded man said.

Sure enough, a man in dark slacks and a golf shirt had exited the house and was coming down the driveway. He had a badge hanging from a lanyard around his neck. I was elated when I saw who it was.

21

The detective's name was Victor Dunn, and he owed me a favor.

Not long after I'd started my new career as a legal videographer, I was trailing a subject — a forty-year-old math teacher — who surprised me one night by driving past a house in a quiet Wimberley neighborhood and firing a shotgun through the living room window. It was a nasty way of saying hello to his ex-wife and her new boyfriend. He might've simply been intending to rattle them, but the boyfriend caught a round of buckshot in one eye, losing vision permanently. My video of the teacher speeding away from the scene made Victor's case a slam dunk. He and I had stayed in touch, off and on, and we'd developed a mutually beneficial working relationship.

We caught up to Victor just as he was opening the door to his plain-vanilla sedan, after he had waded through the throng of news reporters without giving them a comment. Using an artificially cheesy newscaster voice, I said, "Can I get a statement, Detective Dunn?"

He turned, ready to rebuff me, but then he saw me and grinned. He was a lean, short, balding guy in his mid-thirties. Tremendously fit. He ran five or six miles several times a week, and he lifted weights on the other days.

"Hey, Roy," he said. "How ya doing?"

"Better than Tyler Lutz, apparently," I said. "Jeez, that sounded like dialogue out of bad movie. Victor, this is my partner, Mia Madison."

I always enjoy watching the reaction as I introduce Mia to just about any male between the ages of eleven and one hundred. Even the most respectful and well-mannered among them has a tendency to stare, or to even look surprised, like he's thinking, *Is this a practical joke? This supermodel can't really be your partner, right?* Victor managed to keep his gawking to a minimum, probably because Mia was wearing jeans and a fairly modest chambray shirt.

"You still chasing insurance cheats?" Victor asked.

"Until the Astros give me a tryout," I said. "Actually, I had brunch with Lutz this morning about a thing we're working on. My number will be in his phone records, just so you know. One of your guys called my phone earlier today."

"Yeah? What're y'all working on?"

"The Boz Gentry case. Tyler Lutz was his insurance agent."

That statement had the effect I was hoping for. I didn't need to tell Victor who Boz Gentry was — not just because of Victor's line of work, but because Gentry's name had been repeated dozens of times in the news the past few weeks. I could tell from Victor's raised eyebrow that he and his team hadn't yet made the connection between Lutz and Gentry. I had just given him a great lead, and I was hoping to get something in return, assuming Victor had anything to give.

"Interesting," Victor said, drawing the word out.

"Lutz sold Gentry a three-million-dollar life insurance policy just three months before he supposedly died."

"I guess I need to talk to Travis County," Victor said.

"Ruelas has that case," I said. "Amazing. I spoke his name and didn't turn to stone."

Victor grinned again. He pointed a thumb at me and said to Mia, "Think Ruelas says the same thing about him?"

"Of course not," Mia said, "because they are so completely different, right? For instance, Ruelas is snide, but Roy is sardonic."

"I see how that works," Victor said. "Ruelas is hard-headed, but Roy is…determined."

"Exactly. Ruelas is cynical, but Roy is simply realistic."

"Ruelas is obnoxious," Victor said, "whereas Roy has a strong personality."

"Having fun?" I asked.

"Ruelas is impatient," Mia said, "but Roy is keenly focused."

They both laughed. I waited. They laughed some more. Mia bumped me with an elbow.

I said, "If we're done with the witty repartee, can I ask one question?"

"How can I turn down a request like that?" Victor said.

"What happened to Lutz?"

He glanced over my shoulder, toward the reporters, even though there was nobody within earshot. "Off the record."

"Of course."

"Looks like he took a knife between the ribs. Several times."

"Inside the house?" I asked.

"In the doorway. Died on the porch."

"Find the weapon?"

"Nope."

"Got a time of death?" I asked.

"Not yet."

"Who called it in?"

"Wait. Didn't you say, 'One question'?"

"Yes, technically, one question, with a few minor follow-ups. It's because I'm persistent, rather than pushy."

Victor said, "Neighbor's cleaning lady. She said Lutz had asked her about cleaning his place, and they were supposed to talk this afternoon. So she stopped by and found him."

"Got any leads?" I asked.

"Well, I understand this might be linked to the Boz Gentry case in some unspecified manner."

I pointed a finger at him. "You're clever. Don't go changing."

***

"I guess we learned a couple of things, but I'm really not seeing how it helps us any," Mia said.

We were in the Mustang again, driving back to my apartment.

I said, "Maybe we don't see the value of that information right now, but I'm sure, in due time, it will appear even more worthless."

The sun had dropped below the horizon behind us, and the oncoming cars had their headlights on. It was the kind of glorious spring day tailor-made for tooling around at dusk in a classic muscle car with a gorgeous woman at the wheel.

I said, "One thing we know now is that if Boz Gentry killed Tyler Lutz, that means Gentry is still hanging around in this area, rather than in, say, Calcutta or Des Moines."

"True," Mia said. "Here's another if. If Lutz and Gentry were working together, wouldn't Lutz have warned Boz that we were looking for him?"

"Sure, but so what? He already knew the cops were looking for him."

"There's a difference," Mia said. "Ruelas and his crew would've needed Albeck's permission — or a warrant — to search his ranch. Same with his residence. And they wouldn't have been able to get one. No probable cause. You, on the other hand, had no qualms about trespassing to check your hunch."

"Not a one," I said. "And stupid me — I said something to Lutz at our first meeting about not being limited by boundaries as much as cops are."

"Stupid you."

We came to the Y in Oak Hill, which was much less congested with traffic now.

"So if Lutz was involved," I said, "he might've given Boz a heads-up about us, and Boz might've been expecting us to show up at the ranch at some point. So he would've been very conscientious about making sure the house appeared empty."

We both let that sink in for a minute.

"How many *ifs*, *maybes*, and *might'ves* is that?" I asked.

"Does it really matter?" Mia said. "None of it takes a huge leap of faith. Besides, we're good at this sort of thing — filling in the blanks. Hypothesizing. Unless we hear that Lutz was murdered for some other reason, I think it's safe to assume it's related to this Boz Gentry craziness, and that there's a strong possibility Lutz was in on it."

Mia stayed left and went north on MoPac.

"I do, too," I said.

22

"One thing I sometimes forget is that we don't have to figure out who did what, or why. All we have to do is prove that Boz Gentry is still alive. Video would be great, but even audio would work."

Now we were back in my apartment, facing each other from either end of the sofa. My right hand was soaking in a large bowl of ice water that Mia had brought to me, insisting that I take care of my injury. My left hand was wrapped around one of the bottles of beer I'd brought home a few hours earlier. Neither of us had had anything to eat since lunchtime, and I could feel the effects from the one beer I'd already had. Three years without alcohol had lowered my tolerance more than I would have ever imagined. Buzzed from a single beer? What a lightweight.

"But speculating on who might've killed Tyler Lutz could help us do just that," Mia said.

"Well, sure. It's just nice to remember that we don't actually have to solve the crime."

"Except the crime of fraud," Mia said.

"Right."

The TV was tuned to some drama I had never seen before. I wasn't following it. I did notice that virtually every member of the cast was strikingly attractive.

Mia said, "Fraud is an odd word, isn't it? Hey, a rhyme. Odd fraud."

"Are you buzzed?" I asked.

"Like you aren't?"

"It feels nice."

"Can't argue with that," Mia said. She downed the last of her beer, then went to the refrigerator and got us two more. I wasn't going to argue.

"When I was working at the bar," she said, "I could out-drink just about any man in the place."

"I remember," I said. "I spent a few evenings in your company prior to my, uh, legal challenges."

"Well, I know that. I'm just sayin'. You tend to drink more when you work in a bar."

"Do you ever miss it?" I asked.

"What, tending bar?"

"Yeah."

"God, no. Well, I miss seeing some of the people that worked there, and some of the customers, but the actual work? Hell, no. I love what you and I do together. You and me." She frowned. "You and I?"

"Me and you," I said.

"I *know* that's not grammatically correct," she said.

"Is that what we were going for?"

She laughed. "I don't know. So what are our plans for tomorrow?"

"For finding Boz Gentry? I don't know. How about we figure that out in the morning?"

She started to answer, but instead let out a long, open-mouthed yawn.

"Apparently a conversation with me is stronger than Lunesta," I said.

"Sorry. It's almost my bedtime. Oh, before I forget…" She jumped up off the couch. "Let me show you something. Stand up."

I stood. We were about four feet apart.

"I want you to grab me," she said.

"Grab you?"

"Yep."

"I thought you'd never ask," I said.

She rolled her eyes and shook her head. "No, really. Grab me."

"Any particular, uh, part of you?" I asked. "Because if it's up to me, there are a couple of —"

"Imagine you're in a dark alley and you're about to attack me. Do whatever you'd do in that situation."

"I'd start by asking for your phone number."

"Would you be serious for a minute?" she said.

"Okay. Sorry. Just don't hurt me, okay?"

"I won't."

I took a deep breath. "This is weird."

She waited.

I stepped forward and grabbed her around the throat with both hands — gently.

Her response was amazingly quick and effective. She brought both of her hands up and over my forearms, inside my wrists, then swept them outward, breaking my chokehold — and at the same time, she brought her knee up toward my groin, stopping just short of anything important. I instinctively doubled over, even though she hadn't done any damage.

"Whoa," I said.

"Not bad, huh?"

I straightened up. "You took a class?"

"Yep. At the YMCA this morning. I'll be going every Sunday for eight weeks. There's an advanced course after that."

"That was really good," I said.

"Thanks," she said.

"You're a natural athlete anyway. Once you start learning some techniques, look out."

"You should go with me," she said.

"Maybe I will."

"That would be cool."

I looked over at the TV. I don't know why. I wasn't sure what else to do.

"Okay, well, I've got to hit the hay," Mia said. "I'm beat."

"Will it keep you awake if I stay in here and watch TV for a few minutes?" I asked.

"Not at all. I could sleep through a tornado. Thanks again for letting me stay here."

"What are partners for?"

She turned, went into the guest bathroom, and closed the door. I turned off the living room lights and got settled on the couch again. Wanted to catch the news before bedtime.

Then I glanced toward the guest bathroom and noticed that the door wasn't closed all the way. There was still a long sliver of light showing, and I could see Mia in quarter-profile, standing in front of the vanity. She took off her earrings. Took off her necklace. Removed a bracelet.

I knew I should stop watching her.

She leaned over the sink and brushed her teeth. Two full minutes, just as the dentists recommend. Then she scrubbed her face with a washcloth.

The news anchor launched into a story about the Tyler Lutz murder. It included the fact that Lutz was the insurance agent for Boz Gentry, who was suspected of faking his own death for the insurance money. And now there was a quick cutaway to Hays County homicide detective Victor Dunn, who said Boz Gentry was certainly a person of interest in this case.

I was still listening, but my eyes had wandered back to Mia. What kind of voyeuristic creep watches this sort of thing?

Mia patted her face dry. I couldn't move.

The news anchor moved on to a different story.

Mia placed the hand towel back on the ring.

Then she began to unbutton her chambray shirt. I should have said something or made a joke or coughed — somehow made it clear that she didn't have as much privacy as she thought. But I didn't. I'm not proud to admit it, but I watched. I felt like a pre-teen trying to sneak a peek down a girl's blouse, but I couldn't help myself.

Mia slipped her shirt off, revealing a navy-blue bra with tiny rhinestones stitched along the tops of the cups. My palms were actually sweating. I could feel my heart beating heavily. She reached one hand behind her back, unclasped the bra —

I stood up. Some part of my brain forced me to stand up and walk immediately into my bedroom, flicking the TV off as I went. I shut the bedroom door behind me and sat on the edge of my bed, wondering if I'd just made a mistake, because a question finally occurred to me.

What if Mia had left the door open on purpose?

23

The nice thing about a low tolerance for alcohol is that you can get a buzz from three beers and not have a hangover in the morning. I woke at seven o'clock feeling unusually energetic and ready to dive back into the Boz Gentry case. There was also the fact that, based on what Mia had told me about Laura's phone call, that I only had six days remaining before Hannah would arrive for her visit. Assuming Laura didn't flake out again.

I found Mia in the kitchen, her wet hair wrapped in a towel. A long terrycloth robe was covering the lovely torso I had seen last night. I still felt some lingering guilt for watching her as long as I had, but I'd stopped before she'd totally undressed, and that meant I wasn't a total sleazeball — right?

"Morning," Mia said. "Orange juice?"

"We have orange juice?" I asked. I remained on the other side of the pass-through bar.

"We do. I bought some things when I was running errands yesterday. We also have blueberry muffins and some fresh fruit."

"I've heard of fruit," I said. "It's sort of like bacon, but without all the meaty goodness."

She raised the orange juice bottle. "Yes or no?"

"Yes, please," I said.

She poured a glass full and handed it to me.

"Muffin and fruit?" she said.

"Sure," I said.

She placed a very large muffin on a small plate, then used a fork to pull some chunks of cantaloupe out of a plastic tub. She pulled a handful of strawberries from another tub, then slid the plate across the bar.

"Thanks," I said. "This is nice."

"Least I can do. I'm thinking I should probably get a hotel room for tonight."

"Mia, why? Just stay here as long as you need to."

"I don't want to be an inconvenience," she said.

"Nonsense," I said. "Poppycock. Piffle."

"Piffle?"

"I'm stretching the limits of my vocabulary to show how silly it would be for you to get a hotel. Rubbish. Blarney. Codswallop."

"Hooey?" she said.

"Exactly. Stay here. I insist."

"You sure you don't mind?"

"Not even a little," I said.

"I'm hoping to hear from the fire investigator soon, so I can get back into my house."

"You need a good security system," I said. "Some cameras outside."

"I know, I know. I've been thinking about that for awhile."

"Maybe put a fence around your property."

"All of that gets expensive real quick."

"I'll help with any of it. I'm cheap labor. I run on orange juice and fresh fruit, apparently."

"You don't have to do that."

"Far as I'm concerned, it's incumbent on our partnership that both of us remain as safe as possible. These things are a cost of doing business. We can even write it off."

"Incumbent?" she said. "Have you been reading a thesaurus?"

"Impressive, huh?"

"Exemplary," she said. "Even laudable."

"Nice," I said.

"So. Any ideas on how we proceed with Boz Gentry?"

"None whatsoever. You?"

"Hire a psychic?" she said.

"I knew you were going to say that."

Mia and I spent the next hour brainstorming, and eventually we came up with a couple of actions we could take to possibly propel the case forward. Both were risky, but we had more or less hit a wall, so we agreed to do them both anyway. We nailed down the details and tested the equipment we'd need.

Then I took a shower, and when I was done, Mia informed me that Alex Albeck's SUV had left his house fifteen minutes earlier, and it was now parked at an office building in west Austin. Perfect. Gotta love the GPS tracker. Thirty minutes after that, we were in the van, heading west on Bee Caves Road with Mia at the wheel. Traffic wasn't too bad, since rush hour had passed.

We were wearing turquoise-colored polo shirts sporting an embroidered logo on the left breast. The same logo was featured on a magnetic sign on either side of the van.

As cliché as it sounds, we use this type of ruse on occasion — and the amazing thing is that it works. We have a range of uniforms and corresponding magnetic signs that identify us as couriers, plumbers, caterers, or HVAC service technicians. That last one is perfect in the summer, when air conditioning units break down all over town.

In this particular scenario, we were facing a couple of unique challenges. The first was the guard at the gate. What would prevent him from calling ahead to see if we were expected? Our cover would be blown. We had a way around that — we hoped.

The second also involved the guard — and Mia. We had learned from past experience that Mia, unlike me, could only push this kind of scam so far. For instance, it was fine for Mia to conduct surveillance by parking at a curb in an unguarded neighborhood and pretending to be waiting on a homeowner. But pretending to actually unclog drains or chase down Freon leaks for a living? We found that people simply didn't believe that. Not a woman who looked like Mia. It might work in an old episode of *Charlie's Angels* or a soft-porn movie, but not in real life. We knew this because there had been a couple of occasions when Mia, in uniform, had been subjected to such suspicion and disbelief, she'd had to abandon the operation altogether. Then Mia suggested the obvious — that we should go along with gender stereotypes. She should present herself as a delivery person — from a florist. *That* people would believe.

And she was right. She had used the florist uniform only once, but it had worked like a charm. There was, however, one fairly major drawback. Whereas it was normal and even expected to see a plumber's van parked along a curb for several hours, people naturally expected a florist van to come and go in minutes. No problem. That would work for what we had planned today.

Mia turned left on Barton Creek Boulevard.

"Better get ready," she said.

I unbuckled my seat belt and slipped between the two front seats toward the rear of the van. Normally, there would be two more individual seats immediately behind the front seats, but I had removed them long ago and put them in storage, creating a cargo area.

I carefully stepped over the flowers — nearly a dozen arrangements riding on the floorboard in a stabilizer, a large delivery tray with holes for holding vases that we had bought from a real floral supply company. Most of the flowers, on the other hand, were artificial, although realistic enough to withstand all but the closest scrutiny. After all, we couldn't afford to go out and buy a bunch of fresh flowers every time we pulled this stunt. Two of the arrangements were real, and we would deliver both of them, along with cards that read: *Just wanted to brighten your day.* No signature. An anonymous sender. Everyone loved receiving flowers from an anonymous sender. Even guys, although they might not be willing to admit it.

We also kept a can of floral-scented spray in the glove compartment, and Mia gave the air a few short blasts. Amazing how long it took to find a spray that actually smelled like flowers, rather than like some chemist's notion of what flowers should smell like.

Just behind the flower stabilizer was a bench seat, which I climbed over, into the rearmost cargo area. A small space, but I fit in it just fine. Nobody would see me back here.

I peeked over the top of the bench seat as Mia drove at a leisurely pace for another sixty seconds, then turned left onto Chalk Knoll Drive. Twenty yards ahead was the closed iron gate, with the little guard house situated on a landscaped median. Mia pulled right up with no hesitation. I ducked back down into the cargo space.

"Good morning," said a youngish male voice. "Can I help you?"

"I have a delivery on Portofino Ridge. Last name is Williamson."

The Williamsons lived next door to Alex Albeck.

"R and M Flowers," the man said. "I've never heard of that."

"We're a small shop. Just opened late last year." Mia sounded so friendly and cheerful.

"Oh, yeah? How's business?" The guy was already flirting.

"Great, so far. You ever need an arrangement for a special occasion, you let me know, okay? I'll cut you a deal."

"Got a card?" the guard asked.

We did have cards. We also had a website, and a phone number that would lead to voicemail. Because this guard would almost certainly call the number as soon as we pulled away, to verify our authenticity.

"Here you go," Mia said. "That has my direct line on there. I'm Mia. Give me a buzz when you want to do something nice for your wife."

"No wife," the guard said.

"Girlfriend?"

"Nope."

"Really?" Mia said. "Huh." The tone of her voice was intended to convey surprise, or even interest.

"How about you?" the guard asked.

"I don't have a wife or girlfriend either," Mia said.

"You're funny," the guard said. "You know what I mean."

"I am currently unattached, if that's what you're asking," Mia said.

My God. Did two flirting adults normally sound this cheesy?

"In that case," the guard said, "would you, uh, like to go out sometime?"

This guy didn't waste any time. Got to give him credit for that.

"Tell you what," Mia said, "why don't I stop on my way out and we can talk about it?"

"Cool. Let me just buzz the Williamsons real quick."

Not good, because if they didn't answer, the guard would probably ask Mia to leave the flowers with him, and he'd deliver them later.

Mia was quick on her feet. "Oh, you know what?" she said. "It's supposed to be a surprise."

"Oh, yeah? Her birthday or something?" the guard asked.

"I'm not sure what the occasion is, but do you mind if I just go ahead? I don't want to ruin the surprise."

"Well, I'm supposed to buzz beforehand," the guard said, "so I'll just say it's a delivery, without saying it's flowers. That way we won't ruin the surprise."

"That's true, but if it were your grandmother, wouldn't you rather she not know there was a delivery at all until the flowers arrived?"

There was a pause. I'd been in this guy's shoes. When Mia wanted something, it was almost impossible to say no. Sure enough, he said, "Yeah, okay. I don't want to be a party-pooper. You know how to get to the Williamsons' house?"

"Just follow Chalk Knoll and take the first left," Mia said.

"Exactly. I'm Brett, by the way."

"Good to meet you, Brett. I'll see you in a few minutes."

"And we'll talk again?"

"You bet. Back in a sec."

Mia pulled forward, and after a moment, I said, "I think I threw up in my mouth a little."

"Got us through the gate, didn't it?"

"Poor Brett thinks he died and went to heaven. Won't he be in for a letdown."

"Or maybe not," Mia said. "He's pretty cute."

"He sounded about sixteen years old," I said.

"Twenty-five, twenty-six. Somewhere in there."

"So he'd be scoring with an older woman," I said.

"Who said anything about scoring?" Mia said. "And I'm not that much older."

I could feel the van taking a slow left. I lifted my head above the bench seat and saw that we were turning onto Portofino Ridge.

"You can do better than a security guard," I said as I climbed over the bench seat to wait in the cargo area, alongside the flower delivery tray. There was also a canvas tote bag featuring the same R&M Flowers logo as our polo shirts and the magnetic signs on the van. The bag was filled with the items I'd need to complete my task. I was getting nervous. What I was about to do was a felony. The good news was, I hadn't seen a single person yet. No walkers. No joggers. No kids playing in the street.

"Yeah? What could be better than a security guard?" Mia asked.

"Oh, I don't know," I said. "A handsome, witty, intelligent legal videographer, perhaps."

"Maybe I'll meet one someday," Mia said.

"Ouch," I said, just as she pulled up to the curb in front of the Williamsons' house.

24

There are all kinds of useful high-tech gizmos that make our job easier. There were, of course, many brands and models of live and passive GPS tracking devices, like the one I'd attached to Erin Gentry's car. How about a voice-activated audio recorder that looks like a common USB flash drive, a key fob, or a ballpoint pen? Handy as hell.

Covert video cameras were built into all types of common household items: alarm clocks, teddy bears, electrical outlets and adapters, eyeglasses, wristwatches, picture frames, hats (like the one I'd been wearing during my encounter with Shane Moyer), and fake rocks (like the one that had broken open the Tracy Turner case for us last year).

In this instance, I'd be using a camera/DVR combo that looked like a small electrical box you'd find mounted on the side of a house. In fact, it *was* an actual electrical box, minus the guts. It even featured a black-and-red warning sticker that read: DANGER — HIGH VOLTAGE. The camera inside was motion activated, with a three-year battery standby period. Sixty hours of recording time per charge. High-resolution video.

Infrared capabilities for shooting in total darkness. It had a 0.00 Lux low light rating, but I don't really understand what that means, nor do I care. It works. That's the important thing.

What I'd learned from Google Maps was that Alex Albeck had a swimming pool in his backyard — as did most of the homes in this upper-end neighborhood. We had speculated that if Boz Gentry was hiding out at Albeck's house, he wouldn't show his face — except in the backyard. And maybe only at night. He had to go outside for fresh air at some point, right? He'd get cabin fever. Everybody would eventually. Might even decide to go for a swim.

So we'd decided it would be worth the gamble to see if we could get a camera set up back there. There were pitfalls, but we'd concluded that none of them posed a serious problem.

For instance, if Albeck had security cameras around his place, there would be no reason for him to review the video, because we weren't going to break into his home or steal anything from the exterior.

If he had a dog, I'd brought along a can of premium dog food. In my experience, the overwhelming majority of dogs, including aggressive or anxious ones, will stop what they're doing to eat savory chunks of lamb and chicken, smothered in a stewed broth. I think I'd have a tough time resisting that myself.

If the gate to Albeck's backyard fence had a lock on it — and I'd seen from Google photos that he did have a fence — I'd go over it.

And if I got caught in the act? I'd run like hell.

Mia and I exited the van together, wearing our matching turquoise polo shirts, both of us carrying a vase full of flowers. I was also carrying the tote bag containing the covert camera and the tools I'd need to mount it in some discreet location on the back of Albeck's house. There were probably other utility boxes back there, so this one would fit right in.

"If I'm not back in five minutes, save yourself," I said. "Run and don't look back. But think of me from time to time."

"Funny."

She started up the sidewalk to the Williamsons' house, and I proceeded along the street for thirty feet, then turned up Albeck's driveway. What were the odds that two side-by-side neighbors would be getting a delivery from the same florist at the same time? Well, slim, sure, but it could happen. It was happening, wasn't it? That's what anyone watching would think. Seriously, how many average Joes would conclude that we were there on a spying mission? They'd have confidence in young Brett, the guard, who would screen out any potential spies, right?

I marched right up the steps to Albeck's door like I belonged there. Set the tote bag down. Pretended to knock, but didn't. If Gentry was inside, I didn't want to alert him that I was here. I pretended to knock again. Waited for half a minute. Nothing. I picked up the tote bag, stepped down off the porch, and looked around.

If anyone was watching, my body language suddenly said, *Hey, look — a cobblestone pathway that leads to the backyard. A delivery person such as myself should check to see if the resident is back there.*

I followed the curved pathway counterclockwise toward the side of the house. I didn't see any surveillance cameras dangling from the eaves. Along the front of the house, to my left as I walked, was a nicely landscaped bed filled with elephant ears and other plants I couldn't name. Ironic, with me being from a flower shop and all.

I reached the corner and turned, and now I could see the wrought iron fence. Not a privacy fence, which was good, because, for reasons I can't explain, it would seem much more inappropriate for a delivery person to peek through or over a privacy fence.

Still no cameras. No window stickers announcing that the home was protected by such-and-such security system. Didn't mean much. By the time I reached the gate, I could see part of the pool, with patio furniture carefully arranged around it.

I stopped. Waited. I didn't see anybody. I did notice that the gate had no lock on it, which was fortunate. I thumbed the latch and swung the gate open. It made a very faint squealing sound, but nothing to be concerned about.

I left the gate open and continued along the cobblestone pathway. After six or seven more steps, I came to the rear corner of the house, and by then I could see that there wasn't just a swimming pool back here, there was also a hot tub.

And in that hot tub was a woman staring right at me.

***

As Mia would tell me later, Mrs. Williamson was about ninety years old, and the idea that she was receiving flowers from an anonymous sender tickled her to no end.

"Oh, aren't those gorgeous!" Mrs. Williamson was saying, as she accepted the vase, which was just about the time I was pretending to knock on Albeck's door. "Those must be calla lilies?"

"Actually they're Casablanca lilies," Mia said.

"Casablanca lilies?"

"Yes, ma'am. Imported from Holland."

And they were. Normally quite expensive, but we had found them deeply discounted at a florist on the way over here.

Mrs. Williamson made some clucking sounds, showing just how pleased she was as she studied the flowers. "Just wonderful," she said. "Even the vase is lovely." Then she looked at Mia and said, "And look at you. You're even prettier than these flowers are."

"That's so sweet. Thank you."

"Which florist are you with?"

"R and M."

"Pardon?"

"R and M."

"Aranim?"

"R and M." Mia gestured toward the logo on her shirt.

"Oh, R&M! I believe I've ordered from you before."

Not likely, lady.

Mia said, "You'll want to keep them away from direct sunlight and in a cool environment. And please add water regularly. You can also recut the stems every day or two if you'd like them to last longer."

"I'll do that!" She looked over her eyeglasses at Mia. "You can't give me any clue who sent them? Just a hint?"

Mia smiled. "I'm afraid not. I don't even know."

"Well, I guess I should just be glad anyone cares enough about a little old lady to even remember me," Mrs. Williamson said. "I mean, it's not even my birthday."

Mia said, "Okay, I hope you enjoy them, ma'am," and she started to turn.

"Oh, wait, let me get a little something for you," Mrs. Williamson said. "I'll grab my purse."

"That's not necessary, and in fact, we have a policy against accepting tips."

"Are you sure?"

"Yes, ma'am, but thanks anyway, and you have a wonderful day."

"Oh, I will! Thank *you*!"

I froze. Simply stood still for a moment. Maybe the woman in the hot tub wasn't staring at me after all. She had sunglasses on, and a big floppy hat. Maybe her eyes were closed. Dozing. It would be better if I could slip away without any interaction. I could continue with the ruse if necessary and give her the flowers, but it would be better to avoid it. Only one way to find out.

I waved at her. No response.

So I stepped back a few feet. Now I was more or less peeking around the corner of the house, and I was seeing her through the leafy branches of a small ornamental tree halfway between me and the hot tub. If she hadn't seen me before, it was unlikely she'd notice me now.

I could have slipped away, but I waited. Was she alone back here? Was someone going to join her? I wanted to find out, but I couldn't stay here for more than another minute or so. Mia would be back at the van by now. Brett would be wondering what was taking so long.

The woman twitched suddenly, as if jerking awake from a nap. She stretched her arms out in front of her. Yawned. She twisted her torso to her left and picked up a magazine that was lying on the concrete beside the hot tub. Opened it up. The sunglasses must have been too dark for her to read easily, because she removed them, and I finally got a good look at her face. For the second time in 36 hours, I was totally taken aback by who I was seeing. On Saturday evening, it was Candice — Tyler Lutz's receptionist — at Albeck's ranch. And now this.

The woman in the hot tub was Shelley. Boz Gentry's dental hygienist.

25

Mia was waiting in the driver's seat with the engine running when I returned to the van. She could tell by my expression as I approached that I had some big news. I came around to the sliding door, climbed inside, and closed it behind me.

"What happened?" she asked. She popped it into gear and got moving. "Was Albeck home?"

I was shaking my head, still trying to figure out what I had just seen.

"You'll never guess who was in Albeck's hot tub," I said.

"Mickey Thomas, your old friend from Cub Scouts?" Mia said, throwing my joke from yesterday back at me, which I would have complimented under normal circumstances.

"Boz Gentry's dental hygienist," I said. "Shelley."

She glanced at me in the rearview mirror, her mouth agape. "No way!"

"Yes, the same woman who admitted stealing Gentry's dental records is hanging out at Gentry's best friend's house. What in the holy hell is going on here?"

"Did you talk to her?" Mia asked.

"No."

"Did she see you?"

"No, but I snapped a couple of pics with my phone."

"You'd better get in back," she said, because we were getting closer to the guard shack.

I climbed over the bench seat and got into my hiding spot. I felt the van slowing, and then it came to a stop.

"Hey, there," Mia said.

"I was wondering where you were," Brett said, "but then I remembered that Mrs. Williamson is a little, uh, chatty."

"Ah, she's sweet as can be. And she was totally surprised, so thanks."

"No problem. So…it's okay if I call you?"

"Sure, but…"

"Yeah?"

"I need to tell you something right up front. I've found it makes things easier in the long run, because it sorta freaks some guys out. So I'll just come right out with it. I have seven children from previous marriages."

I came *this* close to laughing out loud. I could picture Brett waiting for some indication that Mia was joking, but her face would remain dead serious. It was perfect. She had just ensured that she would never hear from Brett. Ever.

"Wow," Brett finally said, because really, what else do you say in that situation? "That's a lot."

"Four from the first marriage, one from the second, and two from the third. Oldest is twelve, youngest is eleven months. They keep me pretty busy, so it's always nice to have another adult around to help out."

"I, uh —"

"Do you know how to change a diaper?"

Mia turned west on Bee Caves Road. As she drove, we tried to figure out the meaning of what I had just seen — Shelley Milligan in Albeck's hot tub. We didn't come up with much. But we both agreed that it might mean that Albeck was involved in the scam. It was frustrating, because we knew we had several pieces of the puzzle, but we still didn't know how they all fit together.

"If we don't make some sort of breakthrough soon," I said, now sitting in the passenger seat, "we'll have to confront all of these people head on and see what they have to say."

By "these people," I meant Alex Albeck, Shelley Milligan, and Candice the receptionist.

"But we aren't there yet, are we?" Mia said.

"I don't think so. Right now, we have an advantage. We know things they don't know we know."

"Still a lot of blanks to fill in," Mia said.

"True. Like the connection between Albeck and Shelley."

"Dripping Springs is a small town," Mia said. "Everybody knows everybody. Isn't that what Lutz said?"

"Yeah, but even if Albeck knows Shelley — even if Albeck was one of Dr. Wilkins's patients — why would Shelley be enjoying a dip in Albeck's hot tub?"

"And on a Monday morning?" Mia said. "Why isn't she at work?"

"There was a sign in Wilkins's office saying they were closed on Mondays. So we can assume she didn't quit or get fired or anything like that."

"What if Albeck and Shelley are having an affair?" Mia said.

I pondered that possibility while Mia turned right on Highway 71 in the village of Bee Cave.

"Shelley is married," I said, "and she took the money for Boz's file so she could surprise her husband with an anniversary trip. Just doesn't seem likely that she's sleeping with Albeck."

Mia drove past the massive shopping complex called the Hill Country Galleria, which used to be a lush, wide-open field where livestock grazed.

"Okay," Mia said. "No affair. Maybe they're related."

"That's a good theory," I said, "and for that reason, I'll pretend I was thinking the same thing."

"Naturally."

I grabbed my laptop. "Won't take long to find out, and you know who's going to help us?"

"Who?"

"The Mormons," I said.

"What are you talking about?" Mia asked.

"Mormons," I said, "are the most ardent genealogists in the world."

"I've heard that."

"You want to know why?"

"Not really," Mia said.

"It's because they believe they can obtain salvation for their dead ancestors — or any dead person who wasn't Mormon — by baptizing them by proxy into the Mormon faith."

"Wait. What? By proxy?"

"Someone else stands in for the dead person," I said.

"I know what it means, goober. But where do they get the right to decide what the dead person wants?"

"Got me," I said. "All I know is, they trace their family trees way back and baptize all their dead ancestors. Then the entire family can live together eternally."

"Well," Mia said. "Okay."

"They have this huge vault — a repository — built into the mountains just outside Salt Lake City, and it has doors that weigh something like ten or twelve tons, so it's supposed to be able to withstand a nuclear blast. It's climate controlled, and they have millions of rolls of microfilm containing more than two billion names."

"Now you are totally making stuff up," Mia said.

"I'm not, I swear. They've got birth records, death records, marriages, divorces, wills, all that kind of stuff — so they can go back years and years, which allows them to baptize and save great-great-great Uncle Bob and Aunt Sally and all their kids."

Mia turned left on Hamilton Pool Road and continued west.

I said, "The important thing is, the Mormons have made it a lot easier to track your family tree, whether you're Mormon or not. They have an incredible genealogy website. So let me see if I can find a connection between Shelley Milligan and Alex Albeck."

We rode in silence as I surfed. I'd been on the Mormon site often enough to know how to navigate it well, and how to quickly find the information I needed, or to discover that the information I needed wasn't there.

Mia reached Ranch Road 12, went south to Dripping Springs, turned west on Highway 290, and by the time we reached the little community of Henly and turned left on FM 165, I'd found what I was looking for.

It was another twist that I hadn't seen coming.

"Shelley Milligan and Alex Albeck have no family connection at all," I said.

Mia glanced over at me and saw the knowing grin on my face. "But...?"

I said, "You'll never guess who —"

"Roy!"

"Okay, okay. Shelley Milligan is Erin Gentry's aunt from her dad's first wife."

"Holy crap!" Mia said.

"I'm pretty sure Shelley wasn't completely honest with me," I said.

"Ya think?" Mia said. "I'd say you totally got played."

"Maybe so, but isn't it time we stopped dwelling on the past and moved forward with our investigation?"

"Are we still gonna do this?" she asked, nodding toward the windshield. Toward Alex Albeck's ranch. That was the other action we'd decided we could take to propel the case forward — another visit to the ranch. If Boz Gentry was there, he wouldn't be expecting me to show up a second time.

"Now I'm starting to wonder about Erin Gentry again," I said. "Is she involved in this scheme or not? There are too many different possibilities here. I can't even think straight."

"Remember: We don't have to figure out who did what," Mia said. "We just have to prove Boz Gentry is alive."

"That's very wise," I said.

"You said it last night."

"Yeah, I know," I said.

"Right before I kicked your ass," Mia said.

"You're full of piss and vinegar this morning, aren't you?"

"You didn't answer my question," she said.

We were getting closer to the ranch entrance. We could drive past it and keep going. Maybe return to the café at the Blanco Bowling Club and weigh our options. Ponder what we'd learned this morning. Brainstorm some more. See if there was a more logical plan. But I was restless. This case had me feeling like I was standing in quicksand, and I wanted to make something happen.

"What the hell," I said. "Let's do it."

26

Part two of today's agenda went like this: Mia would drop me at Albeck's ranch, and I would take another look around — but I would approach it differently this time. Last time, the house appeared to be empty — and I'm fairly certain it was. No light was showing from any windows at all. The electric meter wasn't moving. I had noted the reading on the meter, and I would check it again, but I didn't expect any change.

Then I would set out to explore the ranch itself. Not all eight hundred acres — just a select portion. It had been Mia's idea, and I had agreed that it was a good one.

This morning, when we'd been brainstorming, she had said, "If Boz Gentry is hiding at the ranch and Lutz warned him we might show up out there, where would Gentry go?"

"Uh, the Amalfi Coast? I hear it's lovely."

"Think about it," she said. "He's an avid outdoorsman. He hunts. He fishes."

I saw where she was going. "He camps. He's a camper."

"Exactly," Mia said.

"He camps just for the fun of it," I said, getting excited. "Even when he's not on the run. He actually enjoys spending time in a sleeping bag on the ground. Even if Lutz didn't warn him about us, Gentry might've been camping on the ranch anyway, instead of staying at the ranch house. It would be like a vacation for him. The weather couldn't be any better for it." I pointed at her. "You, my friend, are more than a pretty face."

"Thanks. Does that mean you are…a happy camper?"

"Well, see, now I have to subtract points for the bad pun."

There were no other vehicles approaching from either direction, so Mia pulled to the shoulder and let me out near the northeast corner of the ranch. I was wearing a dark green shirt and brown pants, so I would blend in with the heavily wooded countryside. Mia drove away while I hopped the fence and disappeared into the brush in a matter of about seven seconds. Then I simply waited to hear from her. It wouldn't take long for her to drive to Blanco and park somewhere.

That was the other smart idea Mia had come up with: We would stay connected via Skype while I searched the ranch, or as long as we had a signal. Mia would be on her laptop, using a screen-recording app to save the video coming from my phone. So if I should happen upon Boz Gentry, all I had to do was aim my phone at him and the evidence we needed to crack the case would be backed up, off site, immediately.

"This way," Mia had said, "if he should take your phone away at gunpoint or something, he won't be able to destroy the video. I'll have it."

"Yes," I'd said, "that would be the important thing in a situation like that. Saving the video. Don't worry about whether I might get shot or something."

"Hey, you're tough, right? I wouldn't be surprised if a bullet just bounced right off."

We'd chosen this particular corner of the ranch for a reason. I couldn't search the entire ranch — not all 800 acres. So we'd tried to think like avid outdoors enthusiasts, hoping we could figure out where Gentry might set up camp. The answer was fairly easy.

Near water.

Google Maps revealed that a strong creek ran through Albeck's ranch, and somebody — Albeck or a previous owner — had constructed a dam at some point. The result was a twenty- or thirty-acre pond — known as a "tank" in Texas — that was located in the middle of the ranch. Satellite view showed a small dock on the east side, complete with a jon boat. Nice little place to catch a few fish for dinner. If I were Boz Gentry, I'd be hanging out around the tank, or somewhere along the creek. And this northeast corner, where Mia had dropped me off, was less than a quarter-mile from the creek.

I expected this outing to take no more than three hours tops. I carried only two pieces of equipment — my phone and my Glock nine-millimeter automatic, currently riding in a nylon holster on my hip. Yes, I was trespassing and I was armed, but I'd decided I didn't want to risk encountering Boz Gentry, a man who might've killed Tyler Lutz yesterday morning, without a weapon.

After twelve minutes of waiting patiently in the woods, I heard the familiar sound of an incoming Skype video call. I accepted, and there was Mia.

"Hey, where's the young Asian girl I asked for?" I said. "Oh, sorry. Wrong web cam."

"You couldn't afford me," Mia said.

"No doubt. You see me all right? It's pretty bright out here."

"Looks fine," Mia said.

"You recording?"

"Yep," she said.

"I have no idea if I'll have a good signal all over the ranch," I said, "but if our call gets dropped, I'm going to keep going anyway."

"Yeah, I know. Just be careful."

"Okay, I'm going to turn the volume down now." I couldn't risk having some unexpected sound coming from my phone, announcing my presence.

"Gotcha," Mia said.

I began my trek, holding the phone loosely at my waist, but pointing the screen forward. The only problem with being on Skype was that I couldn't simultaneously use Google's satellite view to guide my progress. Not a huge drawback, because all I had to do was follow the fence line until I came to the creek. I was no trailblazer, but that wouldn't be difficult at all.

Except it was.

After less than one hundred yards, I hit a grove of cedar trees so thick, it was almost impossible to walk through them without a machete. I struggled forward for about five minutes, gaining some nasty scratches on my arms and face, before I gave up and went back the way I'd come. Why bother? Much easier to go around the grove, knowing it was extremely unlikely that Boz Gentry would be camping inside that grove.

I checked my phone and Mia was still there. Even though my volume was down, she could still hear me, so I whispered, "Going around the trees."

She gave me a thumbs-up.

I walked in a westerly direction, following the edge of the grove. There was an obvious trail here, worn down to caliche — loose limestone soil and small rocks — by generations of wild animals. They didn't like going through the trees, either, apparently. Path of least resistance and all that.

I was moving slowly, quietly, but after walking for just a few minutes, the trees became less dense. In fact, a second trail branched off from the first one and headed north. I followed it. White-winged doves were calling from nearby trees. A light breeze was at my back. It would have been a pleasant hike if I hadn't been looking for a man who might be a murderer.

I kept moving, and after another eighty or ninety yards, I began to hear the faint sounds of water gurgling over rocks. This deer trail was leading straight to the creek, which wasn't surprising. Animals are smart enough to live near water.

I pressed on, through another thin copse of cedar and oak trees, and over a small rise, and when I crested it, I could see down into a wide draw, where the creek was flowing from right to left in front of me. It was actually a very beautiful scene. The water must have been fifteen yards across at its widest point, but it narrowed between two low bluffs and tumbled down a limestone-studded hillside.

Then I spotted the tent.

Seventy yards away. Maybe eighty, at the most. It was constructed from camouflage fabric, and it was tucked between two bush-like cedars, so it would've been easy to miss. Plus, I was almost too startled to realize that, yes, it was really a tent, and it was right there near the water's edge, where we'd speculated it might be. I mean, Mia and I frequently have to take action based on nothing but hunches or guesses, but it's not often that one pays off so quickly and accurately.

I was frozen in place at the top of the hill, and I realized I wasn't aiming my phone in front of me, as I was supposed to. I pointed it down the hill, toward the tent.

And I simply waited. Watching. Looking for any movement. I saw nothing. If Boz Gentry was around, I didn't see him.

It was past noon now, but Gentry could be inside the tent, sleeping. What else was he going to do during the day? He might enjoy camping, but after a few weeks, wouldn't it get a bit tedious? How do you fill your time? Even worse — how do you fill your time when you can't use any sort of electronic device that might lead the authorities to you? No cell phone. No tablet. Maybe he was a reader. Maybe he had a battery-operated TV.

I waited some more, until I felt comfortable moving forward again. Fortunately, the tent was on my side of the creek. I wouldn't have to wade across to check it out.

I slowly turned my phone and checked the screen. Mia's eyes were big and she was nodding. She had seen the tent, too. I turned the phone forward again.

There was no use putting this off. I would have to go down there eventually. If Gentry was in that tent, he'd have the advantage. He could see me coming. In fact, he might be watching me right now. Through binoculars. Or through a rifle scope. I suddenly felt very vulnerable.

I started down the hill toward the tent, picking my steps carefully. Step on a dry cedar stick and it would crack loudly, giving Gentry a warning. Fortunately, the sound of the water flowing through the creek would provide some cover.

Should I pull my Glock from its holster? No. Absolutely not. If I were Gentry and I spotted some trespasser approaching with a drawn weapon, I'd probably feel justified to fire a shot in self-defense.

I continued down the hill. It was steeper than I had originally thought. The ground was mostly caliche, so I had to be careful not to slip.

I was now forty yards from the tent.

And I was having second thoughts. Wouldn't it have been smarter to set up a surveillance camera instead and come back for it later, as we had planned to do at Albeck's house?

Thirty yards.

No movement anywhere in the draw. Not even a bird.

Twenty yards.

I had now reached the more level ground of the creek bank. The tent was to my left, downstream.

I moved closer. Ten yards.

The tent flaps suddenly flew outward. A man in full camo burst out of the tent and marched directly toward me, pointing a handgun, and shouting.

"Get down! On the ground, motherfucker! Right now!"

27

You know what you should do when a man pointing a gun screams at you to get down? You should get down. That's my advice, anyway. Especially if you're trespassing. Especially if you're carrying a gun yourself, and he can later claim that you went for it, even if you didn't. And even more especially if the man might've killed someone else the day before.

So I did get down. I placed my hands on the damp soil and took a prone position on my stomach, attempting to keep the phone in my hand aimed discreetly at the man. Not that it would do much good, because in the two or three seconds before I lay down, as he came toward me, I saw that he had his face streaked with brown and green camo paint. It, in effect, concealed his identity. Was this Boz Gentry? Honestly, I had no idea.

And then I felt him place his hiking boot roughly on the back of my neck.

"Got you this time, numbnut," the man said.

What did that mean? Got me this time?

He leaned over me and I felt him remove my handgun from its holster. I heard him pop the magazine loose, then rack the slide. In my peripheral vision, I saw him fling my gun toward the creek. I heard a splash.

"You owe me five hundred dollars," I said. My voice sounded odd — probably because of the aforementioned boot.

"You're trespassing," he said. "I should pop one in the back of your head and toss you in after it."

"Do that and I'll strike you from my Christmas card list." I have a tendency to be a smartass when I'm nervous. Other times, too.

"Think this is a great time to crack jokes, numbnut?" I felt cold steel on my temple. "How about now? Hilarious, huh? It's just you and me out here. Remember that. All alone."

"Don't forget the wonders of modern technology," I said. "I'm on a Skype call right now. Everything you're saying and doing is being recorded."

I wanted him to know there was a witness to everything that had happened so far, including his threats, and that he'd have to be really stupid to take it any further. Of course, I knew he'd take my phone away — and he did. I felt him grab it roughly from my hand. The boot was still on my neck.

"Yeah, nice try," he said.

He held the phone down low, in my line of sight. The Skype app was still open, but the call had disconnected. I must have lost the signal when I came down into the draw. This, needless to say, was a disappointment. I could only hope that the signal had lasted long enough that Mia had seen the man coming toward me with the gun. If she had, she would have called the Blanco County Sheriff's Office and told them what was happening. If the call had dropped before the man had come out of the tent, then Mia would simply be waiting to hear back from me again. Which would suck.

I said, "My partner knows —"

"Shut the fuck up."

"Valid point," I said. "Were you on the debate team?"

"Don't push me, numbnut. You're a trespasser, and in Texas, that means I can just shoot you if I want to."

"I'm pretty sure that isn't a realistic interpretation of the law," I said.

"Sure is," he said.

"Okay, then. Far be it from me to question the quality of your ninth-grade education."

"This is a nice phone," he said. "Maybe I'll keep it."

"That, plus the Glock, and you'll owe me about twelve hundred bucks," I said. "Of course, that doesn't include airtime, state and local taxes, or my usual handling fee. I can mail you an invoice." I wasn't happy that I continued to sound as if I'd inhaled helium.

"Then maybe I'll just throw it in the creek, too," he said, "and you can suck it. Besides, I told you to shut up."

Unfortunately, since the phone had been active, with the Skype app open, he didn't need to enter my passcode to gain access to my phone. I couldn't do anything but lay there while he explored my personal information.

"Roy Ballard," he said. "What the fuck are you doing out here, Roy Ballard? Don't lie to me."

"I'm a nudist," I said. "I was seconds away from stripping down. Imagine what you missed."

I was stalling, in case deputies were on the way to the ranch.

"You some kind of fag?" the man asked.

"Are there different kinds?" I said.

"Don't be a smartass."

"I wasn't," I said, "but it's possible that your expertise on faggery is more extensive than mine."

He pushed down harder on my neck with his boot.

"You're blowing it, numbnut," he said. "I ain't a big fan of the game warden, but in this case, maybe I'll make a call."

Wait a second. This wasn't making sense. Boz Gentry wouldn't call the game warden. He wouldn't call anyone. I used deductive reasoning to conclude that this man wasn't Boz Gentry.

"You think I'm a poacher?" I said. "I don't have a rifle."

"You were scouting for later," he said. "I'm about sick of poachers, I'll tell you that."

This man wasn't Boz Gentry and he had no clue why I was out here. If he called the game warden, I'd likely get arrested. So it was time to come clean.

"I'm not a poacher," I said. "And if you'll take your boot off my neck,

I'll tell you what I'm doing out here."

"You'll tell me anyway," he said.

"True. But think of all the humanitarian awards you could win if you let me up."

To my surprise, after a few seconds, he removed his boot. Grudgingly. I rolled over and started to stand up, but he said, "Just keep your ass on the ground there."

"What am I gonna do? Run?"

"Only if you wanna get shot," he said.

I stayed on the ground. I could look directly at him now, and even with the camo paint on his face, I could confirm with no doubt that it wasn't Boz Gentry. This man was at least six or seven years older than Gentry. Maybe even closer to my age. If he was one of Gentry's friends, I didn't recognize him. Whoever he was, he still had his gun pointed at me. Semi-automatic. Looked like a Beretta Pico .380. Not that I'm a gun expert, but I'd almost bought one myself, so I recognized it. I was surprised that a dude in the woods with his face painted wasn't carrying something larger. Like an elephant gun.

"Let's hear your bullshit story," he said.

"Who does your make-up?" I said. Couldn't resist. That pissed him off, so before he could reply, I said, "My name is Roy Ballard. I'm a freelance legal videographer. Boz Gentry's insurance company hired me to obtain evidence that he is still alive."

His brow furrowed. Birds chirped. The creek gurgled. And finally he said, "You're a what?"

"A videographer. I try to shoot video of people who are committing insurance fraud."

"And you're trying to find Boz?"

"I am."

"What the fuck for? He's supposed to be dead. Burnt up." He wasn't believing me yet.

"You watch the news?" I asked.

"Fox."

"Anything local?"

"Nope."

"Okay," I said. "The truth is, nobody knows for sure whether Boz is dead, and it's looking like he probably isn't, and I was hired to find him. Since Alex is Boz's friend, I figured Boz might be hiding out on this ranch, and when I saw that tent…"

He shook his head, disgusted. "It's not a tent, numbnut. It's a bow-hunting blind."

I looked at it. "But there aren't any windows," I said. I noticed that he wasn't pointing his gun with as much deliberation as before.

"You shoot through the fabric," he said. "What're you, stupid?"

"Oh," I said. "I'm not a hunter. Were you aware that meat can be readily purchased in stores?"

He ignored the jab and said, "So you thought you'd just invite yourself onto the ranch?"

"Uh, pretty much, yeah," I said. "You friends with Boz?"

"No, I ain't friends with Boz," he said, and it was clear that he didn't want to be.

"Can I ask who you are?" I said.

"Good God," he said. "They really sent the B team, didn't they? You're supposed to be some kind of investigator? I'm Jerry Gillespie, the ranch manager."

My earlier assumption — that the lack of livestock on the ranch meant there probably wouldn't be a manager — had turned out wrong.

"You live here on the ranch, Jerry?" If he did, that would rule out the idea of Boz hiding in the ranch house.

"None of your damn business," Gillespie said.

This conversation was not going the way I wanted it to. And by now, I had a sense that Gillespie was all bluster. He wasn't a hard-ass, even if he wanted to come across like one.

So I stood up. Slowly, but I stood.

Gillespie pointed his gun again. "You sit back down until I decide if you're tellin' the truth."

"I prefer to stand."

"God dammit, I said —"

"Jerry," I said, raising my voice, "you are on the verge of obstructing a fraud investigation. That's a class-A felony punishable by up to ten years in the penitentiary and a fifty thousand dollar fine. Did you know that?"

"But you trespassed!" he said. He'd already lost some of his bravado.

"Doesn't matter," I said, lying. "You know how a game warden can come onto your place anytime he wants? Same thing applies here. I can go anywhere in pursuit of a suspected criminal. Same as a game warden. Same as a bounty hunter. That's the law. So you'd best back the fuck off and answer my questions before I lose my patience. And you'd better put that Beretta away before you get into some serious trouble."

He stared at me petulantly for about five solid seconds. Then he lowered the gun and slipped it into a holster on his hip.

I immediately said, "You live out here or not?"

"I live in Blanco, but I been staying here at the house for about six weeks."

"Why's that?"

"Wife kicked me out," he said. "But she's coming around."

"When was the last time you saw Boz?" I asked.

Gillespie shrugged. "Maybe two months. Not like I keep track."

That would've been shortly before Gentry's alleged accident.

"Out here?" I asked.

"Yep."

Gillespie was going to answer my questions, all right — with as little information as possible. Probably didn't matter, because I doubted he had anything of value to tell me.

"Was he hunting?"

"Nope."

"Then what was he doing?"

"Mr. Albeck and his buddies just hang out here sometimes."

"And do what?"

"Drink beer, shoot guns. Ride motorcycles."

"You hang out with them?" I asked.

"Only when I'm helping 'em gut a deer or cleaning up after 'em."

There was some resentment in his voice.

"They treat you like the help, huh?"

"Boz does. That's what I am. I just do my job. Mr. Albeck treats me okay. So do the rest of his friends."

It was plain that Gillespie wasn't fond of Boz Gentry. I was hoping that would work to my advantage.

"You ever hear any interesting conversations between Boz and Mr.

Albeck?"

"Like what?" Gillespie said.

"Anything that might've had to do with insurance fraud. Something that might've sounded odd when you heard it might make sense now."

"Why the fuck should I tell you?"

"Because if you don't, I'll tell the sheriff you might have information on this case. He'll be up your ass like a first-year proctologist."

He was shaking his head, unhappy that some trespasser was bossing him around. "I don't remember nothing. You saying Mr. Albeck was involved?"

"Not necessarily. I don't know who was involved, or what exactly they were involved in."

He smirked and tried to regain some of his self-respect. "You don't know much, do you?"

"Not as much as I'd like. And, unfortunately, it looks like this conversation is another waste of time. Boz was probably too smart to discuss anything important in front of you, since you're just the manager."

It was a blatant attempt to push Gillespie's buttons. Reverse psychology in its most obvious form. If Gillespie didn't like Boz, this would be his chance to get back at him.

"I do know something," Gillespie said. "More than *you* know, that's for sure."

"Yeah? Like what?"

"Don't have nothing to do with fraud," he said. "It's good, though."

"Yeah?"

I waited. He made a face, like he was weighing whether to spill the beans.

Then he said, "One night during deer season, back in December or January, all of 'em got to drinking around the fire, and Boz said something snotty about Mr. Albeck's girlfriend. The gal he was dating then was a Hooters waitress, and Boz said something about her screwing her customers for tips. You know how you say something like you're just joking? That's what Boz did, but Mr. Albeck fired right back, saying, well, it was better than having a wife who ran around on him — and everybody knew he was talking about Boz's wife."

I had to wonder about Mia's theory that Erin Gentry was having an affair with Alex Albeck, hence her late-night trip to his house the previous Thursday. Had Boz discovered that his wife and his best friend were sleeping together? Had the two lifelong friends managed to work past it? A long shot, but possible. If Albeck was anything like Boz, it wasn't a stretch that the two buddies might've valued their friendship more than they valued the women in their lives.

"Any idea who Mr. Albeck was referring to?" I asked.

"Don't know," Gillespie said. "They both shut up after that, and nobody had the balls to ask any questions. Oh, wait. Mr. Albeck did say one other thing, and it made me think Boz's wife was seeing some dude from East Texas."

"Why's that?" I asked.

"Because Mr. Albeck said something like, 'Don't make me tell 'em about Tyler.'"

28

"What if he really was talking about Tyler, Texas?" Mia asked forty-five minutes later. "Wouldn't that be a coincidence?"

I was back in the van again. Gillespie hadn't had anything else to offer beyond that one fantastic little tidbit. So — after I'd made him retrieve my gun from the creek — I'd hiked out to the road, calling Mia along the way. She had not seen any of my interaction with Gillespie. The Skype call had cut out before I'd gotten halfway down the draw.

"Had to be Tyler Lutz," I said. "Erin Gentry was having an affair with Tyler Lutz. The name 'Tyler' would've been obvious to everyone there except Jerry Gillespie, because he wasn't from Dripping Springs like the rest of them. He obviously thought Albeck was talking about the city. Think of the possibilities — especially if Boz knew about the affair. Talk about a motive for murder."

"But why now?" Mia asked. "If Boz killed Lutz because of an affair, why now? Why not when he found out about it?"

"Maybe he knew he'd be an obvious suspect if he killed Lutz

immediately after learning about it. But if he waited a few months..."

"Interesting," Mia said, "but I'm not sure how any of this ties in to the fraud scheme."

We were almost to the little community of Henly.

"Could've been a love triangle," I said. "Boz finds out, decides to leave Erin, and figures, hey, why not screw Tyler out of three million, then kill him?"

"Yeah, but the money would go to Erin. How would Boz get his hands on it when he's supposed to be dead? I doubt Erin would just hand it over. Besides, it's not Tyler's money."

I thought about it, then said, "Would you stop that?"

"Stop what?"

"Discrediting my theories with reality."

"Get better theories."

She turned right on Highway 290.

"You know, if there were any doubt as to whether the body in the vehicle might be Boz Gentry, this would be a lot easier," she said.

"Yep. Then we could figure Tyler and Erin killed him for the insurance," I said. "Happens all the time."

"But if we're assuming Boz is alive, what if all three of them were working together?"

A Chevy truck zoomed past with a dog in the bed, on top of a mounted tool box. One small swerve and that dog would be on the highway. Made me want to pull the guy over and do cruel things to him with a pair of pliers.

"Walk me through it," I said.

"Okay. We're assuming Boz was angry about the affair, but what if he wasn't? What if he and Erin had grown apart? So Erin starts sleeping with Tyler, and it's obvious she and Boz are headed toward a divorce. Boz doesn't really care, and maybe he thinks, 'Hey, if we're going to end this, why not get rich in the process?' And since the guy Erin is cheating with is an insurance agent, who better to make sure they avoid the obvious pitfalls?"

I pondered it. "Maybe Tyler fell in love with Erin and started to fantasize about killing Boz. Then Tyler could marry Erin, and the cherry on top is that she'd be rich. But Tyler doesn't have the guts to go through with it, so he decides it would be easier and less risky to include Boz in the scheme."

"Could be," Mia said. "Either way, they all three end up working together."

"But why does Erin necessarily have to be involved?" I said. "Boz and Tyler could have brewed this scheme up without her."

"That's true. I could see that. How does Shelley fit in? And what about Candice? Why did she go out to Albeck's ranch on Saturday afternoon?"

"No idea," I said. "But rather than simply wondering what the answers are, you know what we're going to do?"

"What?"

"We're going to go over to Erin's house and ask her."

According to the GPS tracker on her car, Erin had not gone anywhere all day, so we took Bee Caves Road to Riverhills and turned left. As we got closer, I felt an undeniable sense of relief that we were about to confront this case head-on. Yes, I had questioned Erin Gentry four days earlier, but now we were going to interrogate her. Big difference. And we knew some things — or suspected some things — that might make her more willing to talk. If she knew anything. And if she cooperated. She didn't have to answer our questions. She could tell us to go to hell, and she was spunky enough to do just that.

Regardless, I had the feeling this case was either about to open wide, or we would reach a dead end that would force us to give up. That happened sometimes. Not every subject we were hired to watch was actually committing fraud. And, obviously, based purely on the odds, some committed fraud and we simply couldn't catch them.

Mia turned into the Gentrys' driveway, parked behind Erin's car, and we both climbed out of the van. I was wearing my ball cap with the covert video camera, just in case. Who knew what Erin might say, then later deny saying? For that matter, who knew who might answer the door? I could just imagine Boz Gentry opening the door, then slamming it shut again before we could even react.

But, no, it was answered by Erin, who was wearing blue shorts and, just like last week, a bikini top, this one with a floral print. Still no shoes. Her hair was damp. The dog, Blackie, was already barking from the backyard.

"You didn't peek out the curtains this time and your deadbolt wasn't locked," I said before she spoke, trying to set her off balance from the start.

"And didn't you hear the sound of somebody else in the house last time?" Mia asked me.

"Pretty sure I did. Erin, this is my partner Mia."

Mia said, "How you doing, Erin?"

Erin eyeballed Mia without a lot of warmth, then looked at me again. She was still holding the edge of the door with one hand, as if she might close it at any second. "What do y'all want? I still haven't got my money, and I guess you heard Tyler is dead. I figure that'll gum up the works for awhile."

"Your empathy is heartwarming," I said.

"I don't know about that," she said, "but I'm tired of waiting."

I let out a long sigh, as if I'd been working hard and finally reached a point where I could take a much-needed rest. "This has been a tough case, Erin. No doubt about it. But we've just about got it licked. Only question at this point is how many people are gonna get in trouble — how many are gonna go to jail. We'll do our best to help everyone involved, if they come clean. We'll talk to our client and see if they'll go easy — maybe not press charges if there are extenuating circumstances. They usually listen when we vouch for someone. That's why we're here — to see which way you want to go on this."

If she was even the slightest bit rattled, she didn't show it. She flicked her chin toward Mia. "Can I assume she's the brains of your outfit, 'cause you ain't makin' no sense at all. Maybe you drove to the wrong house?"

"She's the beauty *and* the brains," I said.

"I can see that," she said, then shifted gears. "I thought you was trying to help me collect the money. That's what you said last week — that the insurance company wanted you to look for Boz, and if you couldn't find him, they might finally pay up. But now here you are inferring that I had something to do with it. Or am I nuts?"

"Let's just say we've assembled a collection of facts that lead us to that conclusion," I said.

"What facts?" Erin said. "Blackie! Hush!"

The dog went silent.

"Let's start with an easy one," Mia said. "Your aunt, Shelley Milligan, works at the dentist's office where Boz's records went missing."

"So what?"

"I promised Shelley I'd keep this to myself," I said, "but since you and her are kin, I'll let you in on a secret. She admitted she stole those records. She said somebody threatened her and she had no choice. But come on. It's pretty obvious what happened."

"You're doing your best to look shocked," Mia said.

"I *am* shocked, goddammit," Erin said. "You're saying she had something to do with this scheme Boz supposedly came up with?"

"We are," I said.

"She took Boz's dental records? She told you that?"

"She did."

"I don't believe you," Erin said.

"Call her."

"I will," she said. "Soon as you go away."

"When you do, ask her why she was over at Alex Albeck's house this morning."

Her face was blank for a second. Then she smirked.

"You people are ridiculous. You're as bad as the cops. You think you're really smart, but all you've got is a bunch of bullshit."

She knew something we didn't. Something that would make us look incompetent. I hate when that happens.

"What are we missing?" I said.

"My aunt is off on Mondays. She cleans Alex's house for him. She's been doing that for several years."

Oops.

She laughed at my expression. It was starting to remind me of my encounter with Jerry Gillespie. That was the drawback to asking questions and not knowing the answers beforehand.

"She wasn't cleaning," Mia said. "She was lounging around the pool."

"So what?" Erin said. "Alex don't care what she does as long as she gets the place clean. Sometimes she spends the whole day over there. Wouldn't you if you lived in a double-wide?"

Once again, it appeared we were chasing dead ends. I doubted Erin would talk much longer, and she definitely wouldn't answer the door if we ever showed up again, so it was time to place everything on the table.

"Speaking of Alex," I said, "there was a point when we thought the two of you were sleeping together."

"God, you're an idiot," Erin said, appearing genuinely amused. "Why would you think that?"

"Because you went over to his house late on Thursday night," I said.

Her laughter evaporated. "Have you been following me, asshole?"

"I have, yes," I said.

"So you said you were gonna help me, but really you're a liar and a scumbag."

"And some people say those are my finer points."

"Including me," Mia said.

"I am done with you people," Erin said, pointing a finger. "You stop following me. And get off my place right now. You're trespassing."

She began to swing the door closed.

"The affair was between you and Tyler Lutz," I said.

The door stopped moving.

29

The fact that she didn't close the door told me what I needed to know. We had already implied heavy-handedly that she was involved in Boz's scheme, and she'd denied it. So why now would she be hesitant to end the conversation? If she hadn't been sleeping with Tyler, wouldn't she have viewed my last remark as just another outrageous and unfounded accusation? But instead of following through and closing the door, she opened it up again.

Because she wanted to see what we knew.

"Yeah, that's right," she said. "I was banging Tyler."

That was easy.

Then she said, "I was also banging Alex. Hey, and don't forget my Aunt Shelley. We had this crazy lesbian incest thing going on. Oh, and Dr. Wilkins, too. That man is hung like a mule."

"You're cute when you're being sarcastic," I said.

"Well, shit, what would you do in my position? Everybody seems to think I was involved with this stupid con game, so what's one more dirty little deed? I wasn't cheating on Boz, but if you want to think I was, go right ahead. Don't make no difference to me."

I wasn't swayed. We had no hard evidence that Erin and Lutz had been sleeping together — but her sarcasm, followed by the old "You can believe whatever you want" attitude — were classic signs that we were hitting close to home. But could I get her to admit it?

I said, "Erin, seriously, I want you to think about something. It's all but a given that Boz faked his death. And now he's a suspect in Tyler's death. Did you know that?"

"I seen that on the news."

"He can't stay hidden forever, and that means there is eventually going to be a trial. Maybe two trials. So don't fool yourself into thinking this will all just go away. If you were involved, I guarantee that when Boz is caught, he'll flip on you in a heartbeat."

"Happens all the time," Mia said. "Hell, even if you *weren't* involved, he might try to say that you were. And not just in the fraud, but in Tyler's murder, too."

"People get desperate when they're looking at long prison terms," I said. "Boz will, too. And when that trial comes, for your own sake, you don't want to have a history of lying to people. If you get caught in a lie, Boz's lawyers will bring that up and try to blame everything on you. They'll say the entire thing was your idea, and when you deny it, they'll say, 'But look at the lies she's told. She can't be trusted.' And your affair with Tyler Lutz is a good example. Honestly, nobody really cares if you were sleeping with him — it's none of our business. But if you were, you'd better believe the cops will prove it, and it will come up in trial. And both of us — Mia and me — will be called as witnesses, and this conversation right now will go on record. You just said you weren't cheating on Boz, and if that's true, then fine. But if it's not true, now's the time to come clean."

"That way," Mia said, "they can't make you out as both a cheater and a liar. That's one thing jury members really get judgmental about — liars. Once you get labeled as a liar, it's hard for anybody to think of you as anything else."

Erin Gentry was about as tough as they come, but I noticed that the stubborn set to her jaw had softened. The fire was cooling in her eyes.

Mia and I remained silent.

Then Erin gave a very slight nod. "Okay," she said quietly. "Fuck it. Everything is so screwed up. I need a cigarette."

She turned and disappeared somewhere in the house, leaving the door open.

I looked at Mia and made a gesture that said, *Are we supposed to follow her?*

Mia gave me one back that said, *Let's wait a minute.*

So we did wait, and after a few moments, Erin came back, sucking away on a filtered Marlboro. Then she exhaled a long plume of smoke and launched right into it, saying, "Boz cheated on me first. I'm mature enough to know that don't make it right on my part, but that's what happened. I knew something was going on, so I went to Tyler and asked him what he thought."

"Why, uh, talk to Tyler about Boz cheating on you?" I asked.

She frowned like I'd asked a stupid question. Then she realized she'd left out an important part of the story — and I was pretty sure I knew what that part would be. "Because Boz was cheating with Tyler's secretary, Candice."

Outstanding. Another piece had just fallen into place. A small revelation like that isn't quite as rewarding as those moments when you totally bust a fraudster on video, but it was close.

Truth is, Candice had been at the back of my mind since I'd seen her on Albeck's ranch on Saturday afternoon, but I hadn't had time to dig any deeper. There had been the fire at Mia's place, then Sunday had been eaten up by meeting with Lutz, talking to Mia's neighbor Lucian, then driving over to Lutz's house after learning that he'd been killed. But now it was time to take a closer look at Candice.

"How did Tyler find out what was going on between Boz and Candice?" Mia asked.

Erin snorted. "He followed her home at lunchtime and saw Boz over there. When he asked her about it, she totally caved and admitted it. And she cried, if you can believe it. Didn't want to lose her job."

"When was this?" I said.

"January?" she said. "February?"

"And what did you do about it?" I said.

"Kicked Boz out of the house for a couple of weeks. Worthless son of a bitch."

"And how did you end up with Tyler?" Mia asked.

Erin rolled her eyes. "Look. I don't really want to go into a lot of details, okay? I wouldn't say I was 'with' him. I basically slept with Tyler a couple of times to pay Boz back. Revenge sex. Wasn't like I was in love with Tyler. Then Boz came crawling back, swearing he wouldn't do it again, and that was that."

"He stopped seeing Candice?" I said.

"Yeah, and I stopped seeing Tyler."

"Did it help?" Mia asked.

"Did what help?"

"Was your relationship stronger after you both stopped seeing other people?"

"What're you, Doctor Phil?" Erin said. "Boz was still the same old Boz. He can be sweet, but he can also be an asshole. Probably wasn't the first slut he'd slept with. But I'll tell you this much — if this whole fraud thing is true, I'm done with him. And I'm done talking to people — cops, reporters, and both of y'all. Nobody listens to me anyway."

"What do you mean?" I said.

"I keep telling people I had nothing to do with the wreck, or with Boz disappearing — and I don't know where he is or whether he's even alive — but does anybody listen?"

"So he wasn't inside when I talked to you on Thursday?" I said. "He's not in there right now?"

Erin stepped aside, inviting me into the house. "Knock yourself out. Invade my privacy and take a look, if it'll make you feel better."

She didn't look the least bit worried that I might take her up on it. But I'd already learned she was a pretty good actress.

I shook my head.

"Okay, then," she said. "But remember I offered. And from this point forward, you and everybody else can kiss my ass. How about that?"

This time she did close the door.

30

"You believe her?" I asked Mia as she was backing out of the driveway.

"Yes, I'm pretty sure she would let you kiss her ass."

"Well played," I said.

She dropped it into forward gear and gassed it up Riverhills Road.

"I think I do believe her," Mia said. "Do you?"

"Hard not to," I said.

"But there's still one question. If she wasn't involved — if it was just Boz, or Boz and Tyler, or even Boz and Candice — how would he, or they, get the money from Erin?"

I didn't know the answer. I said, "Last week, a fairly well off middle-aged woman approached a bunch of teenagers in a seedy neighborhood and asked if they wanted to kill her husband for five grand. Not discreet about it at all. Didn't even know the kids personally."

"I heard about that," Mia said. "And?"

"Sometimes people do really stupid things — so stupid that you find yourself wondering, 'Can this be real? Can anyone really be that much of an idiot?' And the answer is yes. So maybe Boz was just stupid. Maybe he hadn't thought it through all the way. Maybe he jumped into it without ironing out all the details."

"Where are we going?" Mia said.

"Don't know," I said. "Or maybe you were right yesterday."

"About what?" she said.

"When we were driving to Lutz's house, you wondered if Boz had kept his plan from Erin so that she could get through the police interrogation more easily. She wouldn't be lying, because she honestly wouldn't know anything. She could even pass a polygraph, if they asked. Then, later, Boz would let her know he was alive, and they could take off to some foreign country together with the three million bucks."

"I don't remember saying anything about a foreign country."

"I added that part," I said. "Wouldn't it have to be a given? They couldn't very well plan on staying in the States."

"Except people can be really stupid."

"As a wise man once said."

"Maybe Boz is already out of the country," Mia said.

"Oh, crap. I meant to ask Erin if Boz had a passport."

"I think by the end of the conversation she probably would have told you to stick his passport where the sun don't shine."

"She's a feisty one, huh?" I said.

"Sure is. Cute, too."

I didn't say anything.

"And what is it about a mole on a woman's face that is so sexy?" Mia asked.

I kept quiet.

"And hanging around the house in a bikini top all day," Mia said. "Classy. But I'll admit she looked pretty good in it."

I could feel her looking over at me, waiting for a response.

"She's no Mia Madison," I said.

"Ha. I should hope not."

"Besides," I said, "it's not a mole, it's a beauty mark."

"Semantics," Mia said.

"You hungry?" I asked.

"Changing the subject?"

"So you're not hungry?" I said.

"Starving."

Mia drove west to the village of Bee Cave and stopped at Rosie's Tamale House. There had been a lot of growth in this area, with plenty of trendy new restaurants popping up, but Rosie's — a longtime tradition with the locals — still managed to draw a good crowd, despite the fact that it was housed in a large metal building and had velvet paintings on the walls.

I hadn't been to Rosie's since the previous summer, when I'd briefly dated a woman named Jessica who had played a critical role in the Tracy Turner case. But that didn't last. I'd woken up in a hospital room and found myself relieved that the woman sleeping in a nearby chair was Mia, not Jessica. That told me all I needed to know about that relationship.

"Boz was sleeping with Candice, so Erin paid him back by having sex with Tyler," Mia said. She dipped a tortilla chip into the salsa and wolfed it down. She was going over the details again to spur conversation. We were seated near a painting of a riverboat with red and blue lights built into it, proving there's a fine line between tacky and kitschy.

"Lutz lied to me big-time," I said. "Didn't tell me about any of this stuff. I don't think we can trust anything he ever said. And it makes me wonder if he was involved in the fraud, and that's why he got killed, versus Boz or someone else killing him out of frustration that the money hadn't been released."

"I just can't imagine Boz and Tyler would be anything but enemies after all that sleeping around," Mia said. "Even if Boz and Erin had grown apart or weren't in love anymore, wouldn't a macho guy like Boz be pissed that his wife had had an affair — even if he'd had one himself? That's how guys work, right? It would be a matter of pride and honor, wouldn't it?"

"That's an ugly generalization — but I can't really argue with it."

Our waitress arrived with our dinners — Willie's Plate for the both of us. The dish was named for Willie Nelson, who ate at the restaurant occasionally. I immediately tore into my enchilada. Heaven. I hadn't eaten since breakfast.

"We're doing it again," Mia said.

"Doing what?"

"Trying to figure out the 'why' and the 'who' instead of the 'where.'"

"But you know…" I said.

"Yeah, sometimes the 'why' and the 'who' tell us the 'where,' but we've been trying that approach, and look where we are."

"At the best Tex-Mex joint in central Texas?" I said.

"Sure. But we're here instead of shooting video of Boz Gentry, because we still haven't found him."

"As always," I said, "I'm open to suggestions."

We were quiet for several minutes, just eating.

"I think we're back to speculating as to where he might be," Mia said. "And it's a pretty short list."

"Agreed. Not at Erin's. Not at Albeck's ranch. I wish we'd had a chance to mount that camera in Albeck's backyard."

"Should we try again?" Mia asked.

"At this point, probably not. Even if Erin isn't a player in this, you've gotta figure she's going to call her Aunt Shelley and tell her everything we said, including the fact that we saw her in Albeck's backyard. She might even tell Alex Albeck. He'll know we've been poking around."

"If Boz is holed up in there…" Mia said.

She didn't need to complete that thought. Boz Gentry could stay hidden in Albeck's mansion indefinitely, and nobody could smoke him out.

I said, "Time to talk to Candice, I think. What else can we do at this point? We're running out of options. I'll admit I'm very curious as to why Candice would've gone out to Albeck's ranch. If she was —"

Mia's cell phone alerted. She had the ringer turned off, but someone had left a voicemail. She listened, then said, "Well, that was one of the fire investigators. The lab tests confirmed that it was arson, but I was expecting that. No progress on figuring out who did it. They've interviewed Jens Buerger, Shane Moyer, and those guys, and all of them have alibis that supposedly check out."

"I'd like to hear what those alibis are," I said. I couldn't help being skeptical. One of those lowlifes had to have been the arsonist. I didn't know it at the time, but I'd have a chance, very soon, to judge the quality of one of those alibis myself.

Mia said, "The good news is, I get my house back now."

***

I received some news, too, a couple of hours later.

First, though, Mia came back to my apartment to get her things, and then she left for her house. I offered to let her stay another night, or several, but she declined. I pointed out that her house might still be pretty smelly, but she said she'd live with it. I was honest enough with myself to know I wanted her to stay. Or maybe I just wished *she* wanted to stay.

I simply sat for a few hours and watched television. Sometimes you have to let your mind work on a problem when you're not actively concentrating on it. Let it sort of percolate in your subconscious. Come up with a brilliant idea while you're watching the Astros. That's bullshit, of course. It doesn't really work that way. But it gave me an excuse to set the Boz Gentry case aside for the moment and relax.

Only problem was, I couldn't stop ruminating. Still so many possibilities.

Boz acted alone.

Boz and Erin.

Boz, Erin, and Tyler.

Boz, Erin, Tyler, and Candice.

If we believed Erin and ruled her out:

Boz and Tyler, which didn't seem likely.

Boz, Candice, and Tyler, which also didn't seem likely.

Boz and Candice.

Wait a second. Boz and Shelley?

I was just about ready to go to bed when I heard a text alert on my phone. I figured it was Mia, letting me know she'd gotten settled in back at her place, because she knows I'm a worrier. But then I realized it wasn't "Brick House," it was my generic text tone.

It was from Laura.

The trip is on. It was never Hannah, it was me. I'm sorry. Was just being a nervous mom. Talk soon to finalize the details.

31

As I was walking out to the van the next morning, under a gray sky that threatened rain, a voice said, "Yo, Ballard."

Most of the other residents in the complex had already gone to work, so there weren't many vehicles in the lot. Three spots over from my van was a jacked-up Toyota Tundra, and Shane Moyer was leaning against the driver's door. He appeared to be alone, but I was still going to be careful. I could see both his hands, and the clothes he was wearing — jeans and a faded T-shirt from a rock band called STARZ — didn't provide a lot of options as far as carrying a weapon.

I wasn't happy to see him, but I wasn't surprised that he'd found me. Even a pinhead like Moyer — or any of the other fraudsters I exposed — could use some of the same tools I used to track somebody down. It happened from time to time. The usual result was vandalism to the van, or even my apartment door. Cost of doing business.

I approached him cautiously. If I had to punch him again, I'd do it with my left hand, because my right was still giving me problems.

"You looking for a rematch?" I said. "I just found out I'm anemic, so you might have a chance this time."

"Naw, man, I'm not here for that. Don't be a dick, okay? I came to talk."

Now I was about ten feet away, and I could see that Moyer still had blackened eyes. Some swelling, too, even four days later. Made me proud.

"About what?" I said.

He shrugged. "Cops came around hassling me about the fire at your partner's place. I figure if they suspected me, you do, too, and I came to say I don't want any trouble. I had nothing to do with it. I told 'em I was in Houston on Saturday. And I was. You can ask 'em. Or check it out yourself."

I almost smiled. He was scared that I would come after him.

"Maybe I will," I said.

"The cops got my credit card receipts and phone records. I checked into the Motel 6 on the Gulf Freeway an hour before the fire."

"Only the best, eh?"

"Huh?"

"What about the rest of your Boy Scout troop?" I said.

"They all say they ain't got nothing to do with it."

"But?"

"Like I said, I was in Houston, so I don't know what they was doing. I'm not saying they did or didn't, 'cause I got no idea. I just wanted to make sure you knew it wasn't me. I'm done with that sort of stuff. I'm trying to get my shit together."

"Really?"

"Yup."

"Meaning your life?"

"It's time. You know how much trouble you caused for me with that video you shot the other day?"

"Of course I know," I said. "You were committing fraud, and when you commit fraud, you run the risk of getting busted. It's not some game. You're lucky if you stay out of jail for that. Don't blame other people for problems you created yourself."

"Yeah, yeah, I know," Moyer said. "My lawyer says I'm probably okay since we dropped the claim."

"And let's not forget about the way you came after my partner in the parking lot outside your apartment," I said. "Seriously, do you realize how dumb that was? People get killed for less than that."

I was getting worked up.

"I wouldn't have hurt her," he said.

"If you had —" I had to cut myself off. Take a deep breath. Leave some things unspoken — like what I would have done to him if he had injured Mia in the slightest.

"I know, man," he said, and now he was reluctant to make eye contact. "Between all that and this fire thing, I realized I need to make some changes."

"An all-new you, huh?" I said. "Just like that."

"I don't blame you for thinking I'm full of shit," he said. "But I don't wanna go to prison. Could be you did me a favor. You and your partner both. A wake-up call."

"Maybe you should start this remarkable transformation by finding some new friends," I said.

"Probably."

I nodded my head, then walked closer. It appeared to make him nervous.

"You know who set the fire, Shane?"

"Man, I don't. Really."

Unfortunately, I believed him, which meant he probably didn't have any information for me to badger out of him. I pulled out my wallet and handed him a business card. It didn't list any information that he couldn't find easily enough online. I noticed that his hand was trembling slightly when he took the card from me. Now I was almost a little sad for him.

"My cell number is on there," I said. "If one of your buddies set that fire, I *will* find out, and I *will* take the appropriate steps to make them regret their actions. If any of them goes near her or her house, they will be lucky to live for the next 24 hours. I hope you realize how much I mean that. Do you think I'm exaggerating, Shane?"

He looked at me briefly and shook his head.

I said, "You learn anything useful and want to share it, just between you and me, feel free to call. That's what someone who's trying to lead a better life would do. That's how you redeem yourself for past fuck-ups.

But don't ever — I mean ever — come to my apartment again. You clear on that?"

He tried to look tough for about three seconds. Old habits. Young punks don't like to be dissed, and all that crap. Then he reached out and took the card. "Fair enough," he said.

Thirty minutes later, when Candice opened her apartment door, it took a moment for her to recognize me, and then her expression clouded just enough to be noticeable.

Despite the look on her face, I said, "Hey, Candice. Remember me? Roy Ballard."

"Yeah. Hi."

"And this is my partner, Mia Madison."

"How are you?" Mia asked. "I'm really sorry about what happened to Tyler."

"Me, too," I said. "It's horrible."

Candice was dressed in sweats and a T-shirt, and she wasn't wearing make-up. Obviously she had no plans to go anywhere this morning. Of course, she no longer had a job to go to.

"Thank you," she said. "I just don't even know how to process it."

"Did Tyler happen to tell you why I was meeting with him last week?" I asked.

"Not really, no. Something about the Boz Gentry claim."

"That's right. Any chance we could come inside for a few minutes and talk?" I said.

When she opened the door fully to let us in, a big, gray cat immediately pressed itself against my ankles and began purring insistently. Candice offered coffee, but we both declined. Now Mia and I were seated on a blue floral-print couch. Candice took a matching chair on the other side of a glass-topped coffee table. There was no television in the living area. The cat jumped up beside me and forced itself into my lap.

The apartment was a lot like mine — but then again, many apartments are like mine. Light-brown carpet that hides dirt. Walls painted with beige satin that can be wiped with a damp cloth. Two bedrooms, one bath. A galley kitchen with a pass-through bar. A small patio, on which I kept the obligatory barbecue grill. Totally practical, and boring as hell. Fine if you're a college kid or maybe in your twenties, or if you just need something temporary. But living like this in your thirties, as I'd been doing? I don't know why it hit me right then, but I made a resolution to move out of my place as soon as my lease was up in three months.

"Candice," I said, "We need to be right up front with you about something, okay?"

She nodded, looking earnest. For Mia and me, a lot was riding on this conversation. If Candice had nothing valuable to share — as in Boz's exact location, or at least some ideas where we should look — I didn't know where we would turn next. We'd exhausted the obvious possibilities, as well as some that weren't so obvious. We might just have to give up. I hated giving up.

I said, "You know that Boz Gentry is under investigation for fraud — for faking his death. And now he's a suspect in Tyler's murder. I met with Tyler twice because the insurance company that issued Boz's policy hired Mia and me to find him — to provide evidence that he really is still alive. We've been doing a lot of digging in the past week, and we've learned quite a bit. Some of it is very personal in nature. For instance — and I don't mean to be indelicate — but we learned that you and Boz had an affair."

I paused there. She had been making eye contact, but now she looked down at the carpet. After several long moments, it became obvious that she wasn't going to respond. She was going to let the silence speak for her.

"We're not here to judge you," Mia said softly. "Not that you should care if we were. I mean, you don't even know us. And it's not our business. But we do need to ask you some questions, Candice. Just a couple, and then we'll leave you alone."

Candice looked up now and nodded her assent.

"When did you and Boz first get together?" Mia asked. She was naturally taking the lead, so I decided to stay out of the way. I was glad the first question out of her mouth hadn't been, "Do you know where Boz is right now?" You have to work up to that sort of thing.

"Last fall," Candice said. She grabbed a tissue from a box on the coffee table and dabbed her nose, at the same time saying, "I already told the police all of this. Is Sadie bothering you? She doesn't care for women, but she loves men."

She was referring to the cat, which was purring right in my face. I'd much prefer Lucian's yappy dog Gwendolyn to pushy Sadie. I'm not a big cat fan.

"No, she's fine," I said, because I didn't want to break up the conversation.

"That was smart to talk to the police," Mia said, "but they don't share their findings with us. So please bear with me. Can you tell me how long it lasted?"

"A couple of months. Maybe three or four. It was stupid. I've never done anything like that before. Boz said he and Erin were basically separated and that he was going to get a divorce. I fell for it. And I'm pretty sure I wasn't the only one he was seeing at the time."

"Why did you think that?" Mia asked.

"Just intuition. The way he'd act when his phone would ring, like he was afraid who might be calling. Or contradicting himself when I'd ask where he'd been the night before. Stuff like that."

In other words, Candice had had to endure all the suspicions of cheating that Erin had dealt with. Some people would say Candice deserved it. As for Boz, it appeared he was the kind of guy who liked to fool around with a lot of ladies, and he'd say just about anything to make it happen. Did Erin know that Boz had talked about a divorce? She hadn't said anything to us about that. Most likely it was just another tactic from Boz's playbook.

"How did it end?" Mia asked.

But Candice was rising from the couch. "Sadie, come here." And she came over to grab the cat from my lap. Sadie tried to wriggle free, but Candice walked to the bedroom, dropped Sadie inside, and closed the door. I could immediately hear Sadie's muted meows from behind the door.

"Sorry about that," Candice said, taking her seat again.

"Not a problem," I said. Now I had cat hair all over my clothes.

"I was just wondering how it ended between you and Boz," Mia said, keeping the conversation rolling.

Candice shook her head. I felt I was seeing authentic regret and humiliation. "From what I understand, Erin suspected what was going on, so she asked Tyler if he had seen anything between me and Boz. So then

Tyler followed me at lunchtime one day. I came here, to my apartment, and Boz met me. Tyler totally busted me when I got back to work. He said it was unprofessional to carry on with a client, especially a married client, and it was. I knew that. I still can't believe he didn't fire me."

All of that matched up with what Erin had told us. I was starting to suspect that Boz's scheme had been a one-man operation. Erin wasn't involved. Candice wasn't involved. Alex Albeck wasn't involved. And it didn't seem likely that Boz would conspire with Tyler. There would've been too much animosity between the two of them.

"Did you know Tyler slept with Erin?" Mia asked.

"Yeah, I knew. Boz told me. He was really pissed."

"At Erin or Tyler?"

"Both. I was pretty mad, too, since Tyler was being a hypocrite. Why was it okay for him to see a client if I couldn't?"

"Did Boz ever confront Tyler about it?" Mia asked.

"I don't know for sure," Candice said. "Maybe on the phone. He talked about going over to Tyler's house and kicking his ass, but he never did, as far as I know."

Pretty good confirmation that Tyler almost certainly wasn't tied up in Boz's fraud scheme.

"Did you tell the cops about that?" Mia asked.

"Yeah, I told them everything."

"At any time during those months when you were seeing each other, did Boz ever bring up the idea of faking his own death?"

"Absolutely not," Candice said quickly. "I may be stupid, but I'm not a criminal. I would've told Tyler if anything like that had ever come up."

"Do you have any idea whether Boz is dead or alive?"

She took a deep breath. "I assume he's alive, because that's what everybody is saying. But if he is, there's no way he killed Tyler. That's ridiculous. He just wouldn't do that."

Candice obviously didn't know anything about Boz's whereabouts. Disappointing, but in an odd way, I was sort of relieved that Candice wasn't involved. She seemed like a sweet girl. But I still had questions.

I said, "This past Saturday, I went to Alex Albeck's ranch to see if Boz might be hiding out there."

She looked at me. Despite the circumstances, she appeared amused.

"Saturday afternoon?" she asked.

"Yeah."

"Where were you?" she asked.

"In a deer blind along the main road to the ranch house," I said.

"So you saw me," she said.

"Yeah. And I've been wondering…"

"Why I was out there?" she said.

"Exactly."

"Looking for Boz," she said. "He talked about that place a lot, and how much time he spends out there, so it seemed like a logical place for him to hide."

"But," I said, "I guess my other question is: why? Why would you look for him after he treated you the way he did?"

She started to speak, but stopped, seeming to search for the right words. "Despite everything that happened, I'd like to make sure he's okay. Underneath it all — I realize this is probably hard to believe — but underneath it all, Boz is actually a decent guy. The bottom line is, we all have things we aren't proud of. But that doesn't mean we don't have positive qualities, too. He has a good heart. When you meet him, you can't help but like him."

I was thinking, *Jerry Gillespie would have a different opinion on that.* Maybe Boz only worked on making himself likeable to the ladies.

"Were you in love with him?" Mia asked.

"Oh, God," Candice said, dabbing the corner of one eye. "That's the big question, isn't it? How dumb would a girl have to be to fall in love with a guy like Boz? But I guess, yeah, if I'm being honest, I probably was."

Boz wasn't just a player. He was a heartbreaker. But I couldn't get sucked into feeling sorry for Candice. She was an adult and made her own decisions.

"Can you think of any other places Boz might be hiding out?" I asked.

She contemplated that for a few seconds, then said, "No, I really can't."

"If you *could* think of other places, would you tell us?" I grinned at her, but the question was serious.

"I would, yeah," she said. "I think the best thing for him to do is turn himself in. I don't want him to get hurt."

"I agree," I said. "Nobody wants him to get hurt."

Mia said, "You can't think of even one more place he might hide? With a relative? Some special place nobody knows about?"

Mia knew we had to leave here with something, or our investigation would basically be at a dead end.

Candice said, "Well, the only thing that even comes to mind...Have you ever seen *The Shawshank Redemption*?"

"Sure."

"You remember how the guy broke out of prison and went down to Zihuatanejo?"

I didn't like where this was headed.

"Yeah."

"We were watching it one night — it was Boz's favorite movie — and he said he'd love to do that. Just chuck everything and take off for Zihuatanejo. Live on the beach. Never come home again."

Great.

"Did he seem serious about that?" I asked.

"No, not really, but if anyone would actually do something like that, it would be Boz."

32

We didn't give up, per se. We took a break. A breather. A pause, until one of us had a suggestion as to what we should do next. I did not call Heidi and inform her that her best and favorite investigative team was spinning its tires in the mud. No, I was betting that we weren't quite done yet.

In the meantime, I went to a big-box electronics store and bought four high-definition Dropcam video-surveillance cameras for Mia's house. I was sold when the sales guy showed me how sharp the picture was, and how the cameras streamed encrypted video to the cloud for immediate storage. Perfect. That meant there was no way for a burglar or intruder to get that footage back. You could also receive motion and sound alerts on your smartphone, so you'd know if anyone was on your property or inside your house, and then you could view a live video stream. Amazing. You could even talk to the guy and tell him he'd better get the hell out of there right now. Or just call the cops.

As I connected the cameras via Mia's Wi-Fi network, I tried to ignore the fact that her house smelled like the world's largest ashtray. Regardless, she was obviously happy to be back home, and while I was working on the security system, Mia's handyman showed up and replaced the scorched door between the sunroom and the rest of the house. Mia fed me and the handyman lunch, and then I finished installing the system by mid-afternoon.

Now I had some time on my hands. How to use it, how to use it? Not a tough question.

I found Jens Buerger stocking the breakfast cereal shelves at the super-sized chain grocery store where he worked. It was entertaining to watch his expression sour as he saw me coming up the aisle toward him.

"Hey, look at you," I said. "Back at it, despite that nasty neck injury. And you obviously have a knack for unskilled labor, which means you'll excel at making license plates."

I could tell he didn't get the joke, but still he said, "You wanna keep it down?"

His eyes were darting over my shoulder, watching, no doubt, for a shift manager or department supervisor. A guy like Buerger was probably always on shaky ground at any job he held, and he didn't need his legal troubles to be common knowledge in the workplace. Also, should there be any fraud-related court proceedings in his near future, it wouldn't look good if he were unemployed. I'm sure his lawyer had informed him of that.

"Sure, I'll keep it down," I said, speaking even louder. "I can understand why you're embarrassed, considering the way your fraud scheme collapsed around you."

"What do you want?" Now he was hissing. But he was still putting boxes on the shelves, trying to make it appear that everything was normal.

"Oh, come on. You know the answer to that." I grabbed one of the boxes. "Oh, this one is my favorite. But were you aware that there really isn't such a thing as a frankenberry? Talk about deceptive marketing."

"Are you high?" he said.

"Just on life, my friend. Just on life."

"Yeah, well, I've got work to do."

"Then I won't keep you. Just tell me where you were on Saturday afternoon when the fire started."

"Why should I?" he said.

"Because I can make your life hell."

I could see in his eyes that he badly wanted to challenge that claim, but he knew better.

I couldn't resist saying, "For example, my partner could tell your boss that you said perverted things to her while she was shopping. You were harassing her in the produce section. Very creepy. Better yet, I could say you propositioned me in the men's room. Maybe I could make my complaint anonymously. Bet I could get two or three of my friends to make the same complaint. And if they say —"

He held his hands up, giving in.

"I already told the cops everything," he said. "I have an alibi."

"And I want to hear that alibi myself." I raised my voice again.

"God damn it, you're gonna get me fired."

"We wouldn't want that, would we? I'm a reasonable guy. Just answer the question and I'll take off."

"I was at home watching the Astros, okay? Craig was with me."

I snickered. "Seriously? You and your fellow delinquent provided mutual alibis? And the cops bought it?"

"It's the truth. We ordered a pizza and the delivery dude backed us up. He said we were both there."

Well, crud. I guess it was possible the pizza delivery guy was a liar, but cops can generally spot a lying alibi witness in just a few minutes, and they can just as quickly coerce that witness into telling the truth. If the cops were willing to believe the pizza guy, so was I.

"Bet you were memorable because you didn't tip him," I said. "Am I right?"

"You're an asshole," Buerger said, just barely audible.

"That just leaves Zeke," I said. "What's he got to say for himself?"

A middle-aged woman with some sort of electronic gizmo in her hand had just entered our aisle. She was wearing the same type of red shirt that Buerger was wearing. A fellow store employee — possibly a boss of some kind — which explained why Buerger got noticeably more nervous.

"You said if I answered your question, you'd take off," Buerger said.

"I wasn't entirely honest about that," I said. "Did Zeke set the fire, Jens?"

"How would I know?"

The woman was getting closer, almost within earshot. It appeared she was conducting inventory with the electronic gizmo.

I said, "You'd know because none of you are smart enough to keep your mouths shut. If Zeke did it, he'd brag about it."

"I don't know anything about it — swear to God — and I'm done talking," Buerger said.

Damn it. First I believed Shane Moyer, and now I believed Jens Buerger.

The woman seemed to have noticed our prolonged conversation, and now she was coming this way.

"Crap," Buerger muttered under his breath.

"Can I help you with something?" the woman asked, looking back and forth between Buerger and me.

I gave her a big smile. "My fault," I said. "I tend to ramble on and on, even to total strangers. Can you direct me toward the extra-large condoms?"

Did I really want to drive to San Antonio in an attempt to locate Zeke Cooney and browbeat a confession out of him? No, I did not.

But I drove anyway.

Of the four participants in Jens Buerger's fraud scheme, Zeke Cooney was the one about whom I had the least information. That was because he had lived a nomadic life across the country for the past two decades, and he was known to use aliases. He had moved to San Antonio from Mississippi less than two years ago. I located his house easily enough on the east side of town, after wading through rush-hour traffic on Loop 410.

Zeke was a construction worker — or that's what he listed as his profession whenever he was required to fill out any form requesting such information — but you couldn't tell it from looking at the dump he lived in. It was a rental, but still, you'd think he'd do some basic maintenance. The whole place sagged and needed paint. One window was boarded over. A section of rain gutter had come unmoored and was dangling precariously from the fascia board.

There were no vehicles in the driveway. I parked along the curb and simply sat for a few seconds. He wasn't home. A guy like Zeke would be driving a huge, battered truck, and he wouldn't park it in the garage. Plus, just looking at the garage door — the way the bottom edge didn't rest flush against the concrete — I doubted it was even operable.

So I dialed Zeke's phone number — the one listed in the file from Heidi. I had a spiel ready. See, someone had accidentally driven through my privacy fence this afternoon, and I needed to get it fixed before a big pool party tomorrow afternoon. We'd be celebrating my daughter's birthday, and my wife wanted everything perfect. It wasn't a huge job, but I was willing to pay top dollar to get the repairs done first thing in the morning, which meant I needed someone to give me an estimate tonight. Then I'd give him an address a few miles away — in a nicer neighborhood — and confront him when he arrived.

But he didn't answer. Even worse, the number was no longer in service. Not a good sign.

It was a waste of time, but I went up to the front door and knocked. No response. So I pounded harder. Nothing.

"Lookin' fer Zeke?"

I jumped slightly. Don't know why. The voice came from my right. The neighbor on that side — a pudgy woman in her fifties, wearing a tank top, shorts, and flip-flops — had come out of her open garage and was standing in her driveway. She had a bottled wine cooler in one hand and a cigarette in the other.

"Yes, ma'am," I said. "Have you seen him?"

"Not since this morning," she said. "He packed up a bunch of shit and took off."

And that justified the sinking feeling in my gut.

"Any idea where he went?"

"Nope. You a cop?"

"I'm a freelance phlebotomist."

"Well," she said. "Didn't think you was a cop."

"I'll take that as a compliment," I said.

"You do that, honey." She took a large gulp from her wine cooler.

"My name is Roy," I said.

"Alma," she said.

"When you say he packed up a bunch of shit…" I said.

"Suitcases. Cardboard boxes. Bunch of big power tools all roped down. Looked like the Clampitts' truck when he pulled out of here. I figure we've seen the last of Zeke, and good riddance. That's what I say."

"You didn't like him?" I said.

Alma looked at me as if I were crazy for even asking. "You can probably tell I ain't no high-society snob, but we didn't need his type around here. That man was trouble from A to Z."

"How so?"

"Ain't you ever looked a man in the eye and you could tell he didn't have no conscious at all?"

She meant "conscience," but I wasn't going to quibble.

"Couple of times," I said.

"That was Zeke," Alma said. "Something wasn't quite right in his head."

"Did he live here alone?" I asked.

"Who would live with him?"

"What's he drive?" I asked.

"Big ol' green-and-white GMC truck that must be thirty years old. Got a headache rack and a bunch of toolboxes in the back."

"Tell you what," I said. "If he shows up around here again, I'll pay you a hundred bucks to give me a call."

I pulled out my wallet and handed her a business card.

"Cash money?" she said.

"On the barrelhead," I said.

Alma started shaking her head. "Hell, it don't make no difference anyhow. He's long gone."

I thanked her for her time. She raised her wine cooler in my direction and wished me good luck.

Before I drove away, I checked the mailbox and found at least a week's worth of junk mail and overdue bills addressed to Zeke Cooney and two other names I didn't recognize. I took all of it.

Thunder woke me at three in the morning, followed by a hard and insistent downpour, and it wasn't long before my mind was back on Zeke Cooney.

Just because he had hightailed it, that didn't mean he'd started the fire at Mia's house. Maybe he was running because of the collapse of the fraud scheme. Maybe he was worried that charges were forthcoming. An investigation might force the cops to sort out Zeke's past and fill in any missing holes in his criminal pedigree. How many aliases did he have? Were there any active arrest warrants in other states? Maybe Zeke ran because an avalanche was heading his way.

The entire apartment building shook from an enormous lightning strike that couldn't have been more than a hundred yards away.

I was also fully aware that I was putting more effort into the arson at Mia's house than I would have if I'd been the victim myself. I'd always been that way — protective of my friends and family, sometimes to a fault. When I was a teenager, an insult directed at me might have rolled off my back, whereas the same insult at a friend could very well have led me into a fistfight, whether my friend wanted me involved or not. I'd had to learn how to temper that tendency over the years.

Now, though, it was the circumstances alone that were forcing me to say uncle — both on the Boz Gentry case and on Mia's arson. We'd hit dead ends on both.

But I wasn't totally discouraged yet, because there are times when a case proceeds of its own accord. You're ready to call it quits, and suddenly you learn something, quite by chance, that puts you back in the chase. It is always an enormous relief. Wish for that sort of break and it won't happen. But out of the blue? Unexpected?

Like, say, from a phone call in the middle of the night during a ferocious storm?

The rain was coming down so hard, I almost didn't hear the music. Then I sat up. Yep. I could hear the strains of "Brick House." After what Mia had been through, my first thoughts went toward some sort of emergency. I grabbed the phone off the nightstand and answered by saying, "Everything okay?"

"Yeah, I'm fine," Mia said, sounding excited. "The storm woke me, so I was on the computer, and I saw an alert on Erin Gentry's car. It left her house an hour and a half ago and is now about 45 miles east of town."

"Where, exactly?"

"Just the other side of McDade, but from what I can tell, she's on a little county road, pretty much in the middle of nowhere. Looks like she got a good start before the rain hit. Right now, the car hasn't moved in about twenty minutes."

The obvious question was: Why was Erin Gentry driving around at three in the morning during a massive storm?

Lightning struck again nearby, and the pane of glass in my bedroom window vibrated so loudly I was surprised it didn't shatter.

"Well, hell," I said. "You know what we have to do."

"Now?" she said.

"Unfortunately, yes."

"You want to take the SUV or the van?"

33

She pulled up outside my apartment building in 15 minutes. Even though I used an umbrella when I made the dash to the SUV, I was drenched by the time I hopped inside. The rain was coming down at an angle.

"Holy moly," I said. "Maybe this isn't such a great idea."

"I'll go slow," Mia said. "We've got four-wheel drive and anti-lock brakes."

"And Danica Patrick at the wheel," I said.

As she pulled away — with the windshield wipers furiously trying to keep up with the rain — I removed my laptop from its waterproof case. "I kept tabs on Erin while you were driving over. About two minutes ago, her car started moving again."

Mia didn't reply. There was no need to, and she was busy concentrating on the road.

I checked the tracking software. "She's heading this way," I said. "Coming back the same way she went."

"There's nothing out there, Roy," Mia said. "Where she parked. No houses or other buildings. Nothing."

"Yeah, I noticed that."

The physiography east of Austin was dramatically different than in the opposite direction. Night and day, really.

To the west — to Dripping Springs, and out Bee Caves Road where Erin lived — was the rugged Hill Country, covered with cedars, oaks, yucca, and prickly pear, and layered with thin, inhospitable soil atop limestone or granite bedrock.

To the east was a thin swath of blackland prairie — flat to gently rolling grasslands with rich, deep soil that was much more suited to crop production. And easy digging.

"Which way?" Mia asked a few minutes later. She almost had to shout because of the rain pounding on the glass.

"Same way Erin went," I said. "Interstate 35 to 290."

We had been on the road for about ten minutes and I hadn't seen another moving vehicle. I could hardly see the traffic signals. Mia hadn't yet reached a speed above thirty. I realized I was shivering from my wet clothes.

"Is it handling okay?" I asked. "Do we need to pull over until this passes?"

"No, we're good. Just can't go very fast."

"Go as slow as you need to."

On the interstate, we began to see a handful of vehicles creeping along. When we went east on Highway 290, it was the same — light traffic — but the road here had shoulders, and the majority of vehicles had pulled over to wait until the rain let up. I glanced at the speedometer. We were going eighteen miles per hour, and even that felt a bit reckless.

But we kept going. And I kept silent, so Mia could focus. In the meantime, Erin Gentry's vehicle was roughly three miles away and closing. I watched her progress on my laptop, and I realized we had a decision to make soon.

Mia had been thinking the same thing, because she said, "Follow Erin or keep going?"

Meaning, should we go investigate the area where she had parked? She had obviously gone out there for a reason, and this rain might make it harder for us to figure that reason out. Evidence could be washed away. Evidence? Of what? I was letting my imagination run away with the situation.

"I think we have to keep going, don't you?" I said.

I could see Mia's face in the glow of the dashboard lights. "I really don't know. This is very weird."

"No argument there. But based on our current speeds, we have about five minutes to make up our minds."

"Geez," Mia said. "What was she *doing* out there?"

"I don't know, but if she got out of the car to do whatever it was that she did, there will be tracks. But not for long. Hold on a sec." I jumped over to a weather radar website. "Looks like it's been raining there lightly for awhile, but this big stuff that's right on top of us is headed that way."

"Maybe there's nothing to find," Mia said. "Maybe she was driving to Houston, had second thoughts, pulled over to think for a minute, then turned around."

"Just randomly driving to Houston? At three in the morning? With a storm bearing down?"

"You got a better idea?"

"I rarely do. But say you're right and she was driving to Houston and there's nothing to find where she parked on that little county road. That would also mean there's no reason to follow her, right? What would be the point?"

Mia didn't reply. We were well outside the city limits now — between Austin and the little town of Elgin — and the darkness was overwhelming.

"Not to rush you, but she's about a mile away."

"We have to let her go," Mia said after a moment.

"Agreed."

"Right?"

"Absolutely. And if we don't find anything, remember — it was all your idea."

"And if we do find something," Mia said, "it was all yours."

"Exactly."

We waited. Then, far away on the horizon, headlights appeared. Dim as hell, but they were definitely headlights.

"Erin," Mia said.

"Yep."

The lights got closer. And closer. And then the vehicle was passing us on the other side of the divided highway. I couldn't even see the vehicle well, much less get a look at the driver.

"Maybe we should follow her," I said.

"Goddammit, Roy, we —"

"I was kidding! Sheesh."

"Not a great time to kid."

After ten more minutes, we reached Elgin, known as the Sausage Capital of Texas, for reasons most people can deduce without a lot of trouble. Texans like their sausage.

Even at our slow speeds, we were moving faster than the storm, so the rain was coming down a little more lightly. But it was right behind us, following the same route. Mia was able to goose it up to about forty-five, so, in less than fifteen minutes, we reached McDade, home of the annual McDade Watermelon Festival. Texans like their watermelon, too.

"I have a rough idea where we're going," Mia said, "but I need you to navigate."

"Just a little further up here and you'll turn left on Marlin Street."

She did, and we passed McDade Junior High, plus a bunch of small frame houses on flat lots, and then Marlin Street turned into County Road 142 as we left town. We followed that for maybe half a mile, turned right on Paint Creek Road, then left on Stockade Ranch Road.

Thanks to our slower speeds, the hard rain would catch up to us again soon. I directed Mia through a couple more turns, and eventually the pavement ended and we were on a gravel road.

Mia said, "As the saying goes, we're not at the end of the world, but you can see it from here."

"We're almost there," I said. "One more turn."

The lightning and thunder just a few miles away had once again grown so forceful that you could feel the rumbling in your bones. The storm was catching up to us.

"There are absolutely no lights out there," Mia said, and she was right. If there were any homes or buildings, they were set well off the road.

"Another hundred yards or so," I said. I checked Google Maps, which showed property lines if you zoomed in tight enough. "There are large tracts on either side of the road. We're talking several hundred acres each. Doesn't look like either tract has any buildings on it. We're almost there."

She began to slow.

The gravel road wouldn't show evidence of recent traffic, but the grass on the shoulder would.

"Right there," Mia said.

There was an obvious place where a vehicle had pulled over, creating deep, muddy trenches.

"Just park in the road," I said. "We don't want to make any tire tracks of our own. Leave the flashers on."

The chances of anyone else coming down this road at four in the morning we're almost zilch, and there was room to go around the SUV if necessary.

We always keep cheap rain ponchos in all of our vehicles, so we each quickly slipped on one, complete with the little hood over our head. Better than nothing. I grabbed a couple of powerful flashlights and handed one to Mia. We left all electronics — phones and laptop — in the SUV.

After we stepped out into the road, we used our flashlight beams to inspect the area where the car had parked. The shoulder was sparsely covered with grass, but the majority of the terrain was just dirt — now mud.

"Footprints," Mia said. "That's about where the driver's door would have been."

The prints were not well defined, and the mud was soft enough that it was hard to determine just how big — or small — the shoes were that left the prints.

I used my light to follow the prints toward where the trunk of the car would have been, and then from the trunk toward the fence and the fallow pastureland beyond it. "You see that?" I said.

"Yep."

"What do you see?" I didn't want to influence her opinion.

"Drag marks."

34

The rain began to come down noticeably harder. My jeans and shoes were already soaked.

"This is probably a crime scene, Roy," Mia said.

"We don't know that."

"Oh, come on. You want to explain those marks? Somebody dragged a body."

I didn't know what to say. But it was possible this conversation might someday need to be repeated in a courtroom, and I didn't want either of us to have to lie, so I said, "Could be anything. Won't know until we check it out."

Which was true, technically speaking. If we found what I figured we'd find, the cops could later gripe that we'd contaminated the scene. But I could counterclaim that I didn't know for certain that it was a crime scene at this point.

Mia was shaking her head. "We should've followed the car. Damn it. Then we'd at least know who was driving."

And who might've been dragged, I thought.

"We don't know what we're going to find," I said.

"We should call it in," Mia said.

"These footprints will be gone in minutes," I said. "We need to follow them while we can."

She was torn. I could see that, even in the faint light. Plus, there were some legal nuances she wasn't aware of, but there wasn't time to explain it all right now.

I said, "Mia, look. The tire tracks are already worthless for casting prints. There is no tread pattern. Same with the footprints. They wouldn't even be able to estimate shoe size. And we don't know how far they lead. If they get washed away, even if we do call the cops, they might not be able to find anything. We have to —"

"All right. No more talk. You're right. Let's go."

I didn't waste any time. I led the way, following alongside the tracks, but not on top of them. My feet sank about six inches into the mud with each step. We reached the barbed-wire fence and clumsily helped each other climb over.

"Whatever they were dragging," I said, "it looks like they slid it under the fence."

"Looks like two sets of prints," Mia said. "So one set going in and one going out?"

"I imagine so."

I shined the beam as far as it would reach. It appeared the footprints and the drag marks went in a fairly straight line as far as we could see. So we followed. Ten yards. Then twenty. Then fifty.

My poncho hood slipped backward off my head and I didn't bother putting it back on, because it wasn't helping that much to begin with. Every thirty seconds or so, lightning would split the night, and we could see the landscape ahead of us. But it was all the same. Flat and muddy. A little grass, but not much. A tree here and there.

We kept slogging forward, and it was slow going, but after ten minutes we were at least two hundred yards from the road. At one point, I spotted a yellow cylindrical object about the size of a roll of Lifesavers stuck in the mud. Shotgun shell. It did not appear fresh; the metal on the end was rusted.

"Roy," Mia said.

She had aimed her flashlight well ahead, and it was now shining on a large body of water directly in front of us. I waited, and when lightning flashed, I could see that it was about half an acre in size. Either a natural pond or a manmade livestock tank. Didn't matter, really. What was important — as we discovered when we moved closer — was that the footprints and the drag marks went straight into the water.

We moved within five feet of the edge of the tank. The rain was hitting so hard on the surface, the water looked like it was boiling.

"Now do we call?" Mia asked.

I mulled over our options for a few seconds.

"Roy?"

I shook my head and handed Mia my flashlight. "I'm going in," I said, and I began to remove my poncho.

"You're doing what? Oh, hell no. Are you nuts?"

"That's debatable."

"Roy, come on. You don't know what's in there. It could be dangerous."

"It's just water. Standing water. No currents." I removed my shirt.

"It could be fifty feet deep."

"Most tanks are shallow. Besides, I'm a great swimmer. I swim so well that I sometimes pretend I won a state championship." I took off my shoes, which were so caked with mud they weighed about five pounds each. Then I pulled my wet socks off.

"God damn it, Roy."

"How is it any more dangerous now than if I came out here for a swim on a sunny afternoon?"

Of course, right at that moment, there was a tremendous lightning strike that couldn't have been more than a quarter-mile away.

"Ignore that," I said.

She glared at me. "Don't go beyond voice distance. And not beyond my flashlight beam."

"I won't."

Then I began to unbutton my jeans. "I don't *want* to take these off, you understand, but I don't need the extra weight." And off they came. Now I was standing in the mud in nothing but my underwear. Soggy, sagging underwear. I'm sure it wasn't a good look.

"Well," Mia said, looking me up and down in an exaggerated fashion, "if you don't survive, at least I'll have this lasting memory."

"That's the important thing," I said. I looked at the tank. This was probably a pretty stupid idea. "All right, then," I said.

Mia aimed both flashlight beams at the near surface of the water. I stepped to the edge and began to wade in. The water was cool, but not cold. The bottom of the tank was a layer of mud even thicker than what we had just hiked through, but there were no rocks, sticks, or other debris.

I pushed farther, my bare feet sinking into the mire with each step, and soon I was in water up to my knees, then my hips, then my nipples, and just as I was getting worried, it leveled out. The rain continued to hammer down, punctuated by an occasional lightning strike nearby. I had to wonder what would happen to me if lightning hit the tank directly. Water conducts electricity, obviously, but how far? Would a strike anywhere on the tank be fatal? I'm glad Mia hadn't wondered about that.

"You okay?" she called out. She was keeping both of the flashlights trained on me.

"Fine," I said. "But I think I just found Jimmy Hoffa."

I was forty feet from shore. I realized that slowly walking around wasn't going to cut it. This tank was half the size of a football field, but circular, with a diameter of perhaps 150 feet. "I'm gonna go under," I shouted. "But don't worry. I'll come up every ten minutes or so."

"Not funny, Roy," she yelled back.

"Okay, every thirty seconds. I need to swim along the bottom or we'll be out here all night."

I waited for her to object, and finally she said, "Okay. But *be careful*."

I tried to approach it in some sort of logical manner, so I wouldn't be covering the same ground twice. My thinking was this: If I were going to discard a body in this tank, I'd probably drag it right out to the center, which was about 75 feet out. That way, if the tank began to dry up during a period without rain, the body would remain covered for as long as possible. So it made sense to start my search in the center and swim in circles that got larger and larger. How long would that take? I had no idea.

I slipped under the surface, and the darkness was overwhelming and immediate. I could see nothing — not even my hand twelve inches in front of my face. I'll admit I was a little spooked. I swam toward the center, keeping my hands in front of me, skimming the bottom of the tank as I went. After twenty seconds, I popped to the surface. I couldn't touch the bottom. The water here was about eight feet deep.

Mia found me with the flashlights, though the beams were fairly weak at this distance. I waved that everything was okay. Then I took a deep breath and went under again, down to the bottom, and my hands immediately encountered a floating object that was soft and yielding — almost certainly a torso. Despite the fact that I'd known this was a possibility, I wasn't prepared for it.

I panicked.

I recoiled and began flapping and flailing my arms to reverse my course. I came up out of the water backwards, and I'm sure it was a spectacle, like an underwater creature suddenly erupting to the surface.

"Roy!"

I had the presence of mind to give another wave that I was okay, but I'm sure it was obvious to Mia that something had happened.

"Don't worry," I yelled, and I don't even know why I chose those words. I was still seriously rattled, treading water, trying to keep my cool. Despite the fact that I don't believe in ghosts or spirits, zombies or any sort of undead, I just knew a hand was about to reach up and grab my ankle at any moment.

But I stayed where I was.

Be rational. Calm down. Get ahold of yourself.

It might not be a body. Maybe it was a dead fish. But a fish that large in a tank? And don't dead fish float? I was trying to fool myself. Of course it was a body. But who? Realistically, there were only two likely candidates. Boz or Erin.

"What is it?" Mia shouted.

"I don't know yet. But I found something. Give me a minute."

It was one of the hardest things I've ever done, but I gathered myself and went back down. Slowly. But in less than five seconds, I found the object again.

Jesus.

There was no question now. I was grabbing an arm. And as much as I wished at that moment that the arm was roughly the same size as mine — a man's arm — it wasn't. It was thin. Fragile. A woman's arm. And cold. I forced myself to follow the arm to the torso, and now I knew it was a small woman. Slender. Nude.

With a chain locked around her midsection.

I was already running out of oxygen — anxiety will do that — but I followed the chain and it led to a cinderblock resting in the muck at the bottom of the tank.

I was tempted to pull the body and the cinderblock to the surface, so I could get a look at the face and confirm the identity. But I didn't do it, because I was worried about destroying evidence. I couldn't imagine what evidence I might damage by lifting the corpse to the surface, but just because I couldn't imagine it, that didn't make it an impossibility.

But there was another way to find out.

I followed the chain back to the corpse. It seemed like such a violation, but I did it anyway. I ran my hands along her torso, upward, feeling my way by touch. My hands grazed her rib cage, the sides of her breasts, and then followed her arms to her face. With my air running out, I cupped her right cheek.

Aw, damn.

The mole was there. Small, but I could feel it.

Erin.

I left her where she was, floating in the cool, dark water, while I broke to the surface for air.

35

Pay phones are hard to find nowadays, but Mia spotted one in McDade, on the far edge of the parking lot of a closed convenience store. It was five in the morning and I was shivering so bad my teeth were clattering together.

Earlier, as we'd driven away from the crime scene, after I'd described in detail what I had found and told her why I hadn't tried to lift the body to the surface, I had explained the precarious legal situation to Mia.

"The GPS tracker on Erin's car is illegal," I reminded her. "That means if we call the cops — tell them what we found and *how* we found it — none of it will be admissible."

"But we're not cops. Those rules don't apply to us, do they?" She was, of course, distraught about the situation, but, like me, she had known what we might find out there.

"In this case, yes," I said. "They would be discovering evidence based on illegal activity on our part. In Texas, it's inadmissible — just as much as if they'd used an illegal GPS themselves."

"You're sure?"

"Positive," I said.

It was still raining, but only lightly now, because we were heading west while the storm was continuing east. The worst part was behind us.

"So if a burglar breaks into a house and finds a dead body…"

"Well, that's different," I said. "I don't know if I can explain it with legal jargon, but the burglar wasn't there to collect information on the residents or solve a crime, so what he found would be admissible. Same if a landlord went into a rental property with a legal reason to be there. But if the landlord starts snooping around, like maybe rooting through some desk drawers, and he finds a pound of cocaine, that wouldn't be admissible."

"But if we report it anonymously, it's admissible?" Mia asked.

"Yeah, because the cops don't know we used illegal means to find the body."

"God, that is really fucked up," Mia said.

I didn't say anything. It was the law, that's all. Sometimes the law didn't make much sense, until you did some research into *why* the law was written the way it was. Of course, even then, some laws still didn't make sense. Most did, though, and that was probably as good as it could get.

"Plus," Mia said, "by calling it in anonymously, we avoid getting in trouble."

"True," I said, "but if I thought it'd be better to identify ourselves and tell them exactly what happened — if that would help them build a better case — that's the route I'd want to take. The prosecutor would have to hit me with a class-A misdemeanor for the illegal tracker, and that would probably earn me some probation. I could live with that. But in reality, an anonymous call will put the sheriff on much better ground. He can call the landowner, request permission to search the tank, and go from there."

We reached the city limits of McDade.

"I feel really bad for Erin," Mia said. "She didn't deserve to end up…like that."

"Yeah, I know."

"But she had to have been a part of the scam," Mia said. "Or at least she knew what was going on. And Boz killed her."

"Probably," I said.

"What do you think happened? Why would he do it?"

"Maybe she'd had enough and was threatening to tell the truth. At this point, I'm starting to doubt we'll ever know for sure what really happened — unless Boz gets caught and confesses. Which brings us back, yet again, to the fact that —"

"— we don't have to figure it out," Mia said.

"Right."

"But I have to be honest," she said. "Now I *want* to figure it out. I want to nail the person who killed Erin."

"Yeah, I know. So do I."

That's when Mia saw the payphone and said, "There?"

"Looks good."

"What if the store has surveillance cameras?"

"Park at that vacant lot next door," I said. "I'll wear a hat and keep my head down."

So she did.

I had my phone out and was doing some surfing. "Here's the deal," I said. "I'm not going to call 9-1-1, because I don't want to speak to a live person. Instead…" I trailed off for a moment as I searched the website for the Lee County Sheriff's Office. "Perfect," I said. "I'm going to call the sheriff's secretary's number and leave a voicemail. It'll be waiting when she gets to work in a couple of hours."

"Aren't you worried about them having a recording of your voice?"

"I'll disguise it," I said.

"How?"

I grinned. "I can't believe I'm about to say this, but…there's an app for that."

And there was. Since I wasn't using my phone to make the call, I had to record the message on my phone, then play it into the mouthpiece of the pay phone. One extra step. No big deal. I chose the mode that made my voice sound like a robot. Tinny. Mechanical. A monotone. But very easy to understand.

"Four miles east of McDade, on Stockade Ranch Road, about one mile north of Paint Creek Road, there is a pasture on the right-hand side that has a barbed-wire fence with red T-posts. Look for an orange piece of

surveyor's tape tied around the top strand. Roughly two hundred yards east of that tape is a livestock tank, and approximately in the center of that tank you will find a woman's body, held down by a chain around a cinderblock. The body was placed there at about three-thirty this morning by an unidentified person driving a car owned by Erin Gentry of Travis County. Her husband is Boz Gentry. If you don't recall that name, Google it or talk to Detective Ruelas at the Travis County Sheriff's Office. There were track marks indicating that a single individual dragged the body from the car, parked on the shoulder, to the tank."

As we continued driving, something occurred to me. I said, "We have to remove the tracker from Erin's car. Soon. Right now might even be best."

Mia didn't say anything.

"You hear me?" I said.

"I did, yeah. I'm thinking about something else."

I waited.

Finally Mia said, "Will Ruelas be able to get a search warrant for the Gentry house now?"

She had a mischievous expression on her face. Odd, because Mia isn't generally mischievous. Playful, sure, but not mischievous, because "mischievous" implies a willingness to do things one shouldn't do, and that's not Mia's style. She's smart. Grounded. Determined. But she stays within the lines. She is usually the voice of reason calling me back from the edge. Maybe this case had pushed her beyond her normal limits.

"Absolutely," I said.

"How quickly?" she asked. We were entering the Austin city limits. It was still dark out, but the eastern sky behind us was now clear of storm clouds and starting to lighten with the coming sunrise.

"That will be their next step," I said.

"Will they search it today?"

I tilted my head back and forth, thinking. "I'd say tomorrow is much more likely. We've got three different counties working on this — Lee, Hays, and Travis. It'll take them awhile to share all of their information. Plus, Ruelas won't rush it, because it's such a high-profile case. He'll want to put together a very thorough and well organized search — one that no defense attorney can pick apart later. So he'll do it first thing tomorrow morning. He'll write the affidavit today, get it signed, then search tomorrow. Why? What are you getting at?"

"What if," she said slowly, "we search the house first?"

I let out a snort of disbelief. "Uh...pardon me?"

"You heard me," she said.

"Yes, I did, and it's taking me a second to process it."

"I'll wait. But if we're ever going to figure this mess out, the evidence — if there is any — will be in the Gentry house."

"You realize what you are suggesting is majorly illegal?" I said.

"Of course. But we have to go over there anyway to get the tracker, so..."

I've never seen a more fuck-it-all expression on her face.

I said, "You understand that trespassing is peanuts compared to breaking and entering?"

"I'm aware of that fact," she said. "We wouldn't take anything or compromise the police investigation in any way."

"Searching the land and the tank outside of McDade was questionable, but this..."

"I know."

She had to know which way I'd go. I'm not a patient man, and my impatience often manifests itself as a tendency to take risks or stupid shortcuts. It'll probably bite me in the ass someday. I was hoping it wouldn't be today.

"If we're gonna do it," I said, "we'd better do it now."

36

We drove past the Gentrys' driveway. Reconnaissance, but we couldn't see much through the trees. The tracker told us that Erin's car was back home again.

"You nervous?" I asked Mia.

"Are you fucking kidding me? Of course I'm nervous. I get nervous when I drive through a yellow light. What if Boz is there? Or whoever was driving the car?"

"Had to be Boz," I said. "Can't imagine he's still there, though. He wouldn't murder his wife, then go home and hang around — not a man who was already on the run."

"But how would he have left? On foot?"

"I seem to recall that he owned a motorcycle. Wouldn't surprise me if he took off on that."

Mia did not appear convinced.

"I'll do it alone if you want me to," I said.

"Nope. One of us needs to be the lookout. Besides, it was my idea."

She found a place to turn around. I was glad it was a weekday in a quiet, semi-rural area. We hadn't passed another vehicle — or seen another human being — since we'd turned off Bee Caves Road.

The plan was simple.

Drive right up to the house as if we belonged there — like we'd come by to question Erin again. Hope to find a door or window unlocked. Then walk right in, as bold as you please. But we'd decided we wouldn't force our way in. That might throw the investigators in the wrong direction if they saw signs of a burglary.

When we reached the driveway the second time, Mia turned in. The caliche driveway wouldn't hold tire tracks, so that was a plus. We wouldn't leave tracks or ruin any existing tracks.

When we were halfway up the driveway, I could see Erin's Ford Focus. Mia stopped in the same spot where I had parked on my previous two visits. We immediately exited the SUV and headed toward the door.

"In and out," I said quietly.

"I know, I know."

No sign of anyone inside the house. Fortunately, the dog was not barking yet. But if he barked, so be it. I doubted that would raise any red flags for anyone within earshot. They had to be used to it by now.

Mia led the way up the steps and onto the porch. She rapped on the door with her knuckles. We waited fifteen seconds. Mia rapped again — more firmly this time. Still nothing. Mia banged very hard on the door. Not a peep. I reached out and tried the doorknob.

Yes.

Unlocked. I swung the door open.

"Hello?" I called out.

The place was silent.

"Erin?" I said. "Boz? Anybody?"

Dead quiet.

We both stepped inside, our senses on full alert. I closed the door, and then we waited another minute. Not a sound other than the humming of the refrigerator. We waited another full minute, and then I said, "Let's do it."

We'd decided that the search itself would be based around the answer to one question: Which single item is more likely than any other to reveal valuable information about a person's daily activities, deepest secrets, desires, and fantasies?

Some people might say it's a person's cell phone, and I think that day is coming, but for now, in my opinion, it's still the computer.

That's where a married guy hides his porn.

Or where a married woman hides her online purchases.

Or where a married couple intent on committing insurance fraud would leave behind traces of their scheme.

So we'd decided to forget everything else in the house and focus on finding Erin's computer. I knew she had a computer, because I'd noticed an Internet dish on her roof during my earlier visits. While I was searching, Mia would simply stand by the front windows and keep watch. If anyone pulled in or came up the drive on foot, we would quickly abandon the search and step back onto the porch, using the excuse that the door had been wide open when we'd arrived.

My search took less than thirty seconds. I found a Mac on a desk inside a small bedroom that functioned as a study. The screen saver was an ever-changing collage of various snapshots, mostly of Erin and Boz.

I woke the screen up and got busy. This wouldn't take long, because I wasn't going to sift through her emails, documents, and photos right now. There wasn't time for that. Instead, I took the shorter, more intelligent route. I copied the entire hard drive, using an expensive high-speed cloner I'd bought at the electronics store. Amazingly fast.

Then we wiped any fingerprints we'd left and got the hell out of there, only stopping briefly outside for me to slide under the Ford Focus and grab the GPS tracker.

Blackie must've woken up, because he began to bark as we got back in the SUV.

We went to Mia's house. The smoky smell had dissipated quite a bit even since the afternoon before, when I installed the surveillance system. I was beat, and I could tell that Mia was, too. Long night. Going to be a long day, most likely. We had a hard drive to dig through.

"Want something to eat?" Mia asked.

We were sprawled on either end of her couch, taking a break. It was still early — only eight-thirty — but the Lee County Sheriff's Office would already be bustling with activity.

"Not really. Not right now. But don't let me stop you."

"No, I'm all right. Roy?"

"Yeah?"

"Is there any chance you're wrong?"

"Always, but about what specifically?"

"Any chance it wasn't Erin in the tank?" she said.

I shook my head. "It was her."

Mia's lips were tight and her face seemed paler than normal. Maybe it was just the lighting. She said, "It just seemed wrong to leave her there. I struggled with that."

"I know. So did I. But the sheriff will recover the body, and then they'll catch whoever put her in that tank. We did the right thing."

We had her television tuned to a local channel with the sound down, and the radio dialed to an AM news/talk station. We'd know as soon as any news broke.

"How will they go about it?" Mia asked. "Same way you did?"

"I'm not real sure," I said. "They might drag the tank, but I suspect they'll send in a diver, or maybe a couple of divers. I don't know if they'll be able to see in that water during the daytime, but even if they can't, it won't take them long to find her."

We sat quietly for several minutes.

Mia said, "Hey, what if the sheriff's secretary is on vacation?"

That thought left me cold for a moment. Then I said, "I imagine there'd be a temp in there for the week."

Mia nodded.

We went quiet again. After a few minutes, my eyelids began to droop.

Mia said, "When they listen to that voicemail — and then they contact Ruelas — he's going to know it was us. Who else would it be?"

I had already thought of that. I knew it when I mentioned his name in the voicemail, but I wanted the Lee County sheriff to know what he was dealing with as quickly as possible. Ruelas could fill in a lot of blanks. They could work together. I would wager that Ruelas was a lot more cooperative with fellow law-enforcement officers than he was with me, and I couldn't blame him for that.

"Doesn't really matter," I said. "They can't prove it was us. If they contact us, we won't answer any questions. Besides, regardless of the message I left, Ruelas would suspect that it was us anyway. At lunch the other day, he guessed that I had a tracker on Erin's car."

"Did you admit it?"

"Hell, no. But he'll assume we did, and that that's how we found her, so he'll keep his mouth shut about it, because it's in his own best interest. Goes back to that admissibility thing."

Mia chuckled. "If it was any other cop but Ruelas, I'd say you're being a cynic. But you're probably right."

That was followed by a long stretch of silence, and then I opened my eyes, realizing that I had dozed off for several minutes. Mia was curled up on her half of the couch and her eyes were closed. Her breathing pattern told me she was asleep.

I grabbed one of the throw pillows and stretched out on the floor. I lay there, just thinking.

Where in the holy hell was Boz Gentry? The truth is, it's almost impossible for anyone to fake his or her own death and get away with it, even in the short term. There is always somebody else who knows the truth, and that person eventually breaks. Or, like Erin and maybe Tyler Lutz, they get killed before they break.

I found myself hoping again that the body in the tank wouldn't be Erin. I liked her, to be honest. She wasn't the warmest young woman one might encounter, but at least she was authentic. I wondered what she was like in a normal situation — say, meeting for happy hour, as opposed to being grilled from all sides about possible involvement in her husband's stupid scheme.

I kicked my shoes off and closed my eyes.

Shelley was standing in a corner, watching and nodding, as Erin had a set of pliers buried in my mouth, preparing to pull a molar. I knew I was dreaming, but that didn't make it seem any less real.

"Just get a good hold on it and yank," Shelley said. "Don't worry — he won't feel a thing."

But I would feel it. I could tell that the drugs hadn't taken effect yet. This was going to be horrible, but I didn't have the ability to sit up and object. I couldn't move.

"He's scared," Erin said somewhat apprehensively. "I can see it in his eyes."

"Nonsense," Shelley said. "He won't even remember it."

Now Erin put her hand on my shoulder and squeezed it, saying, "Roy?" She was testing to see if I could respond. "Roy?"

And then I began to come out of it, remembering that I was sleeping on the floor of Mia's living room. That would be Mia's hand on my shoulder, gently waking me — but it wasn't. There was no hand at all, and no voice murmuring my name. I opened my eyes and I was alone. The couch was empty. Mia must've woken and gone into her bedroom or some other part of the house.

I slowly sat up, trying to clear my head. I glanced at the clock and was surprised to see that three hours had gone by. The radio was turned off now. But the TV was still on, with the volume down.

And I froze when I saw the face on the screen. A driver's license photo. They'd found Erin Gentry's body.

37

I grabbed the remote and turned up the volume, while simultaneously shouting for Mia. She came from the hallway that led to her bedroom, her hair ruffled from sleep, and I wordlessly pointed toward the TV, where a reporter was now standing along a stretch of road — recognizable to me even though I'd never seen it in the daylight — and melodramatically addressing the camera.

"— are not saying how long the body has been in the tank or how they knew to look for it at this location. One thing we do know: Erin Gentry's friends and family members are mourning the loss of this young woman — and wondering if her death has anything to do with the alleged fatality of her husband, Boz Gentry, last month in a car accident. That case is still under investigation by the Travis County Sheriff's Office, and it took a strange twist just three days ago, when Tyler Lutz — the Dripping Springs insurance agent who provided Boz Gentry's life insurance policy — was stabbed to death in his home by an unidentified assailant. At this point, there are still lots of questions, and not many answers."

They cut to a taped interview with an older uniformed man identified by a caption as the county sheriff.

"We're in the early stages of the investigation and have been in touch with several other law enforcement agencies in the area. Meanwhile, if anyone has any information, we would really appreciate it if they would give us a call."

Someone off camera — a reporter — asked a question that was not audible.

"No," the sheriff said, "the landowner is not a suspect. He allowed us out here without a warrant, and he has no connection with the deceased whatsoever. What we have here is a piece of property that is used as a day lease for dove hunters, which means there have been hundreds of people out here in just the past few years. All of them are familiar with the property itself, and with the proximity of the tank to the road."

Dove hunting. That explained the shotgun shell I had seen in the mud last night. Boz Gentry was a hunter. So was Alex Albeck and most of Gentry's other friends. I didn't know much about dove hunting, but I knew that the agricultural flatlands east of Austin were good dove hunting territory.

Had Boz Gentry hunted that property before? I was pretty sure landowners were required to keep lease records. There would probably be a paper trail that would answer that question. I had a feeling that the answer was yes, and that when Boz had needed a place to dispose of Erin's body, the tank had come to mind.

When the news report ended, Mia repeated what she had said last night. "We should have followed the car. That's my fault."

"It is not. We both made the decision. We assumed Erin was driving the car. How could we have known what was really happening? Besides, if we had followed the car, we probably wouldn't have found the body. That tank is more than 200 yards from the road, and the tracks would've been gone. We would have driven out there and found nothing."

She didn't say anything. She was still staring at the TV.

"Mia?"

Now she looked at me.

"Second-guessing yourself is a waste of time," I said. "Take it from an old pro. You'll just drive yourself crazy."

I grinned, just to make her grin back, and she did.

"Yeah, okay," she said.

"You hungry yet?"

"Not really."

"Okay, then what say we take a look at that hard drive?"

I am admittedly weak in the area of computer forensics, and by "weak" I mean that I don't know what I'm doing. This is not a skill I employ often in my line of work. But that didn't mean I couldn't search the cloned version of Erin Gentry's hard drive in a sensible, methodical fashion. I had all day. Literally. And the next day. And the day after.

And Mia would be helping, because we made a second copy of Erin's hard drive for Mia to explore. She was working on her desktop computer in her home office, while I set up on her couch with my laptop.

What to do first? Start with the obvious. Browser history, of course. Erin's preferences were set to maintain her history going back a full year, which was convenient. I started on the date of Boz's "death" and went backward from there. I spent a solid hour checking the websites Erin — or anyone else using the computer — had visited.

Tedious doesn't begin to cover it.

Erin liked to browse a lot of online shops. Hundreds of them. Clothing. Shoes. Purses. Home furnishings. A lot of high-end stuff. She appeared to spend hours every day just surfing. This seemed to be as true eleven months ago as it was one month before Boz Gentry disappeared. It wasn't new behavior, so she wasn't necessarily browsing with the thoughts of a big financial windfall in her future. If she had ever visited a single website that discussed insurance fraud, her history didn't show it.

Emails were next.

There weren't as many as I would have guessed. Maybe she was more of a texter. I scanned a bunch of them until my eyeballs were tired. Then I used the search bar to hunt for keywords, such as "insurance," "fraud," and "Lutz." There were plenty of emails back and forth between friends and family members discussing the situation — not just the alleged accident and Boz's "death," but the denial of benefits and the resulting police investigation. But not a trace of anything that might reveal a conspiracy, or even a one-person crime on Boz's part. And no discussion of Boz's affair with Candice or Erin's affair with Tyler Lutz. Didn't mean much. She could have deleted incriminating emails immediately after she sent or received them.

"How's it going in there?" I called out.

"Glad we don't do this every day," Mia called back.

It went on from there. There are thousands of places on a computer where a person can hide a file or folder. And I'm pretty sure there are software programs that can hide those items in such a way that a guy like me could never find them. Or a person could leave a folder in plain view, but use password protection strong enough that it would take an expert to gain access.

Would Erin do that? Would she have known how? She didn't strike me as a tech-savvy power user. What about Boz? I hadn't seen any indication that he regularly used that particular computer.

At about two o'clock, Mia said, "Just sent you an email. A photo."

"Pornography?" I asked as my laptop dinged with an incoming mail.

"Ha. Pretty close."

I clicked the email and took a look. "Yowser."

It was a selfie of Tyler Lutz and Erin Gentry on a speedboat. You could only see Tyler's face and bare shoulders, but Erin was several feet behind him, lounging, stomach down, on the front deck of the boat in a thong bikini and no top.

"Is this the only one you've found like this?" I said.

"Yeah."

"Where'd you find it?"

"In the Mail Downloads folder."

"So Lutz emailed it to her," I said.

"I guess so. I'm not sure how that works."

"Me neither."

There were people I could call who knew a lot more about searching hard drives than we did, but at this point, I preferred to keep the investigation limited to ourselves.

"I've looked through her photo library in iPhoto and I haven't found that particular picture," Mia said. "So she probably didn't intend to keep a copy."

"I haven't found squat," I said. "Hungry yet?"

"Getting there."

"Want me to order a pizza?" I said.

"Sure."

"Pepperoni and green peppers, right?"

"Ah, you remembered," Mia said.

It arrived 45 minutes later. We took a break to eat, and then we went right back to it.

As time wore on, I was having to spend more time on search tactics that were less likely to pay off, like rooting through individual folders within the hard drive, one by one. It would have been easy to hide some photos or a document in one of the thousands of folders on a hard drive. I'm sure the forensics technicians who do this for a living know a hundred tricks to find that sort of thing, but I had no such advantages.

I realized with surprise that it was almost ten o'clock, and I was exhausted.

"Maybe we should call it a night," I said.

Mia didn't reply.

"Mia?"

"Oh, God, we're stupid," she said.

"Speak for myself," I said.

"I found it, Roy. It's here in an email."

I quickly got up and walked into her office. She had been sorting through emails again, and she had one very long email open on her screen.

"When you send an email, it ends up in the Sent folder, as you'd expect," Mia said. "If you go in and delete that email from the Sent folder, you might think it's deleted —"

"But it goes into the Trash folder," I said.

"Exactly. It stays there until you delete it, or until it is deleted automatically after a certain number of days, based on the settings you choose."

"Beautiful," I said. "What do we got?"

"Looks like Erin sent this email to a second address she used. I guess she figured the cops would eventually find it if something happened to her. I haven't read it all yet." She turned the screen slightly in my direction.

38

If anybody finds this it means something bad has happen to me, and that means it's time for me to tell the truth about everything that's gone on, and at this point I have no reason to lie. First off, I had no idea what Boz was going to do. He never said a word to me about it, and then a cop showed up at my door that night telling me Boz had died in a car wreck. I thought it was true just like everybody else. When Boz signed up for all that life insurance he said it was because Tyler told him it was a good idea so that I would be taken care of if anything happened to him. Boz wasn't always the best husband and we had our ups and downs, but I really thought he was doing the right thing for once. Should of known better.

So anyway Boz supposedly died or everyone thought he did, and then the detectives came around saying not so fast. They couldn't proof that the body in the truck was Boz, so that meant I wasn't going to get any insurance money anytime soon, and they started asking me a bunch of questions. It was obvious they thought it was all a big scam that me and Boz cooked up. I know I'm no angle, but I wouldn't ever do anything that stupid or crazy. I didn't know what to think, was Boz dead or alive? So then I come home from the lake one afternoon a couple weeks later and Boz is inside the house waiting for me, which just about scared me to death. He had been hiding out at Alexs ranch (Alex didn't know that) and then he came over here on one of the motorycles they keep out there. So I'm going to write everything he told me and what happened before the accident.

It started when I figured out that Boz was sleeping with that girl Candace that works for Tyler. So I told Boz to get the hell out of the house and he did. After that, even though Tyler isn't exactly my type, me and him started to fool around. I did it to get back at Boz and it worked. I've never seen him so jealous and I decided he deserved to suffer for awhile. But then one night I said something to Tyler about how mad I was at Boz and Tyler made a joke about killing Boz for the life insurance. The thing is, he said it like a joke but I could tell that he really meant it, you know what I mean? I'm not proud of this but I laughed about it and we started talking abnout really doing it, or just pretending we were, like in a movie. But then Tyler came up with this entire plan and everything. He said he would need to sufoccate Boz or use a stun gun on him so there wouldn't be any signs of what happened after the wreck and fire. He wasn't kidding! He said we could get married after that and we'd be rich.

So I was freaking out pretty bad and when Boz came over one night with a bottle of Jim Beam I gave in and slept with him and told him everything that had happen and what Tyler had been talking about. I cried so Boz wouldn't get mad at me but boy did he get mad at Tyler. He was going to go over there right then and kick his ass but he passed out instead. When he woke up he was in a really bad mood but it suddenly went away. I didn't know why at the time but I later learned he liked the plan too and he was going to force Tyler to be his partner in it. If Tyler didn't go along, Boz was going to tell the cops that Tyler had been planning his murder. So those two geniusses come up with a plan to dig up a body from a cemmatery and pretend it was Boz in the crash. I truely couldn't make anything up that dumb if I tried. So they watched the news until some poor guy died who was about the same heigth and weigth and age as Boz. They didn't tell me who it was, but I know it was out by Round Mountain because they said it would be easier to dig a body up at a cemmatery out in the country.

Then Tyler said there were some other things they'd have to do to fool everybody, like getting rid of Boz's dentist records. That way even if the DNA tests didn't match, those tests take a really long time and maybe by then we would have gotten the money and could be long gone. Boz said my Aunt Shelley didn't know he was the one who offered her money for the dentist records. That part I believe.

Anyway, after Boz showed up at home again, I tried to talk him into giving up and I told him that a good lawyer could probably get him probation for his stupid idea. But he kept hoping they'd pay me the insurance money and then we could take off. He had fake passports for us and everything. He said we'd go down to Bolivia in Mexico like Butch Cassidy and the Sundance Kid. I told him to remember how it turned out for them. Plus I said Bolivia is a country by itself, its not in Mexico. Anyway, Boz is stubborn and wouldn't give up and I didn't want to turn him in and I'll admit it sounded pretty good to run away with three million dollars and live on a beach. So we kept waiting for the money but they wouldn't pay it.

Boz and Tyler strated to argue about why I wasn't receiving the money, and Boz would tell me that maybe it was some trick that Tyler was pulling, like he was cheating us somehow. So I would hear them on the phone yelling, and the next thing I heard Tyler was dead. That totally freaked me out. Boz denied doing it but I didn't believe him. He would come and go on the motorcycle mostly at night, and he was gone when Tyler died, so he didn't have an alibi as far as I was concerned.

It wasn't long before I started wondering what might happen to me. I was the only person still alive who knew what Boz had done, not just the fraud but the murder. I don't really think anything will happen, but Boz has a temper and I guess nobody expects to be murdered, right? Maybe you'll find this after we're long gone with the money, in which case I won't really care.

One other thing, when Boz and me were arguing about this mess, I recorded a video on my phone and he didn't know what I was doing. It's a file on my computer called "blackie chasing squirrel".

Maybe I'm letting my imaggination run away with me. I hope nobody ever reads this, I hope I'm just being paranoid and Boz won't really do *anything to me. But if something does happen to me you can bet it was Boz who did it.*

39

Mia finished reading just a few moments before I did, and when I was done, I said, "Wow."

We had hit a gold mine. Not just evidence that would solve our case for us, but beyond-the-grave testimony against Boz Gentry in two murders.

Mia didn't say a word, but instead did a search for the file — which was buried deep in a folder we would have never located — and played the video.

It wasn't a heated argument — just some bickering between Erin and Boz about what Boz should do. Exactly as Erin had said, she had pushed for Boz to turn himself in. He refused. He wanted to wait and see if the life insurance money would be disbursed. The remarks they made in the seven minutes of video were more than enough to establish that Boz Gentry had staged his own death, that Tyler had been his co-conspirator, and that Erin had had nothing to do with it.

We watched it again. I noticed the second time around that Erin had managed to aim the camera at a nearby TV at one point, and on the screen, sound muted, was an Astros baseball game. Clever of her. The game would establish beyond any doubt that the video was shot *after* Boz disappeared.

When the video ended, Mia said, "That really is remarkable. When Ruelas and his crew find this stuff — the email and the video — will they be admissible?"

"I'm pretty sure," I said. "Can't think of a reason why they wouldn't be."

I took a seat in an armchair in a corner of Mia's office, near a window overlooking the small backyard.

"So this case is closed," Mia said.

"Looks that way. Kind of anticlimactic, huh?"

"Honestly, that doesn't bother me a bit. Just glad it's over."

I was thrilled that we were done, with days to spare before Hannah arrived for her visit.

"From a practical standpoint," I said, "we've got a small problem. We can't give any of this stuff to Heidi."

Mia started to ask why not, but she figured it out. "We wouldn't be able to explain where we got it," she said.

"Nope. If we give her a copy, she'll be obligated to tell Ruelas what she has and how it came into her possession, since it's evidence in two murders."

"And it's also evidence of our little excursion inside the Gentry home," Mia said.

"Right."

Mia leaned back in her chair and crossed her arms. "Well, that sucks," she said, "but Ruelas will find the note and the video, and Heidi won't have to pay the claim. Same result."

"Yeah, I know," I said. "Except it's a little irksome that Heidi will think Ruelas solved it, when it was really us."

Neither of us spoke for several minutes.

"She might even wonder if it was worth hiring us in the first place," I said.

"Heidi?" Mia said. "That thought will never cross her mind."

"It might," I said.

"Roy?"

"Huh?"

"What random idea is bouncing around in that crazy little brain of yours?"

"Nothing, really. Except, you know, it wouldn't hurt to let Heidi know the real situation. It would be nice, after all, to be recognized for our hard work on this case. Our doggedness and determination. Our ingenuity. Our —"

"Okay, yeah, I won't argue with any of that," Mia said. "But how would we go about it?"

"Seems pretty simple," I said.

Heidi answered on the third ring.

"What are you wearing?" I said.

"More than my husband is," she said. "Would you rather talk to him?"

"Tempting, but no. We have business to discuss."

"Yeah? What's up?"

I paused for a moment. "I need to speak to you in somewhat vague terms. And it might be best if you didn't ask any questions."

"You are being weirder than normal," she said.

"Thanks. You've always respected my hunches, haven't you?"

"I don't think we've ever discussed your hunches."

"I had a hunch you'd say that," I said. "I also have a hunch that very soon — in the next day or two — Ruelas will inform you that he has indisputable evidence that Boz Gentry is still alive. This evidence will include a video."

"Okay. If he..." She stopped talking. She remembered — no questions.

I said, "My hunch tells me that he wouldn't have found the evidence without a tip from an anonymous source. Of course, Ruelas being Ruelas, he almost certainly won't mention that fact. But I figured you'd want to know."

"An anonymous source," Heidi repeated. It wasn't a question. "I hope this hunch is accurate," she said. Still not a question.

"Rock solid," I said.

A few minutes later, when I hung up, Mia had a lingering expression of doubt or discontent.

"What?" I said.

"Something just doesn't feel…finished. You know what I mean?"

"It's because Boz Gentry is still on the loose," I said.

"Is that it?"

"He's still out there, and it doesn't seem right that we were able to wrap up the case without ever actually locating him."

Maybe I'm a small person, but when I left Mia's house, I couldn't resist making one more phone call. I was gratified that Heidi would know exactly who had solved the case, but I also wanted Ruelas to know. Not just the anonymous tip that led to Erin's body — he already had to know where that had come from. But I also wanted him to know we'd beaten him to the video evidence that proved Boz Gentry was alive. Why? What did it matter if Ruelas knew?

Like I said, maybe I'm a small person.

He answered with a warm and courteous, "What do you want?"

"I'm guessing you'll be searching the Gentry house tomorrow morning," I said.

"What business is it of yours?"

"None, really, but if you get a minute, pet Blackie for me, okay? He's the barking dog in the backyard. I understand he likes to chase squirrels."

It was perfect. When he found the video file, he'd know exactly what my remark meant. But there was nothing he could — or would — do about it.

"What the hell are you babbling about?" he said.

"He likes to chase squirrels," I said. "You'll see."

"Have you been drinking?"

"Good luck tomorrow," I said.

40

Things went exactly as we'd guessed, and it was easy to follow the progress on the news. The Travis County Sheriff's Office searched the Gentry home and found evidence that Bosworth Gentry was still alive. He was also a suspect in the murder of his wife and his former insurance agent.

Further, based on what Erin had said in her note — that Boz and Tyler Lutz had dug up a body from a Round Mountain cemetery — the cops were able to determine whose body it was. Just some poor college kid who had died in a car wreck earlier in the spring.

Eventually, the headlines died down. I never heard from Ruelas. I managed to put Boz Gentry out of my mind and find other ways to keep myself busy over the next few days.

First, I finally broke down and went to a minor-emergency clinic about my hand. X-rays said it wasn't fractured. Ice it twice a day, the doctor said. Take ibuprofen. And use that hand as little as possible. Yeah, right.

Then I began preparing my apartment — and myself — for a visit from a 14-year-old girl. I wasn't sure exactly how to do that, but I started by upgrading my cable TV subscription. Was that a mistake? We were, after all, going to spend 30 days together. There would be some downtime. Couldn't be on the go every minute.

Speaking of which, I'd had some ideas as to how we could occupy ourselves, but now I began to assemble an exhaustive list of activities and events. Places to go, things to see. Swimming holes. Nearby state parks. Barbecue and Tex-Mex restaurants. Museums. Art galleries. Horseback riding. Camping. Laser tag. Concerts.

Then I cleaned my apartment. Not just a cursory once-over, but a thorough, top-to-bottom, wall-to-wall cleaning of every square inch. I dusted, mopped, scrubbed, vacuumed, swept, polished, laundered, and Windexed. It drove home the fact that I was an incorrigible slob.

Next, I laid in a healthy supply of fresh fruits and vegetables, plus various juices and soft drinks, and even a few snack items, such as chips and cookies. Nothing too junky.

Finally, I felt I was ready, with time to spare, and that was a good thing, because life was about to take an unexpected turn.

Every so often, my mind would wander to Zeke Cooney. I was still hoping I might be able to track him down. Not right now, but maybe after Hannah's visit was over. How far would a guy like Cooney go? A hundred miles? A thousand? Was he worth the effort? Would I be able to connect him to the arson at Mia's house?

I wasn't even sure where to look. Zeke Cooney didn't strike me as a Facebook kind of guy. He wasn't going to tweet or text or write a blog. He probably had no idea those things even existed.

Then I remembered his mail.

I had emptied Cooney's mailbox when I'd visited his rental house in San Antonio. Sure, technically speaking, stealing mail is a federal crime, but Cooney had abandoned it, right? I was simply lowering the burden on federal employees by decreasing the volume of nondeliverable mail.

The morning after finishing my preparations for Hannah, I retrieved Cooney's hefty stack of junk ads and overdue bills from the van and began to go through it all. No surprise that Cooney owed several credit card companies a total of nearly thirty thousand dollars. He owed a hospital in Louisiana more than eighty thousand dollars. Didn't say what for, but a single aspirin can cost $20, so maybe he had a hangnail. Several of the bills threatened legal action.

A small cable TV operator in Hattiesburg, Mississippi, was trying to collect nine hundred from a man named Pete Hopper. Was that one of Zeke Cooney's aliases? And how does anyone rack up nine hundred in cable TV service before his service gets cut off? Then I noticed that the bill was for a single month. What the hell? I flipped to the second page — where pay-per-view orders were itemized — and I saw that Pete Hopper had watched nearly a thousand dollars worth of adult entertainment. Class act.

The phone number listed for Hopper on the bill was the same cell phone number I'd had for Cooney — the one that was now out of service — so it was a safe bet that Pete Hopper and Zeke Cooney were one and the same. I had already known Cooney was a scumbag, but these new revelations were pissing me off. Why is it so easy for a guy like Cooney to abuse the system and walk away unscathed from a mountain of debt?

After I'd sorted through the mail, I jumped online and began conducting searches for Zeke Cooney and Pete Hopper. At this point, I couldn't be certain which name was authentic and which was an alias. Maybe both names were aliases.

Intuition told me that instead of starting with a general Google search, I should check the sites that carry mug shots, which have become more and more numerous. These sites operate in such a way that if you surf too long, you feel the need to take a shower afterward. See, if your mug shot is featured on a site, you have the option to request its removal, but it'll cost you several hundred dollars. How is that not blackmail? I surfed over to one of the most popular mug shot sites and plugged in the name Zeke Cooney. I was rewarded with immediate success. Zeke had an impressive and wide-ranging criminal history.

It can be depressing to view a collection of mug shots for a career criminal over the span of his or her lifetime. In the early shots, they often seem almost amused to have been arrested. It's a lark or a bit of whimsy. It'll make a good conversation starter at a party. But their expression in subsequent mug shots becomes progressively more bitter or hostile. Or, like Zeke Cooney, they appear completely indifferent. *Got arrested again. Who the fuck cares?*

Nearly twenty-seven years earlier, Cooney had had his debut arrest — for driving while intoxicated in Escambia County, Florida. That led to another arrest less than a year later for driving with a suspended license and failure to carry proof of insurance. Well, sure it did. Wasn't that the way it always worked? I could just hear the objections Cooney probably raised at the time. The system was rigged against a guy like Zeke, see? How was he supposed to work if he couldn't drive? How was he supposed to pay his fines if he couldn't work? That's why he eventually turned into a thief and con man. It wasn't his fault.

He had three arrests for possession of marijuana, two for possession of methamphetamine, one for fictitious license plates, a whopping five for theft by check, and then a biggie: he'd been busted seven years ago for sexual assault. I wondered what had happened with that case. Would he be out now if he had been found guilty? Doubtful. He had either walked or pled to a lesser charge.

I was about to do a search for Pete Hopper when Mia called. She cut right to it, saying, "I just sent you a link. They think Boz Gentry crossed the border yesterday afternoon."

"The Mexican border?"

"Yeah, in Laredo."

"They're sure it was him?"

"I'm looking at a frame from a video right now and I'd say it's him."

Her email arrived and I clicked the link, which led to a short piece on a local news website posted less than an hour ago. First thing I saw was the photo. I found myself leaning toward the screen for a better look.

"Damn," I said.

"You agree it's him?" Mia asked.

"Him or his long-lost twin, yeah. He's looking right at the camera. Where was it?"

"A few blocks from one of the bridges."

I quickly scanned the brief text, but there were no helpful details. Facts were scant. Authorities were reviewing additional video for footage of Gentry actually crossing the bridge to Mexico.

"Guess he's following through with his original plan," I said. "Fleeing the country, except without the three million dollars."

"And without Erin," Mia said.

"Well, yeah."

There wasn't much else to cover on that topic, so Mia said, "How's it going over there?" She knew I'd been getting ready for Hannah's visit. I couldn't believe my daughter would be arriving tomorrow. Thirty hours from now, to be precise.

I didn't tell Mia that I was still trying to track down Zeke Cooney. I'm aware that my vengeful streak can be a bit disconcerting, and the news might upset her. Instead, I said, "The apartment's ready."

"Are you?" she asked.

I started to make a wise-ass remark, but instead I said, "Yeah, I am. Can't wait."

I focused my attention back on the website and conducted a search for anyone named Pete Hopper, which was obviously a more common name than Zeke Cooney. But it was unique enough that the list of resulting hits was fairly brief. I scrolled downward and the photo of the fourth man on the page was Zeke Cooney.

Cooney's Pete Hopper alter ego had only one arrest listed, six years ago in Daphne, Alabama, for criminal mischief. That charge covers a lot of ground, ranging from class C misdemeanor to a first-degree felony, depending on what sort of act was committed. This mug shot site didn't contain specifics, so I logged into an archival newspaper site. Quickly found a daily called the *Baldwin County Press*. My search for "pete hopper" returned a single hit:

DAPHNE MAN ARRESTED AFTER CAR FIRE

That got my attention. The article was no more than two hundred words long, but the gist was clear. "Pete Hopper" had had some sort of dispute at a bar with another man named Foster. It almost led to a fistfight, but other patrons broke it up. Hopper left shortly thereafter, and ten minutes later Foster's twenty-year-old Buick Skylark went up in flames in the parking lot. Hopper was the only suspect. He denied any involvement.

Wow. What were the odds? Zeke Cooney — a.k.a. Pete Hopper — had a penchant for setting things on fire. I saved a copy of the article.

I was about to broaden my search to see if Hopper had been convicted, but my phone interrupted me again. I checked the caller I.D. and saw a number I didn't recognize. I almost always let unknown callers route to voicemail, but something told me to answer this one.

"This is Roy," I said.

"It's Shane Moyer."

"You got something for me?"

"I just heard from Zeke. I know where he is."

41

Considering my line of work, and that I live in an enormous state, I'm used to driving. A lot. The thought of jumping in the van and covering two or three hundred miles on a moment's notice is nothing to me.

Ten minutes after I ended my call with Shane Moyer, I was on the road to Port Arthur, Texas, which was about 20 miles southeast of Beaumont, which was about 80 miles east of Houston. I had no idea why Zeke Cooney had chosen Port Arthur, but I didn't care. Why does a man who has wandered the Gulf Coast for twenty years choose any place in particular? Steady work? He likes the ocean?

According to Moyer, Cooney was staying at the Motel 6. There was only one in Port Arthur, so that made things easy. I left at ten-thirty and arrived at just after three o'clock that afternoon.

I had no plan. Maybe Cooney would simply admit what he'd done, and then I could punch him in the face. Knock out a few teeth. If he didn't admit it, well, what then? Punch him anyway? Even if he didn't set fire to Mia's house, he probably deserved it for something else he had done.

Shame on me. That was a copout — the kind of rationale a small-minded redneck uses to justify the execution of someone who might not be guilty.

The Motel 6 was near the intersection of two major highways. Three stories tall — a long, rectangular box painted in the familiar tan-and-rusty-orange color scheme. Clean, but stripped of any visible frills whatsoever, except for a small pool on the north end. Hard for a motel in Texas to make it without a pool. The parking lot was sparsely filled with aging cars and trucks — workers' vehicles, dirty and battered. One thing did surprise me: The doors to the rooms were accessed via interior hallways. Didn't that make it a hotel instead of a motel? That presented a problem for me.

On one side of the motel was a small retail store that sold safety apparel — not unusual for a blue-collar city that revolved around the oil refining industry. Almost directly across the highway was the public library, but I was willing to wager they didn't get much traffic from the motel.

It wasn't until I turned the corner to the rear of the motel that I spotted Zeke Cooney's truck — backed into a spot beside a dumpster, just steps away from a glass door leading into the motel. Why walk farther with your belongings than you had to? There was still a mountain of random belongings strapped down in the bed of the green-and-white GMC with the headache rack and the tool boxes.

I parked two spots over from the truck and pondered the situation. If the doors to the rooms had been outside, as they were with most motels, it would have been easier to determine which room was Cooney's. He'd park as close to his room as possible. But the interior hallways made it difficult. And the three floors.

Think logically. Figure it out.

Cooney was an experienced traveler. He'd stayed at hundreds of cheap motels, and he knew that not all of the rooms were created equal. He would ask for a first-floor room, and because the motel wasn't even close to full, he'd get it. He would ask for a room on the rear side of the motel, away from highway traffic noise, and he'd probably get that, too. He would ask to be as far from the pool as possible — again because of the potential noise — and that was why he was parked on the south end of the motel. He'd want a window looking out at his truck, for security purposes, and he'd want to be as close to an entry door as possible. All of these things narrowed it down greatly for me, and that meant I'd have to knock on fewer doors. Maybe just one — the room with the window two yards from the tailgate of his truck.

I exited the van and locked up. I was wearing a loose button-down shirt that allowed me to carry my handgun holstered on my hip with a minimal bulge.

Was I about to do something incredibly stupid?

Nearly twenty years ago, my closest friend was sucker-punched by a bully at a party and needed eight stitches over his left eye. The next night, I went looking for the bully with an aluminum baseball bat. Didn't find him. Probably fortunate for both of us. To this day, I wonder how I would react if I spotted him in a crowd. I have no doubt there would be an impulse to injure him severely. Could I resist?

For better or worse, that's the way I feel when someone close to me is harmed or even placed in danger. I want to punish the transgressor. Get revenge. I've discussed this topic with many male friends, and about half of them begin nodding their heads in agreement before I even ask if they can identify with my violent primal urges. The other half looks at me as if they should be concerned for their welfare around me.

I yanked opened the door to the motel and stepped inside. Let my eyes adjust to the difference in light. Then I started down the hallway. There wasn't anyone in sight. The check-in office was at the other end of the hallway.

The thing that was propelling me forward was the fact that Mia could have been in the house when the fire had started. She could have been napping or taking a shower. Death from smoke asphyxiation comes quickly. Whoever set the fire needed to pay. And for a guy like Cooney, a prison term wouldn't do much good. He wouldn't change. He'd get out eventually, and then what? Who would he harm next?

Third door on the left. I stopped when I reached it. Stood there for a moment. I could hear the TV. Someone was inside the room. I was aware that I was breathing more heavily than I had been just moments earlier. Not hyperventilating, but not far from it. I could feel my heartbeat in my temples.

My plan was simple. Tell him who I was. Accuse him of the arson. See how he reacted. I'd be able to tell if he'd done it. If the answer was yes? I hadn't worked it out that far. But I knew I wouldn't walk away. I knew I'd take action. I was starting to wish I'd brought a baseball bat instead of a Glock.

I reached out and knocked on the door.

At this point I was a jumble of emotions. Anger. Fear. Even some guilt. Should I be here? I knew Mia would answer that question with a firm "no."

I knocked again, and at the same time my phone gave the alert for an incoming text.

I waited. There was nothing to hear except the murmuring voices coming from the TV. Maybe the room was empty after all. Maybe Cooney had walked to a nearby restaurant or bar.

I grabbed my phone and saw that the text had come from an unknown number.

U asked abt my camera. Still wnt 2 see vid?

I didn't understand? I had no idea who this was from or what it was about. A spam text? But it seemed —

The door to the motel room swung open, and there was Zeke Cooney, wearing dirty jeans and nothing else. It appeared he had just woken up. Eyes red, hair disheveled, crease marks on his face from the sheets. He wasn't a big guy, and he might've been closing in on 50 years old, but his torso was lean and well muscled.

"Yeah?" he said, and there wasn't anything friendly about it. Jens Buerger had taken that photo of Mia and me in the parking lot at Trudy's, but he must not have shared it with his buddies, because Cooney didn't seem to recognize me. I was just the guy who had ruined his nap, and that was enough to piss him off.

But I couldn't put the text out of my mind. Video from a camera? And then realization washed over me. Oh, man. I had completely forgotten. The house in Tarrytown, down the street from Mia's place. They had a security camera aiming at the street. I'd left a note.

Now Cooney made an impatient gesture with his arms, like *Are you going to say something or what?*

"Sorry," I said. "Wrong room."

***

I didn't reply with a text. I called from the parking lot, before I'd even made it back to the van.

A man answered by saying, "This is Tom."

I tried to sound as friendly as possible. Casual. Didn't want to scare him away. "Hi, Tom. This is Roy Ballard. You just sent me a text."

"Oh, hey, right. The note. Sorry it took me so long to get in touch. I was out of the country."

"You're probably wondering what I want," I said. I had reached the van and now I climbed inside and closed the door.

"Well, yeah," Tom said. "But I heard about the fire at the house down the street, so…"

"That's my partner's house," I said. "Her name is Mia Madison. Do you know her?"

"We haven't met, but, yeah, I've seen her around. What line of work are you two in?"

"We investigate insurance fraud, mostly."

I asked whether his security camera had been active on the day of the arson, and if it was the type of camera that backed up to a DVR or to the cloud. He answered yes to both questions. Great news.

"I'm going to ask for a big favor, Tom. I'm out of town at the moment, but I'm hoping you can check your archived video on that date and see if a man jogs past your house a few minutes before the fire at Mia's place. That would've been about 12:15 or so. He was probably wearing blue shorts and a white T-shirt. He might've been carrying a water bottle."

"You think this guy in the blue shorts set the fire?" Tom asked.

"Well, I wouldn't say that. We just don't know. So I'd like to see if he's on your video, and if he is, can you email a clip to me?"

"Oh, sure," Tom said. "I have a Dropcam and it's super easy to do something like that. Just give me a few minutes to go through it."

Perfect. Dropcam was the same brand of surveillance camera I'd bought for Mia's house.

"I really appreciate that, Tom," I said. I gave him my email address.

"You help me catch this guy and I'll buy you a beer. Or perhaps an entire brewery."

Some people fumble around with fairly simple tasks involving technology, while others can dive right in and get it done in minutes. They just seem to pick new things up quickly. Mia, for example, was one of those people. When we first partnered, I noticed that she had the kind of intuitive mind that enabled her to understand the various surveillance devices and software programs we used on a regular basis.

I was hoping Tom had the same ability. Would I really hear back in a few minutes? Or would it be a few hours?

I waited.

If I was lucky, the man in the blue shorts would be on the video. If I was luckier, the video would be sharp enough to identify the man as Zeke Cooney.

Then…what?

Should I still confront him, or would the video be enough for the arson investigators to make an arrest? Would it qualify as probable cause?

Ten minutes passed. Then fifteen. I took that as a good sign.

If Tom knew what he was doing, it would take him just a few minutes to narrow the video down to the right date and time, watch it, and see if the man in the blue shorts appeared. Then it would take just a few more minutes to extract and export the five or ten seconds in which the man appeared. Then Tom would email it, which would take a few more minutes, and then I would hear the sweet chime of an incoming email. If Tom knew what he was doing.

Twenty minutes had passed now.

Before we'd hung up, I had made it clear that I was sitting in my van, specifically waiting to hear back. Tom had said he'd get back to me one way or the other. He'd send me a text if there was a problem, or if the man in the blue shorts did not appear. I was beginning to think I should send him a text and see —

Then I heard it. Incoming mail.

Subject: Video clip
Hope this is useful. Let me know if you need anything else. Please
tell Mia I'm sorry about her house.
— Tom Delaney

The attached MPEG file was less than two megabytes. I double clicked and it opened with no problem. The time indicator showed that the video was 58 seconds long. I was looking down Tom Delaney's driveway toward the street. The quality was surprisingly good. Crisp. In focus. Colors were vivid.

Eleven seconds elapsed with nobody moving on the screen. Then a figure appeared from the right. A man in blue shorts and a white T-shirt, carrying a water bottle, and wearing a ball cap and sunglasses. He was walking, not jogging, on the near side of the street. Average height. Average weight. Was it Cooney? One of his partners? It was impossible to tell.

Then the man actually stopped right at the foot of Delaney's driveway. He was winded from his jog. He lifted the water bottle and took a long drink. There was no gasoline in that bottle. Never had been.

The man removed his cap to wipe his forehead. He was bald. Not balding. Bald. Completely. There wasn't a hair on his head. It wasn't Cooney. It wasn't Moyer or Buerger or Evans. It was just some bald dude jogging. He put his cap back on and walked right out of the frame.

Well, damn.

It didn't mean Cooney hadn't set the fire, but it meant the most promising piece of evidence had turned out to be worthless. It wasn't evidence at all. Lucian, Mia's neighbor, had said the man had had dark blond or light brown hair, but witness testimony was notoriously unreliable.

I reached out to stop the video and then I paused.

Another person had just entered the frame from the right-hand side, carrying a soft drink can, and walking briskly. With purpose. The way someone would walk if they'd just set a fire and needed to leave the neighborhood quickly.

And I knew immediately who it was.

42

As I drove back to Austin, Mia and I spoke for at least an hour on the phone, going over all the details of the case, and finally understanding how some of the missing pieces fit together.

Then, just before sundown, we met in the parking lot of Candice Klein's apartment complex.

I wasn't beating myself up anymore, as I had been when I'd left Port Arthur. I'd felt so gullible, but as Mia had pointed out, it's impossible to see into someone's soul. If a person — in this case, Candice — has a freakish ability to lie convincingly, in the absence of any contradictory evidence, why wouldn't you believe her? I had certainly believed her. So had Mia. And, actually, there *was* other evidence — the fact that I had seen Candice at Albeck's ranch — but I'd incorrectly interpreted that as proof of her innocence rather than evidence of her involvement in the scam.

We made our way quietly up the concrete staircase and paused at the top of the landing on the second floor. Candice's door was less then ten feet away. Light was showing through the closed blinds in the window beside the door. We stepped to the door and listened. Silence.

No sense in waiting. I pulled my phone out and dialed her number. A few seconds later, we could hear her phone ringing inside the apartment. Then she answered, and I felt a sense of relief. We'd figured there was a good chance she'd gone down to Mexico to meet up with Boz Gentry.

I wasn't going to give her a chance to lie again. "Hey, Candice, it's Roy Ballard. Mia and I are standing outside your door right now. We had a few more questions, but Mia convinced me it was rude to show up without calling. So I'm calling first."

Now she knew that we knew she was home.

She let out a sigh, as if this were an imposition. "Can it wait until tomorrow?" she said.

"It won't take long," I said. "Just a few minutes and we'll be out of your hair."

"Let me change clothes. Just a sec."

She hung up.

We waited. She wouldn't be exiting through a back door because she didn't have one. Besides, she didn't know it was time to run.

She opened the door about a minute later, wearing yoga pants and a large, loose, pink sweatshirt. Her hair was in a ponytail and, like last time, she had no make-up on, but she had a great complexion without it.

"I was just about to go to bed," she said.

"Sorry to bother you," I said.

"Mind if we come inside for just a minute?" Mia asked.

Candice reluctantly opened the door and let us in. This was important, because we wanted to see if there were any signs that she was about to leave town. The cat, Sadie, immediately appeared at my ankles, purring and rubbing. Great.

"I don't have any coffee," Candice said.

"That's okay," Mia said.

"Got any Dr Pepper?" I asked.

"I'm afraid not," Candice said.

"But you like Dr Pepper, don't you?" I said.

"What?"

"Never mind," I said.

"I don't mean to be rude," Candice said, "but I'm really beat. Why exactly are you here?"

We were still standing near the front door, but I took a few steps and sat on the sofa, and Mia followed and sat beside me, so Candice felt obligated to sit in the upholstered chair she'd occupied the last time we'd been here. The damn cat wasted no time hopping up into my lap.

"Guess you heard about Boz," I said. "Down in Mexico."

Candice nodded.

Mia and I had discussed at length the best way to approach Candice. We'd agreed to go at her head-on.

"What surprises us," Mia said, "is that you aren't down there with him."

Candice frowned, just a little. Playing confused. "What're you talking about?" she said.

"Candice," I said, "you're very good. Seriously. Most people aren't skilled liars — at least not face to face. But you've got a knack for it."

"What the hell?" she said, her voice rising. "Why are you saying that?" Now she was pretending to be appalled and offended. Indignant, like I had some nerve talking to her that way.

"Because we have video of you one block from Mia's house, just a minute or two after you started the fire."

Candice sort of jerked her head and her eyes widened, but no words came out.

"You're wondering if I'm bluffing," I said. "Let me assure you that I'm not. I can show you the video on my phone, if you'd like."

Mia said, "Right before we knocked on your door, we emailed the clip to a long list of people — to the arson investigation team, and to the detectives investigating Boz's alleged death and Tyler's murder. It was tempting for us to stay out of it and let them question you, but when some twisted bitch tries to burn your house down, you take it a little personally."

Now Candice came right back up out of her chair, angry and glaring. "I have no idea what either of you are raving about and you need to leave. Right now."

Neither of us budged. The cat decided I wasn't giving her enough attention, so she hopped down and wandered into the bedroom.

"I'm guessing when the cops subpoena your credit-card and debit-card records, they'll see that you bought a gas can and a small quantity of gas that very morning," I said. "A woman like you doesn't keep a gas can handy, because why would you? You don't have a lawn mower or anything like that. And you wouldn't have siphoned gas from your car. So you bought it. Then you carried that gas in a Dr Pepper can. We could see it in the video."

Candice was stone-faced.

"Not a lot of gas, but more than enough to start a fire," Mia said.

"It would've been easy enough for you to toss that can out the window when you were driving," I said. "But I bet you tossed it into a trash can in the parking lot across from the Hula Hut. I bet they don't empty those trash cans very often, and I bet your Dr Pepper can will still have your fingerprints on it."

"See, we think you were working with Boz from the start on this scam," Mia said. "But Tyler didn't know Boz had another partner. There was no reason to tell him. But we got at least one thing wrong: Boz wasn't planning to leave the country with Erin, he was planning to leave with you. At first."

Candice was beginning to appear rattled. It was dawning on her how bad this situation really was.

I said, "He was hiding out here in your apartment for the first few weeks, right? Waiting for the insurance money to be released? Originally, we assumed Erin had to be involved — at least afterward — because she was the beneficiary. But then we finally realized the money would be put into a bank account that Boz and Erin shared, which meant he'd still have access to it, even though he was supposedly dead. He could go online and transfer it to another account — probably a foreign account — one that Erin didn't even know existed. By the time she figured out where the money went, you and Boz would be long gone, too. Of course, some of this is speculation on our part, but are we close?"

Her only response was to cross her arms and try to look petulant.

"Unfortunately," Mia said, "The plan went south. The cops started to wonder if that was really Boz in the wreck, and they started investigating pretty hard, and you knew they'd eventually come around and ask you some questions. They'd learn about your affair with Boz, so they'd be watching you. Might even tap your phone or get a warrant to search your place. So Boz decided it would be better if he stayed somewhere else. He came up with the idea of hiding at Alex Albeck's ranch house. Seemed perfect, because the house is usually empty this time of year. Alex isn't out there often except during hunting season."

I said, "Only problem is — and I don't think you know this — is that Alex's ranch foreman is staying at the house right now. Had a little tiff with his wife and she kicked him out. So sad. That meant Boz was screwed. He didn't have a house to stay in, and he didn't want to risk camping out, because the foreman might stumble on him."

I could tell that Candice's mind was racing as she processed this information.

"You didn't know any of that, did you?" I said. "You thought he was staying at the ranch, but after a certain amount of time, you started to worry about him. To wonder if he was doing okay, or even if he had high-tailed it without you. I'm guessing you didn't have disposable cell phones — you never anticipated needing any — so you couldn't call to see how he was doing. Then I showed up to talk to Tyler, and that's when you really started to worry. You were probably listening right outside the door, so you heard the conversation. You knew I was going to try to find Boz. You heard me open my big mouth and say cops have boundaries that don't apply to me as much, or words to that effect. You're smart enough to know that meant we might decide to search Alex Albeck's ranch."

Mia said, "So you came up with a plan to get us out of the picture. You tried to burn my house down. You thought we'd be too busy trying to catch the arsonist to focus on Boz."

Candice didn't try to deny any of this. I sensed that she realized it was futile at this point. She simply remained silent.

Mia continued. "Then, that afternoon, you went out to Albeck's ranch. Not just to check on Boz, and because you missed him, but to warn him about us. Only problem was, Boz wasn't there. There was no sign of him at all. That must've freaked you out a little. Where the hell was he?"

"You know where he was, Candice?" I asked. "Did he ever come clean about that?"

She glared at me.

"He'd gone back to Erin," I said, shaking my head. "And she actually let him stay. Man, that dude must talk a good game. Why do women continually fall for his bullshit?"

It was plain from the pained expression on Candice's face that she hadn't known this.

"He betrayed you," Mia said. "Yes, he was originally planning to take off with you, but he changed his mind. He was trying to convince Erin to run away with him, with or without the money."

"That's not true," Candice said in a small voice. "Boz loves me." She still seemed so convinced of that fact. Ridiculous.

"Maybe so, maybe not," I said. "If he does, why is he in Mexico while you're sitting here alone?"

She started to say something, but decided to keep quiet instead. Why did I have the feeling that something wasn't quite right? That I was missing an obvious clue?

"Believe it or not, I actually feel a little sympathy for you," Mia said. "I think you got duped by Boz. He took advantage of you, and you got involved in his crazy scheme because you loved him, despite the fact that he was a proven liar and cheater. That's incredibly stupid, but I can sort of understand."

Candice's expression of stubborn resolve was finally beginning to waiver. I sort of wished the cat was still in my lap so I'd have a reason to look somewhere other than Candice's sad face.

"On the other hand — the fire at my house — that was all you. Nobody asked or told you to do that. You came up with that all by yourself. That means you are a dangerous woman, and I'm going to do everything I can to make sure you get locked up for it."

Right there, after that remark from Mia, was when we should've left. We had the evidence that would almost certainly convict Candice for arson, and that should've been enough. But hindsight is 20/20. I had no way of knowing what I was about to say would drastically alter the future.

I said, "What we're going to do, Candice — in case you're thinking of leaving town — is wait outside and keep an eye on your place. All night, if we have to. I imagine the cops will be here soon — by morning at the latest — to ask you some questions. They might even have a warrant for your arrest by then."

I didn't know it yet, but I had just pushed it too far. I wasn't worried about Candice or what she might do. She was showing no signs of doing anything rash. She was resigned. Defeated. She wasn't going to throw herself at me and try to scratch my eyes out. But Candice wasn't the problem.

Boz Gentry was. Because right then he emerged from Candice's bedroom with a handgun.

43

I'll admit I was speechless for several seconds, and because neither Boz Gentry nor Candice said anything, the room was silent, except for the cat's insistent mewing.

Jesus, the cat.

I'm such a dumbass. That's what I'd missed. I should have wondered why Sadie had left me alone. She'd gone into the bedroom, where Boz had been hiding, because she preferred him to me. Seemed every female fell under his spell.

Finally I said, "Oh, hey, it's Boz Gentry. Speak of the devil. I was —"

"Shut up," he said. "Either of you talks again, you're dead."

Boz was aiming the gun, a revolver, directly at my head from about eight feet. Close enough to ensure he wouldn't miss, but far enough that I couldn't make a sudden lunge. Mia and I remained still and quiet. Boz Gentry had already killed two people. He had no reason to stop now. I don't carry my Glock on a regular basis, but I wished like hell I was carrying it right now.

"Baby, you got any rope?" he said over his shoulder to Candice.

"What?"

"We need to tie 'em up and get the hell out of here."

Candice didn't move.

"Candy!" Boz barked. "Baby, we gotta get moving."

"I don't have any," Candice said. "It's true, isn't it? What they said?"

The cat was still rubbing against Boz's shins, purring loudly. He kicked her away, but she came right back.

"They're liars," he said, his eyes locked on mine as he sighted down the barrel. "We don't have time for this."

"Where were you when I came out to the ranch?" Candice said. "You weren't there."

"Baby, please," Boz pleaded. "Not right now."

He was fidgeting with the gun — anxious and on edge — and I didn't like it. Men in Boz Gentry's mental state rarely made logical or compassionate choices. He'd kill both of us to get away.

"You were with Erin," Candice said, starting to cry. "Admit it."

"Baby..." Boz said.

"Tell me the truth, Boz. For once. Be a man and tell the truth."

"I had to go somewhere," he said, clearly becoming angry. "I went home. Where else was I supposed to go?"

"You were going to leave with Erin, weren't you?"

"No, baby. We're running out of time. The cops might already be on their way."

"Do you have a passport, Candice?" I asked.

"What?"

"Shut up!" Boz said. I could see his finger tightening on the trigger.

But I couldn't shut up. Candice had already said she didn't have any rope, and I knew Boz wouldn't leave us here alive, unrestrained. He'd kill us. That's why I had to take a chance. I had to turn Candice against Boz for good. He wouldn't kill her, too. She was his only hope for escape.

So I repeated myself. "Do you have a passport?"

"Boz got a fake passport for Erin," Mia said. She knew what I was doing, and she wasn't going to let me take all the risk by myself. I'd never been more proud to be her partner.

"Quiet!" Boz yelled.

"But he didn't get one for you, Candice," I said. "Did he?"

Boz took one step closer and pointed the revolver with more conviction. His mouth was twisted into a grimace. "I've got nothing to lose," he said. "You understand that?"

"Boz?" Candice said. She sounded pathetic.

"I have a passport for you in the car," Boz said.

"That might be his biggest lie yet," I said.

If he was going to shoot — right here, in the apartment, for all the neighbors to hear — he'd shoot now. But, instead, he made a move as if he wanted to strike me with the butt of the revolver. He thought better of it and stayed where he was, out of my reach.

"He killed Erin," I said.

"That's a lie!" Boz shouted.

"Because she was pressuring him to turn himself in," I said. "They probably argued and he lost his temper. Before that, he killed Tyler."

"Boz?" Candice said.

"That's why he came back to you," Mia said. "He can't make it on his own. He's too recognizable. But you aren't."

"I came back because I love her," Boz said.

I could feel the sweat dampening my armpits. My heart was racing wildly. I was willing Candice to do something, anything, to distract Boz and give me an opening. If she'd just go into the bedroom, lock the door, and call 9-1-1. Or, the opposite — get angry and lash out at him.

"Candice," I said, "he knows he might have a chance on the run if you're with him. But alone, his chances are zero."

"He went down to the border, then came back for me," Candice said. Still holding out hope. "He could've left."

"He went down there to throw the cops off," I said. "He never planned to actually cross. He knew they'd catch him, even with a fake passport. I should've realized that myself a long time ago. He has to stay in the States, at least until the search cools down. For that, he needs you."

Boz said, "You people are really limiting my options here, you know what I mean?" He was almost laughing from sheer stress and desperation. We'd backed him into a corner. He was starting to crack under the pressure. At that point, I was convinced he would kill us all, if he could, and flee in Candice's car.

"I have duct tape in my van," I said. "You can use that."

"Where are your keys?"

"In my pocket."

Boz nodded and made a "give me" motion with his free hand. I tossed him the keys.

"Candy," he said. "Go out and get the tape."

She didn't respond. She didn't move. I could see the turmoil on her face. The indecision.

"Candy!"

She was balking. She wasn't prepared to go on the run with a man who'd killed two people. And I believe she was also frozen with fear. Too paralyzed to even see her way out. *Our* way out.

"Go ahead, Candice," I said, giving her a reassuring nod. "Get the tape. It'll be all right."

And right then, something changed in her eyes. She understood. She walked up beside Boz and took the keys.

"Where's the tape?" Boz asked.

"Glove compartment," I said.

Candice walked out of the apartment without a word and closed the door behind her. We waited in silence.

Thirty seconds passed. A minute.

I let the clock continue to tick without pointing out the obvious — that Candice wasn't coming back. It was to our advantage to let as much time transpire as possible. So I tried to distract him — and fill in the last hole.

"Only thing I can't figure out," I said, "is why Erin, or you, or both of you, drove over to Alex's house on that Thursday night. Did Alex know about your plan?"

Boz had no reason to answer — or not to answer. "Not at first, no. He didn't know a thing. Don't you try to screw him over on this."

"I won't," I said. "Sounds like he wasn't involved."

"I went over there to ask for money. He didn't even believe it was me at first. Then he said to turn myself in and he'd hire a lawyer for me. But he wouldn't give me any money. Some best friend."

"So he —"

"Shut up," Boz said. He finally seemed to understand what was happening with Candice. He said, "Both of you — get over there." He wanted us to move away from the windows so he could take a look and confirm his suspicions. We both willingly complied, moving to our right along the wall.

"She's called 9-1-1 by now," I said. "The cops are on their way."

I hoped that was true. I hoped Candice had actually made the call, rather than simply taking off to save her own hide. And I hoped there had been a patrol unit so close that the officer was already pulling into the apartment complex. I hoped all of those things, right at that moment, because I didn't yet know that it wouldn't matter if a cop was outside or not. Everything would be settled within these four walls. Quickly. Violently. In a manner I wouldn't have expected.

Boz Gentry was trying to step toward the windows while keeping an eye on us. Moving laterally.

And he tripped over the cat.

It happened so quickly — and it looked so comical — that I almost didn't have time to react. Boz Gentry tried desperately to stay on his feet, but Sadie had wrapped herself around one of his ankles like some sort of feline ankle weight.

It became apparent that Boz was going to take a tumble, and he did what most people would do in that situation. He let go of the gun so he could use both hands to break his fall. Or maybe he had the presence of mind to release the gun so he wouldn't accidentally pull the trigger and execute himself. He hit the carpet and the gun bounced a few feet in front of him.

In situations like this, you don't have time to weigh the pros and cons of various courses of action. You spontaneously react. And in this case, Mia and I did the same thing, at the same time. We both hurled ourselves at Boz Gentry and landed on him as he was still on his knees. Our combined weight on his back knocked him flat, and I heard him grunt from the force of the impact.

But he was still reaching for the revolver with his right hand. I grabbed his arm in an attempt to slow him down, but I was using my injured hand, and it was too weak to get a solid grip. Gentry was lean and strong — and fueled by massive amounts of adrenaline. His fingertips brushed the butt of the revolver, and he stretched further, managing to wrap his hand around it. I couldn't let him swing the gun around in this direction.

I was so focused on the gun, I had no idea what Mia was doing — until Gentry let out a piercing shriek and let the revolver go. Mia had just dug her fingernails into one of Gentry's eye sockets. He began twisting his head from side to side in an attempt to shake free.

Mia continued her assault, and in the meantime, I managed to snake my left arm — my good arm — around Gentry's throat. I began to squeeze as hard as I could. Was I breaking delicate bones? Crushing his windpipe? I didn't care. Gentry was kicking and flailing, using every last ounce of energy, while making some unsettling guttural grunts and moans.

And then, as if someone had flicked a switch, he went limp. Totally out cold. Mia quickly sprung to her feet and grabbed the revolver. We were both gasping for air.

"You okay?" she said.

"Yeah. You?"

She nodded her head at Gentry. "You're going to kill him." I hadn't relaxed my grip, and it was tempting to keep it that way until the son of a bitch turned blue.

"Roy," Mia said. "Come on."

I relaxed my headlock just enough to let him breathe, but I wasn't going to completely let go until the cops arrived.

I looked around for the cat, but she was nowhere to be seen. I made a mental note to buy her about ten pounds of fresh salmon.

44

I got to the airport an hour early, simply because not being there when her plane arrived would've left an impression on her that I could have never erased. I figured I already had enough work ahead of me on that front. I was the father who had allowed her to be abducted, and that was a hurdle I might not ever be able to overcome completely.

I would have liked to have met her right as she exited the gate, but security regulations prohibit that nowadays, so we'd agreed to meet at the baggage carousel, downstairs. I found an out-of-the-way seat and waited.

Forty minutes.

My right hand ached. My arms were sore. My back was stiff. I hadn't realized until this morning how much of a physical struggle it had taken to subdue Boz Gentry.

The police — Austin cops, not Travis County deputies, since we'd been inside the city limits — had arrived at Candice's apartment in about four minutes. That's when the tedium began: Going down to the station to tell the entire story over and over to an APD detective. I'd given her everything, but, of course, they always want to make sure every last detail is nailed down. They want to make sure a witness's story matches up every time he tells it. I told her to call Ruelas at TCSO. Call Victor Dunn at Hays County. Call the Lee County Sheriff. But she kept asking questions. Finally, at two in the morning, I'd had to say sorry, but I'm done. It's time for me to go home and sleep, because I have a big day tomorrow. We'll have to pick this up another time. Mia was in another room telling another detective all the same details. When she saw me in the hallway, she called it quits, too.

Thirty minutes.

When I'd woken up, Heidi had sent a short and sweet text.

Well done, Roy. Enjoy every minute with your daughter.

About a dozen journalists and reporters had left voicemails. I knew some of them pretty well, but I didn't return any of their calls. No way. Not right now.

Twenty minutes.

I fidgeted and watched people grab luggage from a flight that had arrived from Atlanta.

Then, over the noise of hundreds of travelers passing to and fro, I heard my phone ring. It was Ruelas. Tempting to let it go to voicemail, but I answered.

"I have just a few minutes to talk," I said.

"They just grabbed Candice Klein in Dallas," he said.

I wasn't even sure how to feel about that. Part of me didn't even care. Part of me wanted Candice to get away. And still another part wanted her to serve serious time for the arson at Mia's house.

"Thanks for letting me know," I said. "I'll tell Mia." I didn't ask any questions. The details of Candice's capture could wait.

"Jeez, where the hell are you?" he said, because of the background noise.

"Picking someone up at the airport," I said. He didn't need to know the particulars.

"Yeah, okay, anyway," he said. "Just wanted you to know about Candice. And good job with all that."

Good job with all that?

Was this really Ruelas? Was he actually doling out some praise? I expected to look out a window and see a pig taxiing on the runway.

"Thanks," I said.

"And I met that dog, Blackie," he said. "You were right. He likes to chase squirrels."

There was a tone to his voice, acknowledging what my strange phone call to him had meant a few days ago. I had beaten him to the evidence. He knew that. But he didn't sound bitter. He actually sounded amused.

Ten minutes.

"Listen," I said, "my daughter's plane is going to arrive in just a few minutes…"

"Your daughter?"

He knew all about my daughter, and what had happened to her years ago. He was a cop. Of course he knew.

"Yeah, she's visiting for a month."

"Well, I won't keep you then," he said.

Then I surprised myself by saying, "Maybe you'll get a chance to meet her." Really? Had I just said that?

"That'd be cool," Ruelas said. "Give me a call sometime."

And he hung up. I sat there, stunned, wondering what had just happened. While I was holding my phone, it rang again — the Commodores singing "Brick House."

"Hey," I said.

"Hey, back," Mia said. "Have you heard?"

"About Candice Klein? Yeah, Ruelas just called."

"It's already on the news. Figured you'd want to know. You at the airport?"

"Yep."

"How you feeling?" she said.

"Possibly the most nervous I've ever been."

"Understandable. But, Roy?"

"Yeah?"

"Can I give you some unsolicited advice?"

"Of course you can."

Five minutes.

"It's time to focus on the future, not the past," Mia said. "You've atoned for your mistake, and then some. Many times over. You can't let it follow you around forever. You are one of the finest men I know, Roy. I hope you know that. You have to forgive yourself, and if you do, I promise that Hannah will forgive you, too. Make it a clean slate, Roy, starting right now. You deserve that."

I didn't want to, but damn it, I was starting to cry. What kind of tough guy sits in an airport and cries? Mia knew what was happening, so she simply waited. I realized right then that I was going to tell her very soon how I felt about her. Not right now, on the phone, but in person. No more waiting.

"Thank you, Mia," I said. "I hope you know how much that means to me."

"You bet. See you tomorrow night?"

We'd planned dinner, so Hannah and Mia could meet.

"Absolutely," I said. "See you then."

We hung up.

Two minutes later, Hannah's flight touched down.

ABOUT THE AUTHOR

Ben Rehder lives with his wife near Austin, Texas, where he was born and raised. His novels have made best-of-the-year lists in *Publishers Weekly, Library Journal, Kirkus Reviews,* and *Field & Stream. Buck Fever* was nominated for the Edgar Award. For more information, visit www.benrehder.com.

OTHER NOVELS BY BEN REHDER

Buck Fever
Bone Dry
Flat Crazy
Guilt Trip
Gun Shy
Holy Moly
The Chicken Hanger
The Driving Lesson
Gone The Next
Hog Heaven
Stag Party
Bum Steer